THE THOMAS *Flair*

E.J. RUSSELL

Cover art: Cate Ashwood, cateashwooddesigns.com
Professional Beta Reading: Leslie Copeland
Edited by Meg DesCamp, Sue Brown-Moore

ISBN: 978-1-947033-20-7

First edition
July 2020

Contact information:
ejr@ejrussell.com

THE THOMAS Flair

E.J. RUSSELL

FOREWORD

When I wrote the first draft of *The Thomas Flair*, the COVID-19 pandemic wasn't even a blip on anyone's radar because the novel corona virus hadn't appeared anywhere on the planet. We were all going about business as usual, and (at least in my case) eagerly looking forward to the 2020 Tokyo Games.

Then things changed.

As of this writing, the Tokyo Olympics have been postponed to 2021, but the pandemic isn't close to being contained. I thought very long and hard about what to do with this book. After several months of waffling, I decided to move forward as if the 2020 Summer Games still happened as planned.

My decision was based partly on the fact that we don't know what the next year will bring—the 2021 Olympics might be postponed as well. But what ultimately pushed me to publish the book as it stood was hope: hope that we'll be able to return to a normal world, a *better* world, and things that give us joy (like the Olympic Games) will once again be part of our lives.

That being said, any sports romance has an element of fantasy about it—fictional teams, fictional athletes, fictional results. In *The Thomas Flair*, I've altered the results of the 2016 Games as well as inventing the outcome of the 2020 Games-that-might-have-been for the purposes of my story. Although I reference some public figures—like the late Kurt Thomas, who invented the move that inspired my title, and Tim Daggett, a member of the 1984 US gold medal men's team who is a regular commentator at gymnastics meets—the novel's story and characters are completely fictitious and are not intended to represent any real person.

So… let the Games begin.

CHAPTER ONE

Rio, 2016

Sol Ashvili lifted onto his toes and craned his neck, searching the crowd in the Rio Olympic Village Plaza, but it was pretty much a lost cause. A gymnast like Sol couldn't hope to see over a basketball player or around a weightlifter to find another gymnast.

But miraculously the crowd parted for an instant and Sol glimpsed the person he'd been searching for.

Tony Thomas.

In the ambient light from the big screen monitor, Tony's smile was brilliant white against his brown skin, his signature bleached curls topping his high-top fade like a crown. Tony turned to say something to Luiz Fonseca, one of the Brazilian gymnasts, and when he threw back his head to laugh, exposing the strong column of his throat, Sol's mouth dried. *Beautiful.*

Sol downed the last gulp in his water bottle and dropped the empty in the nearest recycling bin.

Tonight. I'm telling him tonight.

The Rio evening was pleasantly warm and a little humid, but Sol shivered anyway, longing for the parka he'd left at home in Colorado.

Yeah, admitting to your best friend that you've been in love with him for years was a sure-fire way to spawn terror-induced chills.

Hadn't he waited long enough, though? He'd been crushing on Tony almost since the day they'd met, before he'd even realized he was gay. He'd walked into Central Gymnastics as a quaking ten-year-old whose body had been hijacked by diabetes, and the first person who'd greeted him was Tony, two years older and impossibly cool even then.

Sol dodged the last clump of athletes that separated him from his target—swimmers or divers, judging from the eau de chlorine fragrance—as Tony held up a "just a minute" finger to Luiz and dug his phone out of his pocket. From the way his grin faded, Sol knew exactly who must be on the other end of the text.

Tony's fucking father.

If the guy hadn't been the size of a Humvee—former linebacker, and he never let Tony forget what a huge disappointment he was for taking after his petite Senegalese mother rather than his beefy white self—Sol would have drop-kicked the asshole to Mars for the way he treated his son. Sol had never known Tony's mom. Breast cancer had taken her before the boys had met. But Tony kept a picture of her with him as a toddler tucked in his gym bag. They had identical brilliant smiles and tight black curls, and if Tony's skin was a shade lighter, it was an equally rich and gorgeous brown.

Tony caught sight of Sol and grinned. "Having a good time?" He tipped back his own water. "Living the dream, right?"

That grin might have fooled everybody else, but he'd been Sol's best friend for nine years, and Sol kept a mental scrapbook of every one of Tony's expressions. *Because I've seen them all.* And been mesmerized by each of them from that very first moment.

Something's wrong.

But Sol couldn't come out and just ask, not with Luiz standing right there—and the way Luiz's gaze kept flicking from Tony's lips, down his body, and back again, set Sol's teeth on edge.

"Solly, you know Luiz, right?"

Sol forced himself to smile. "Of course. Congratulations on your silver on rings today."

Luiz lifted his cup in a toast. "I reward myself with Coca Cola. For now." He cocked his head, dark brows lifting in an undeniably handsome face. Sol could appreciate Luiz's looks objectively, but subjectively? *I'm Tony-blind.* "You are here but not competing?"

Sol shrugged. "Alternate. They didn't need me, but it's still the Olympics, right?"

"Hey." Tony nudged Sol with an elbow. "I always need you. Wouldn't know how to face the judges without my Solly there to cheer me on."

Sol snorted. "Yeah, right. You did fine at OU for the two years before I got there."

Luiz's brows rose in inquiry. "OU?"

"University of Oklahoma. We're both on their NCAA gymnastics team. Go, Sooners!" Tony grinned and held up his fist for Sol to bump.

Luiz grimaced at his Coke. "Would you like to go somewhere else for a drink with a little more kick? Rio is my home, so I know all the best places."

Sol glanced sidelong at Tony. Would he accept? He had two event finals tomorrow—parallel bars and high bar—the only member of Team USA to make it into more than one. But Tony shook his head.

"No, thanks. I'm heading back to the dorm. Gotta rest up for tomorrow."

"Then you, Sol. You have not his excuse. As you say, this is the Olympics." Luiz's smile was crooked and sly. "Now that my competition is over, it is time to party."

Sol shook his head. "Thanks, but I'll head back with Tony. I don't really drink."

Tony gave Sol the side-eye. "You sure, Solly? Don't bail on my account."

"I'm sure." He offered his hand for Luiz to shake. "Congratulations again on your medal."

Luiz ignored his hand and brought him in for a hug and a back slap. "*Obrigado*." He retreated a step and grinned. "Maybe tomorrow I can change both your minds about that drink."

Tony laughed. "Could be. We'll see how things go."

The two of them threaded their way through the crowd. Despite Tony's declaration about needing to rest, he seemed in no hurry, ambling along with his hands in the pockets of his shorts.

Tell him. Tell him now.

"There's something—" Sol's voice was nothing but a croak. He cleared his throat, but before he could spit out his confession, Tony chuckled.

"You can be pretty oblivious, Solly."

Sol frowned as they flashed their credentials at the guards to pass into the Residential Zone. "About what?"

Tony's grin glinted in the soft glow of a streetlight. "He was hitting on you."

Sol whipped his head around as though some guy might leap out from behind a palm tree. "What? Who?"

"Luiz, you idiot."

"Hello? I'm pretty sure he was hitting on you."

Tony shrugged. "I'm not the one he wanted to party with tonight."

"Only because you've got a competition tomorrow."

Tony sighed. "Yeah, about that." His steps slowed to a stop in the shadow of a banner with the Games' logo. "Do you resent it, Solly?"

Sol frowned, trying to make out Tony's face in the dim light. "Resent what?"

"That I got moved up from alternate instead of you."

"What?" Sol gripped Tony's shoulders, noting the tension that turned his muscles into concrete. "No, of course not."

"But it was always our dream to make the team together. To go to the Olympics together."

"And we did." Sol gestured to the paved walkway that meandered through the athlete's apartment complex. "Here we both are."

"But—"

"The one I feel sorry for is John Sinclair. If he hadn't torn his Achilles a week before the Games, he'd be here and both of us would be sitting in the stands."

"It could just as easily have been you they tapped. Probably should have been." Tony peered up into the dark velvet sky. "You're more consistent than me."

"Yeah, but they needed somebody to match John's strength profile—p-bars, high bar, rings. That's not me. Now if they'd needed somebody on floor ex or pommel horse?" He shrugged. "Maybe. But you've got two years' more international experience, not to mention two years' more muscle mass. I mean you qualified for two event finals. Obviously the coaches knew what they were doing."

Tony narrowed his eyes. "You're sure?"

"Absolutely."

Tony's shoulders lifted as he took a huge breath. "Okay, then."

"I wish I could be down on the floor with you tomorrow, though."

Tony's smile was a crooked shadow of itself. "Me too.

They walked along in silence for a few minutes, Sol trying to work up the courage to speak, until Tony's cell phone chimed in his pocket. He pulled it out and even the shadow smile disappeared.

"Text from your dad?"

Tony sighed. "Yeah. Big surprise, huh?"

"Let me guess. He's giving you advice about tomorrow that's a direct contradiction to what the coaches say?"

"He hasn't gotten to that part yet, although I'm sure it's coming." He tucked his phone back into his shorts without responding. "His current song and dance is how Matt shouldn't be celebrating his medal. It was only a bronze, and to Glen Thomas, nothing short of gold is good enough."

Sol let his steps take him closer to Tony—not close enough to touch, but not far enough away to escape the scent of citrus body wash on Tony's skin. *Dammit.* "Considering that's the only medal the men's team has scored at the Games"—he nudged Tony's ribs with his elbow and lifted an eyebrow—"so far, anyway, that seems a little harsh."

"Yeah, well, that's my dad. He couldn't resist adding a dig about how we men should be ashamed that the women's team wiped up the floor with their competition while we dropped to fifth."

"The women just performed outstanding gymnastics. It's not like they tackled their opponents and knocked them off the balance beam or blocked a release on the uneven bars."

"Dad probably thinks the rules should be changed to allow it. Full-contact gymnastics."

Sol chuckled. "I think your dad's idea about how gymnastics competitions work is a little skewed by his football mindset."

"Gee, you think?" Tony's voice was dryer than chalk dust.

"Well, never mind him." Sol bumped Tony's shoulder with his own as Team USA's dorm loomed in front of them. "You ready for tomorrow?"

Instead of flashing his grin and puffing out his chest with his usual pre-competition confidence, Tony bit his lip, his gaze sliding away. "Are you sure you don't hold it against me? If they'd chosen you, the *team* might have medaled."

Sol gave Tony a *get-real-dude* stare. "Unlikely. Besides, despite how your dad feels about the lamentable lack of body-checking in gymnastics, the team medal doesn't rely on one person. It's a group effort. And you know as well as I do that anything can happen up there on the podium. That's the nature of our sport."

Do I tell him? What if he doesn't feel the same? Will it psych him out even more?

The haunted look in Tony's dark eyes decided Sol. *I'll wait until after he competes tomorrow, after the medal ceremonies.* Because despite Tony's weird lack of confidence—and since when did Tony Thomas doubt himself?—Sol was convinced Tony would be wearing at least one medal if not two at the end of the day.

"You can do something for me, though," Sol said slowly.

Tony turned to him eagerly, as if he were hoping for Sol to assign some kind of penance. "Anything, Solly. Just name it."

Sol leaned in and patted Tony's chest. "Kick some ass, Tony. Show everyone that famous Thomas flair. For me. For you. For all of us."

The sea of faces in front of him, the lights, the noise, the *voices* —God, the shouting—that had followed him since the second medal ceremony sent Tony's head reeling. He only wanted one voice, one face, and it would be hours before he could see Solly again.

It had just felt so wrong—with Sol there but not there, training with the team but not competing at Tony's side, centering him, inspiring him, letting him fly.

But during Sol's little pep talk last night, Tony had been certain he'd wanted to say something else. *I can only hope it's what I think it is. What I want too.* That hope did more than anything the coaches, or the other guys on the team, or his fucking father could do to inspire Tony.

It had gotten him through both event finals, both medal ceremonies, all the subsequent interviews. It would get him through the awkward conversation with his father, which was inevitable since he didn't have the excuse of training or competition to avoid him anymore.

Sure enough, dear ol' Dad was waiting for him in the broadcast center lobby when Tony finished taping his last televised interview.

Tony sighed and trudged over to where his dad stood, arms crossed, glaring at him as if Tony had just gotten expelled from school rather than winning two silver medals at the fucking *Olympics*.

"Dad. Been waiting long?"

His father didn't move. "You didn't answer my texts."

"We aren't allowed cell phones on the competition floor."

"That doesn't account for the rest of the week." He grabbed Tony's arm and led him to a more central location, where everybody could see them together. Tony wanted to dive behind the nearest potted palm. "You need to show appreciation to the right people, Tony. People who matter. People who can do things for you."

Tony lifted an eyebrow. "People like you, Dad?"

"To start with." He glared at the medals hanging around Tony's neck. "You could have been more aggressive today. Tried to get at least *one* gold."

Tony's jaw dropped. "Seriously, Dad? I wasn't exactly picking daisies out there. My scores were higher than in any of my other rounds."

His father narrowed his eyes, obviously considering whether that made any difference in Sports According to Glen Thomas. He grunted. "I'll grant that's a point. You posted the scores when it mattered."

Tony stared at his shoes. "It mattered more in the team competition."

"Don't be naïve. You'd have shared the spotlight with everyone else then." He scowled at a group of men that included the team coach and the US men's high performance director. "I told them to put you on all the apparatus so you'd qualify for the all-around. I see I'll have some heads to crack about that."

Tony's insides turned to ice. "What are you talking about?"

He didn't spare Tony a glance, his gaze focused on the group that had started migrating toward the exit. "I called the head of the selection committee as soon as Sinclair was on the way to the hospital and told them in no uncertain terms that you should be named to the team." He huffed in disgust. "They were considering Ashvili, of all the ridiculous choices. I reminded them where their loyalties lay. Who their biggest donors were."

Tony clenched his fists, his nails driving into his palms. "What the *fuck*, Dad?" He'd comforted himself with Sol's words, that he was the best choice because his skill profile matched John's most closely. But if his position on the team was nothing more than the result of strong-arm tactics by his father, the old-boy sports network flexing its aging muscles, then Tony really had let the team down. But worse, he'd let Sol down.

"It's called negotiation, son."

"It's called bullying, Dad."

He chuckled as if Tony were being childish. "You'll never get anywhere in the world if you don't understand leverage." His head came up, and he squinted at the group across the room. "And I need to go apply a little more. Wait for me here." He swaggered across the room as if he owned the place and pushed himself into the circle, slapping the head coach on the back with a hearty laugh.

Tony turned away before he could see more evidence that his place, his relative success, his fucking *medals* had more to do with his father's influence than his own ability. *This could have been Solly. This* should *have been Solly.* Sol might not be the flashiest gymnast on the planet, but he was the most consistent.

A petite woman with a blade of a nose and a wild aureole of curly dark hair approached him, her smile fading as she studied his face. "Mr. Thomas? I'm Ori Hirsch. Is this a bad time?"

Only the worst. "No." His smile might be totally fake, but he knew it was convincing. Over the years, he'd had plenty of practice pretending his father wasn't a manipulative asshole to perfect it. "What can I do for you?"

She smiled, her slightly crooked front teeth giving her narrow face a cockeyed sort of charm. "It's more what I can do for you." She handed him a business card. "I'm a sports agent. What are your plans for after the Games?"

Tony glanced over his shoulder, where his father was yukking it up with the bigwigs, probably trying to convince them to give Tony something else that he didn't deserve. "Not much at the moment."

"I know you've got one more year before you graduate from the University of Oklahoma. But..." The way she drew out the last word snapped Tony's attention back to her.

"But?"

"Have you considered going pro? You'll lose your NCAA eligibility if you do, of course. It would take your career in an entirely different direction."

A different direction? Away from his father? Away from entitlement? *Away from Solly?* God, how could he lose Sol? *But how can I face him now?*

He grinned down at her. "Tell me more, Ms. Hirsch. I am all ears."

***

Sol hadn't stopped grinning since Tony had nailed his p-bars routine. He'd intended to escape the arena in time to catch Tony after he ran the gauntlet of the press in the mixed zone. That way they could catch the bus back to the Olympic Village together before Tony got dragged off to post-competition interviews.

But he hadn't wanted to miss a single minute of Tony's *second* medal ceremony, so he'd gotten caught in the crowd. By the time he'd fought his way outside, Tony had been long gone.

One way or another, this is happening. Tonight. Sol was determined to make use of the free condoms the Games had handed out like Halloween candy, although he doubted he'd get a chance to see Tony before the team's publicity engine chewed him up and spit him out. When Matt had won his bronze medal on pommel horse two days ago, he hadn't staggered back to the team suite until nearly three in the morning. *I don't care. I'll camp out outside Tony's door all night if I have to.*

So when he finally caught the bus to the Residential Zone and returned to the team's suite, he parked himself in the hallway next to Tony's room. *He'll be back, eventually. It won't be that long.*

But hours later, his ass numb from sitting on the floor, he was startled out of a half doze by a teammate stumbling over his feet.

"Sorry." Ron, Tony's roommate, grinned goofily down at Sol as he wavered outside the door, his keycard nowhere near the lock.

Sol knuckled his eyes. "What time is it?"

"I dunno. Morning?"

"What?" Sol wrestled his cell phone out of his pants pocket. Almost six. *Shit. I need to check my levels and eat.* He pushed himself to his feet as Ron finally opened his door and staggered inside. A series of thumps had Sol peering inside to make sure he hadn't tripped on the usual clutter the followed Tony anywhere and knocked himself silly.

But Ron wasn't sprawled on his bed, waiting to be ambushed by a monster hangover. Instead, he was tossing things into a suitcase on one of the beds.

Tony's suitcase. Tony's bed.

"Ron? What's going on?"

"Oh." He blinked at Sol then squinted at the open suitcase. "Packing up Tony's shit. Wait." He snatched a T-shirt out of the case and tossed it over his shoulder. "That's mine."

"Why? Tony—"

"Gone."

Sol clutched the doorframe, his belly jolting like he'd misjudged a dismount landing. "What do you mean he's gone? He was fine."

Ron gaped at him, then burst into giggles. "Not *that* kind of gone. I mean—" He hooked his thumbs together and flapped his palms to mock a bird in flight. "Hopped a plane back home." He snorted. "With his new *agent*."

"Agent? What? He's going pro? But that means he won't be NCAA eligible for his last year at OU. If—"

"Don't ask me, man." He snagged a pair of shorts and rifled them into the suitcase. "I'm just the bellhop."

Sol head spun. *Right. Levels. Eat.* But as he hurried to his own room, he shot a quick text to Tony.

Sol->Tony WTF, T? You're bailing on the Sooners?

But although Sol kept his cell phone practically glued to his hand all morning, shooting additional texts to Tony every half hour—okay, every ten minutes—Tony never responded. Not that day, and not the next. Finally Sol broke down and called him. *Voicemail, dammit.*

And the next time he called, the number had been disconnected.

CHAPTER TWO

Arvada, Colorado, 2020

Breathe. Balance. Keep rhythm steady. One skill at a time.

Sol kept his focus on the pommel horse, trusting his body's muscle memory and the hundreds of times he'd run this routine in the past season.

Scissors. Flairs. Russian circles. Fly up to a handstand. Aaaand stick the dismount.

Yes! No errors. He allowed himself a surreptitious fist pump as he crossed to the chalk bucket to recoat his hands. Now, if he could just do one more perfect pass before the end of training—

"Sol."

Sol winced at the sound of his coach's voice. Xiao never raised his voice in anger, but his gymnasts could always tell when he was annoyed by the bite in his tone. "Yes?"

"How many times have you repeated that exercise?"

Sol turned back to the chalk, making sure his hands were covered. He didn't want to get another rip. Not now. Not so close to heading off to Colorado Springs to train with the rest of the national team.

Not so close to the Olympics.

"A few. The last with no errors. If I can do one more—"

"No more."

Sol's head jerked up. "What? But, Xiao—"

"If you haven't counted, I have. That makes seven. You and I both know that big numbers are not your friend. And have you looked at the time?"

Sol glanced at the clock, high on the gym wall. *Shit.* "Sorry. I didn't realize it had gotten so late. The transition from flairs to circles was giving me trouble, and—"

"Enough for now. Center yourself. Eat if you need to. We'll talk afterward."

Eat. Talk. Yeah, no point in arguing, because Xiao was right, as he usually was. Sol couldn't remember the last time he'd lost track of his schedule. He'd been nine when diabetes had reprogrammed his system into something that couldn't maintain itself without outside intervention. Starting gymnastics—the discipline, the routine, the proof that he still had power over *something* about his body—had helped him manage his condition. He *never* let his control slip like this.

The looming Olympic team selection must be freaking him out even more than he thought.

But as he headed to the locker room, he admitted to himself that was only *part* of his problem.

It's those damn flairs. Sol had resisted putting flairs in his exercises for four years. Not because he couldn't do them—at twenty-three, although he was strong and fit, he hadn't started building up the heavy muscle mass that older gymnasts developed, so he was still able to move easily on the horse where balance, agility, and finesse were as important as strength.

Xiao had been urging Sol to put flairs into his routine almost the instant they'd returned from Rio. "It is never too early to start preparing for the *next* Olympics," Xiao had told him. "You must prove your value to the team. You have the potential to be an all-around champion. Floor and pommel horse will, I think, be your specialties, but not—" Xiao had fixed him with his patented coach's stare. "—if you resist adding such an important component."

Sol's stubborn streak—the same stubborn streak that sparked his quick rise in gymnastics, the same stubborn streak that had made him buckle down and learn to manage his diabetes—had kicked in, however, and until this season, he'd refused to add the skill. For one reason and one reason only.

Tony Thomas.

It was stupid. Tony hadn't invented the move—it was the legendary *Kurt* Thomas, back in the seventies, who'd invented it, first on horse and then on floor. The gymnastics Code of Points didn't even call them Thomas flairs anymore—they were just *flairs.*

But every time Sol executed the skill, that name echoed in his head because Tony had always joked that flairs were *his* signature move. *"How can I resist when they're named after me?"*

After Tony jetted out of the Olympic Village to turn pro and transform his individual success into adrenaline-fueled celebrity, he'd quit the team, quit school, quit gymnastics.

Quit me.

And Sol, hurt, bewildered, adrift, hadn't been able to face flairs since.

He sighed and trudged into the locker room to wash his hands and grab his glucometer. *Yikes.* Xiao was right to have called him on his tunnel vision. His levels were way off. He grabbed some apple juice from his bag to boost his blood sugar for the moment. He needed his post-workout protein snack too —he needed that regardless of stupidly losing track of his carb timing. *Home's only twenty minutes away. Should I wait until then and have a regular meal?* No. Xiao had said he wanted to talk, and he kept a stock of Sol's preferred supplements in the coaches' office.

So Sol grabbed a fresh set of sweats out of his bag and ducked into the gym's shower room. After sluicing the sweat and chalk off himself, letting the hot water pound on his lower back where it ached, he started to feel more centered, but his muscles twitched with fatigue. Oh, yeah. He needed that recovery protein. He dried off, dressed, and returned to the gym.

Xiao wasn't waiting for him by the pommel horse, nor anywhere else on the gym floor. It was late enough that all the other gymnasts, both the high-level athletes and recreational classes, had cleared the apparatus. A clump of teens—boys and girls from the mid-level competitive teams—were clustered around a boy holding an iPad.

Sol recognized the kid, one of the boys he was mentoring. *Jason is going to get his ass kicked if Xiao finds him with electronics in the gym.* For everyone's safety and privacy, Central Gymnastics had a strict rule that no electronic devices were allowed in the locker rooms, and only coaches were allowed them on the gym floor. Sol glanced around. Still no sign of Xiao or any of the other adult coaches. As a peer coach, though, he knew his responsibilities.

He strode toward the kids. As he drew nearer, he could hear voices coming from the device. *Man, the speakers on those things are really good.* Sol couldn't make out the words yet, but at least one voice pinged his familiarity buttons. *If they've been taking video of the coaches or of other kids in the gym...*

"Jason! I hope that's not what I think it is."

Jason bit his lip, then jabbed the Home button to kill the video. "It's nothing bad, Sol, honest."

"Looks like an iPad to me."

"Well..." Jason glanced down at the device in his hand. *Let's see how he spins this one.* "It's just a new model Etch-a-Sketch, Sol, honest." "Um, yeah."

"You know the rules. You could be suspended for bringing that into training."

"But I didn't! Everybody was already done. I wasn't *filming* anybody. Not even any selfies. We just wanted to watch *Quinn's Ringside.*"

Sol checked the clock. 9:30, time for the live stream of the popular Olympics-themed webcast. "You can watch it when the episode is uploaded to Quinn's channel."

"But then we'd have to wait!"

Sol lowered his chin and glared at Jason from under his eyebrows. "But then you wouldn't be violating gym rules and getting your butt suspended from the team a week before a meet."

Jason glowered at Sol, but flipped the cover over his iPad and shoved it into the bag by his feet. "It's not fair. We were only *watching*. That's not hurting anybody."

"Unfortunately, when it comes to gym rules, you have to keep to the letter, not the spirit." Sol suppressed a wince at his self-righteous tone. He'd been straining the bounds of the rules himself tonight by not adhering to his own training plan. But a *plan* wasn't a *rule*. Precisely. Still, he couldn't give the kids too much grief.

He waited until all the younger gymnasts had collected their bags from either the locker room or the cubbies next to the door by the restrooms, then turned out the gym's overhead lights, leaving just the safety lights on. He walked down the short hallway, ready to head upstairs to the coaches' office to find Xiao. He'd only planted one foot on the stairs, though, when he heard Jason say something that froze his muscles.

"... Tony Thomas. I can't believe—"

"What did you say?" Sol lunged around the corner, startling the group of kids in the middle of the lobby.

Jason gulped. "I wasn't complaining, Sol, honest. But Quinn's interviewing Tony Thomas tonight, and I really wanted to see it live." He sighed. "By the time we get home, the live stream'll be over."

"Duh, Jason." Kayla, one of the level eight girls, rolled her eyes. "Just watch it on your phone once your dad picks you up."

Jason wrinkled his nose and said something about his phone's lousy screen resolution, but Sol wasn't listening anymore.

Why would Tony be on Quinn's Ringside? True, Quinn Urquhart had practically made a second career out of following Tony from one outrageous exploit to another. Not that Sol would know much about that (as long as he kept his denial firmly in place). But *Ringside* was about the Olympics and Olympians.

Tony's an Olympian. A double silver medalist. Maybe the show was about past Games. *Yeah, that must be it.*

It couldn't be because Sol had put flairs in both his pommel horse and floor routine and *conjured* Tony back into Sol's consciousness.

Get over yourself, Ashvili. Everything Tony does is not about you.

Sol snorted, startling some of the kids into glancing at him wide-eyed. If Tony had cared about their friendship, about Sol, about the *more* that Sol had been starting to believe their friendship was evolving into, then he wouldn't have bailed four years ago, with no word since.

Maybe it's time to let everything I *do—or don't do—not be about* him.

But despite the need for his protein shake, despite Xiao waiting for him upstairs, once the last of the kids trailed out the door, leaving the lobby empty, the itch that was constantly with Sol, the itch to know more about what Tony was doing—even though Tony's antics made Sol cringe most of the time—grew until he had to scratch.

Just like I always do. Damn it, why couldn't he leave Tony in the past where he belonged?

Sol's heart whispered the answer, but his brain refused to listen. Nevertheless, he slunk back through the shadowed gym and pulled out his cell phone.

As he straddled the bench in front of his locker, he rationalized his pathetic lapse like he always did. *It only makes sense to keep up with* Quinn's Ringside. Somehow, Quinn always got the earliest news about Olympic competitors. Maybe she'd spill something about how the new rules were predicted to change the competition. *Get real, Ashvili. If that was the only reason for the episode, why would Tony be the featured guest? He hasn't competed since—*

Sol froze, his finger about to touch the Ringside app. Tony *had* competed, although not at any of the meets that Sol had attended. OU finals and graduation had derailed Sol's Tony Thomas obsession for a few months, but he'd heard Tony had signed on with the notorious Andrei Nicolescu to get back into competition form after three years of training for other activities altogether. What if, under the new rules, Tony had qualified for the Olympics not by team, but *by name*?

That won't matter. The other guys on the national team had been training for this for years, the program at the US Olympic and Paralympic Training Center molding them into a unit, into Team USA. Bringing an outsider like Tony in, even if he had picked up a qualifying berth, would be disruptive to the point of disaster. The coaches wouldn't do that.

Would they?

Sol braced himself and launched the app just as the opening credits ended.

Quinn's wide-cheeked face, crowned with her signature braided locs, filled the screen. "Good evening, everyone. And welcome to *Quinn's Ringside*." She grinned, teeth blinding white against her crimson lipstick. "Have I got a treat for you tonight."

And there was Tony—his laughing eyes, his fade tipped with a shock of tight platinum curls, his glowing brown skin a match for Quinn's—so beautiful he made Sol's heart stutter.

Sol had to pinch his quad—hard—to remind himself that Tony didn't give a good goddamn about Sol, or their friendship, or gymnastics. If he forgot that—Tony's abandonment, his obvious thirst for the spotlight, the way he chased one risky stunt after another—Sol would be in danger of falling in love with Tony all over again.

Too bad I've never really fallen out.

CHAPTER THREE

Seated across from Quinn in her high-end studio, Tony stretched one arm along the back of the leather couch as she finished her intro. He winked at her assistant, a seriously cute guy with a geeky hipster vibe who'd always had a bit of a crush on Tony—not that Tony would do anything about it. He valued his relationship with Quinn too much. She'd been a stalwart supporter, sympathetic yet fair, ever since Ori had set up that first post-Rio interview.

So Tony naturally delivered good content for her every time. But even good content wouldn't offset being a dick to her staff, and Tony knew himself. He'd definitely be a dick. He was always a dick to anybody he dated—whatever their gender identity or orientation—because none of them were ever the one he wanted.

But I burned that bridge long ago. Maybe it's time to move on.

Despite the cushy sofa, Tony shifted uneasily, the heat of the studio lights making sweat prickle on his nape. Moving on wouldn't be so easy if his plans played out. And if they did—

"Tony Thomas." Quinn turned to him, smiling and regal, her chin tilted at the perfect photogenic angle. "Welcome back to *Quinn's Ringside*."

Tony pushed aside his worries and grinned back at her. "Great to be here, Quinn. Thanks for having me."

"Believe me, it's my pleasure. You're one of my favorite guests, on any and all of my shows."

"How many is it up to now, Quinn?" Tony winked at her. *Always give your host a chance to hype their own stuff.*

She lifted an impeccable eyebrow. *Oh yeah. She knows what I'm doing.* "Well, since you asked…"

Quinn turned to the camera and launched into a charming spiel about her impressive information dynasty, well-rehearsed yet still fresh because the woman was a pro. Yeah, she knew how to market her brand, and the material she delivered was high quality all the way.

She turned back to Tony. "You're no slouch yourself, Tony. You've got over one million subscribers on your Xtreme Bucket List channel—"

"One point two million. But who's counting?"

Quinn laughed and crossed her legs, flashing the red soles of her Louboutin pumps. "Who indeed? Maybe by the end of this show, it'll be one point three."

Tony shook his head, shooting her one of his patented *get-real* looks. "Don't sell yourself short, Quinn. With your viewership, *XBL* may break two million easy."

"Flatterer."

"I tell it like it is."

"Then tell me this…"

Oh boy. Here it comes. Tony steeled himself for a hard question, because as fair as Quinn was, she was still a journalist who depended on readership and viewership to keep her relevant.

"Have you gotten any flack for… this?" One of the images from his shoot with ESPN's Body Issue flashed on the screen behind Quinn—the color shot of an L-sit on the parallel bars. He was naked, of course—a requirement of the Body Issue—although given the lighting, and with the camera angled from below and to the side, the muscles in his arms and legs were thrown into relief, the tattoos on his shoulder and chest shadowed, the curve of his bare flank gleaming in the light.

The studio audience *ooohed*.

Tony grinned at them. "Not that one, no." He quirked an eyebrow at Quinn. "You're not going to show the other—"

The projection changed, and the audience hooted and clapped. Tony put his hand over his eyes and pretended to be mortified, because this one—the one that had gone viral—was a full back shot, his bare ass on display as he did a swing on the pommel horse.

"I can't believe you went there, Quinn." He peeked at her from under his hand. "Isn't this a family show?"

"I think pretty much everyone who's ever opened a social media app has seen that one, Tony. And it's a beautiful shot, you've got to admit that. Perfectly embodying the beauty of the athletic form, which is what the Body Issue is all about. I do have a question, though."

"Only one?"

She leaned forward, a wicked glint in her coffee-dark eyes. "How long did it take them to get that shot without any naughty bits swinging into view?"

Tony laughed, because that *had* been a problem. "Long enough." The audience groaned. He pointed at them. "Hey. That wasn't a double entendre, folks, so minds out of the gutter." He faced Quinn once more. "Seriously though, the equipment in men's gymnastics can be, shall we say, tough on the body? We had to work to find skills that wouldn't cause undue trauma to my more delicate bits." He nodded at the screen. "For instance, I couldn't do scissors over the horse dressed like that."

Quinn winced. "No, I don't expect you could."

"And high bar as a photographic subject was right out." He waggled his eyebrows at the audience. "Centripetal force can't be fought, am I right?"

Half the audience clapped and the other half booed good-naturedly. Tony saluted them with a grin and turned back to Quinn. "Any more tough questions, ma'am?"

"Always." She leaned back in her chair and folded her hands on her knee, a sure sign she was getting ready to pounce. "*Ringside* is all about the Olympics, and you've got two medals from Rio."

Tony managed to keep his smile in place. *Because I've had four more years to practice.* "Yes, that's right." Two medals that should have belonged to somebody else, proof of how he'd failed the team. *Failed Sol.* Although in his father's eyes, the failure would always be about the medals' color, not whether Tony had stolen the opportunity to win them.

"After Rio, though, you stepped away from competition for years, at least in gymnastics. Why is that? Did you become disillusioned with the sport?"

Tony fought the deep sofa cushions and sat up, his blood firing with a familiar crusading zeal. "Absolutely not. I fell in love with men's artistic gymnastics when I was seven years old, and I love it still."

Quinn's expression turned sly. "It seems not everyone in the USA feels the same, though. At least not about the men's side. It's the women's team that gets the glory and the endorsement deals."

"Yeah, well, they deserve it. They're Olympic champions, multiple world champions. They've worked damn hard, and many have paid a price they should never have been asked to bear. I don't want to take anything away from them. But I don't think Americans have a true appreciation of the men's program. The number of colleges that field varsity NCAA men's teams has shrunk to sixteen. There are eighty-two women's programs."

"Why do you think that is?"

"The truth?"

"Of course."

Tony arranged his face into a perfectly serious expression. "It's the uniforms."

That surprised a laugh from Quinn. "The uniforms? Seriously?"

"Did you know that it's written in the rules, the official Code of Points, that men can't wear black uniform pants? Black socks?"

"No, I didn't."

"Think about it. White socks aren't sexy. Neither are those baggy short-shorts that fan out like skirts when we twist on a vault. And as for our competition shirts..." He turned to the audience again. "Would you be more likely to watch a gymnastics meet if we competed shirtless?"

He grabbed the hem of his polo and cocked an eyebrow at Quinn. She grinned and nodded, so Tony ripped off his shirt—to the wild applause of the audience—and struck a cheesy bodybuilder pose.

"To be successful in men's gymnastics, you have to be strong, so if you're talking about guns?" He flexed his biceps. "Absolutely got you covered. But compared to, say, divers? We're at a huge eye-candy disadvantage. Divers are up on their board or platform, bare-chested in those tiny tight trunks. And swimmers are always getting high-tech upgrades to their suits, and water sheets off their muscles every time they climb out of the pool. Gymnasts? We're covered in chalk and wearing stirrup pants that weren't even cool in the sixties."

Quinn tapped a perfectly manicured finger on her knee, the red polish matching both her lipstick and her Louboutins. "Interesting point. So you think the low of popularity of men's gymnastics is because of what you're wearing?"

"Well, there's our size too. Most gymnasts are on the short side." Tony stood up, gesturing for Quinn to rise too. Since she was nearly six feet tall—taller with her crown of locs and stiletto heels—she towered over him. "I'm five-eight, so I'm on the tall side for my sport, but compared to swimmers, or God forbid, basketball players?" They both sat again. "A female Olympian once likened us to cuddly little Ewoks." Tony scrunched up his face. "Dead unsexy, let's face it."

"I've heard that some scientists believe that gymnastics actually impedes growth because of the extreme stress on your bodies."

"That might be. But it's also true that the taller you are, the tougher it is to be a top-level gymnast because it's harder to propel a longer body through the exercises." He shrugged. "It's just physics. So are you a good gymnast because you're short, or are you short because you're a good gymnast? The jury's still out."

Quinn nodded. "Although you migrated away from the gym after Rio, you certainly weren't idle when it comes to competition. *Dancing With the Stars. American Ninja Warrior.* A different challenge every week on your XBL channel."

Tony shrugged again. "What can I say? I'm an adrenaline junkie, and I love the thrill of competing."

"You had surgery last year. Was that from a bad high bar dismount?"

Tony snorted, because it really was ridiculous. He'd had injuries over the course of his gymnastics career, of course. Every gymnast did. You couldn't avoid it. But that's not how he'd torn his ACL. "Nope. Bad skydiving dismount." He tapped his knee. "But it's 100 percent now."

"And you're back in the gym. Back competing now."

"Yes I am. I'm working with Andrei Nicolescu."

Her eyebrows rose. "The former Romanian champion?"

"That's the one. He's tough, but that's what I needed. He got me back into competition shape."

"Have his methods changed the way you compete? I noticed that you've got a new habit now—you close your eyes and tap your chest right before you salute the judges to begin each exercise. You didn't do that before Rio. Can you tell us about that?"

Tony didn't let his smile waver, but he wasn't about to go into details. By now, he was a master at evasion—he'd been doing it for half his life. "Gymnastics—all sports really—are as much a mental game as a physical one. Almost any athlete you talk to will tell you they've got some routine, some talisman, some habit before they compete. I don't think any of us go so far as to dance naked around a sacrificial fire at midnight, but you never know."

She spread her hands in a *there-you-have-it* gesture to the audience. "Well, whatever your method, it seems to be working, based on the results of the last qualifying events. I understand your Olympic dreams aren't over yet."

Tony cursed to himself. He didn't want the news to come out this way. It wouldn't endear him to the other men vying for an Olympic berth—especially Sol. But he should have known better: Quinn had the most extensive information network in the business.

"Don't jinx me, Quinn. Didn't we just talk about superstitions?"

"And don't be coy, Tony. Your performance at the World Cup apparatus events puts you in the top rank on high bar and still rings. That's a huge achievement for someone who's been away from the sport for so long."

Tony sighed. "Thank you, Quinn." *Might as well bite the bullet.* "I'm incredibly honored to have been invited to train with the national team at the US Olympic and Paralympic Training Center in Colorado Springs. But as for my personal Olympic dreams? That's up to the coaches and the committee, because even though gymnastics depends on the work we do as individuals, the Olympics is focused on Team USA." He looked directly into the camera. "And just like the rest of the guys, I'm all about the team."

All about the team.

Sol let his cell phone screen go black. If Tony was so team oriented, why did he run away after Rio? Sol scrubbed a hand through his hair, his belly clenching worse than after one of Xiao's killer ab workouts, because that wasn't the real question, was it?

The real question, the one that still plagued Sol every day, was *why did he run away from* me?

After Tony changed his cell phone number, Sol could have gotten it from one of the other guys on the Olympic team, but he couldn't make himself ask. Because then someone would wonder why Tony hadn't bothered to give it to the guy who was supposed to be his best friend.

Sol sighed and pushed himself off the bench. His parents always accused him of being stubborn, and they weren't wrong. His mom had chivied him like a flustered hen with a wayward chick, asking why Tony never stopped by when he was in town anymore, why Sol never talked to Tony, why Sol never *mentioned* Tony, when they'd always been so close, when Sol had followed Tony to the University of Oklahoma program, even though Tony was two years ahead of him.

"Talk to him, Solomon. He must miss you as much as you miss him. Stubbornness shouldn't get in the way of a friendship."

But Sol never tried, because even though he didn't have Tony's number, Tony had his. And it wasn't stubbornness, not entirely. Sol was so bleached with shame that he hadn't even merited a goodbye text that he just couldn't. His fear of rejection ran deep—all the way back to the knowledge that his biological parents had put him up for adoption. And although his adoptive parents—his *real* parents—were the best ever, that first hit of *not good enough to keep* still lingered.

Sol had harbored the hope that when Tony came back to campus in the fall, the two of them would have a chance to reconnect. But after losing his NCAA eligibility when he went pro, Tony hadn't even returned to OU to finish his last academic semester. Sixteen credits short of his degree and he'd bailed, just like he'd bailed on gymnastics. *Just like he bailed on me.*

Yeah, Tony was a freaking *expert* on bailing. When they'd first started training together right here at Central Gymnastics, years before Xiao had joined the coaching staff, if one of his exercises wasn't going well, Tony would stop in the middle instead of powering through. No matter how much the head coach at the time—a man who believed the louder he yelled, the more likely his gymnasts were to listen—had hollered that Tony needed to learn how to finish an exercise after an error, just as he'd have to do in competition, Tony continued to stop mid-routine after any mistake.

Tony had told Sol that if the routine wasn't perfect, the rush at the end just wasn't the same.

He'd gotten better, of course, at least when it came to finishing his routines at meets. But apparently he'd channeled all of his bailing behavior into his personal life—and then into his gymnastics career.

The more Sol thought about it, the more his stomach roiled. The guys on the national team, the guys Sol had been training with for four years, the ones he'd be training with again next week—all of them were committed to the team, to putting Team USA on the podium at the Olympics. Every one of them deserved a spot on the team, even though, with the new rules, there were only four team spots to fill, plus the two additional individual quota spots.

The fact that Tony might fill one of those spots because of his World Cup performance meant that one of the guys who'd shown up for every practice, *consistently* busting his ass, could get bumped if the selection committee decided to go with Tony.

Tony. The only veteran of the Rio Games other than Sol—and Sol had only been an alternate. Did Olympic experience outweigh loyalty? Should it? What was best for the team?

Sol's hands were shaking as he shoved his phone in his bag. *Shit. Recovery protein. I forgot.* He hoisted the bag to his shoulder and walked out of the locker room.

When he got upstairs, Xiao was the only one in the coaches' office. He was on the phone, but he glanced up at Sol, then looked pointedly at the bilious green shake sitting on his desk. *He must still be mad if he picked the kale-flavored powder. Ugh.*

Sol grimaced and mouthed *sorry*. He picked up the cup and started to back out of the office, but Xiao motioned him to sit in the chair next to the desk.

"Yes. I understand. Thank you." Xiao hung up, but didn't speak immediately. Xiao's patient wordlessness made Sol squirm worse than the loudest tirade from the former coach.

"I'm sorry."

"It is not me you should be apologizing to. You hurt no one but yourself when you ignore your body's needs." Xiao studied Sol with his dark, solemn eyes, his hands completely still on his chair arms. "This is not like you. What's the matter?"

Sol gulped down about a third of the nasty kale shake. "Apparently Tony Thomas is angling for a spot on the Olympic team."

Xiao nodded calmly. "This should not be a surprise. He's been competing at qualifying events all season."

"Never at the ones I've been at." Sol glared at his feet. Was that on purpose? Did Tony want to avoid Sol so badly—for some reason that Sol couldn't fathom—that he couldn't even stand to be in the same arena?

"Of course not. You were competing with the team, at team events. He was competing individually, at the apparatus events. But none of that should affect how you approach your own training and self-care."

Shouldn't it? "I know. I'll get my shit together by next week. Even if… Even if…" Sol slammed his empty cup into his open palm, spattering green drops onto his sweats. *Damn kale.* "He doesn't deserve to be there with the other guys who've worked so hard to make the team."

"He has worked hard also. His routines have some of the highest start values of any but the Japanese."

"Assuming he lands them," Sol muttered.

"What was that?"

Sol leaned back in the chair, the slats cutting into his shoulder blades. "You didn't join the coaching staff until after Tony left. You haven't seen how he'd bail when an exercise wasn't going exactly the way he wanted."

"I didn't see that this season."

Sol's gaze shot to Xiao's face. "You've been *following* him?"

A tiny smile curved Xiao's lips. "I follow everyone. How else can we strategize if we don't know our own talent pool as well as that of our opponents?"

"'We'?"

Xiao inclined his head. "I have been asked to assist at the USOPTC. I'll be going with you next week."

"Really?" Xiao deserved the spot. He'd been in the Chinese training program before his parents had immigrated to California when he was in his teens. He'd never pursued competitive gymnastics in the US, choosing to follow a sports training and coaching path instead. "That's... that's great. I mean it. And it'll be great to have you there."

Xiao placed his hand, palm down, on the desktop near Sol's arm, as close as he ever got to touching any of his athletes without permission. "Will your history with Mr. Thomas interfere with your preparation? Your training?"

Would it? It already had, hadn't it, since Sol had avoided doing a basic skill for three years just because it had been named for somebody who shared Tony's last name—and wasn't even related. But he couldn't lie to Xiao. That wasn't what their relationship was based on.

"I don't know. I hope not. But he could be a disruptive influence." *Hell, he's already a disruptive influence, if only in my head.*

Xiao studied Sol's face. "He won't be sharing quarters with you at the Training Center, if that's what you're worried about."

God, that hadn't even occurred to him. What kind of nightmare would that be? "But what if he makes the team? We'll all be in the same suite in the Olympic Village."

"You are anticipating trouble again. You must treat this as you've learned to treat your routines—focus only on the moment, on the skill at hand, not on the next one coming up nor on the one just past. You cannot control the choices of the selection committee, nor can you control Mr. Thomas's behavior. Railing against his mere presence hurts nobody but you, and *you*, you can control. So I suggest you begin to do so." He nodded at the empty shake cup. "Are you stable enough to drive home?"

Sol nodded. Stable enough to drive home? Sure. Stable enough to train in the same gym as Tony Thomas?

Not in a million years.

CHAPTER FOUR

Standing in front of the USOPTC, Tony grinned up at the phone atop his selfie stick.

"Good morning and welcome to the Xtreme Bucket List channel. Take a look at where I am, Xtremists!" Tony panned to show Pikes Peak and then back to the entrance of the Training Center. "That's right. I'm in C. Springs, about to head inside for the next big item on the list: training with the US national men's artistic gymnastics team." Tony hunkered down on the sidewalk, assuming a serious expression—not hard to do with his insides feeling like they were banging around his ribcage. "Now some of your XBL comments over the last few months have been skeptical that stepping away from the BASE jumping and slack lining and free climbing isn't extreme enough, that I should be living up to the promise of the channel and going for the big thrills, the big risks. All I can say is, seriously, dudes?" He made a get-real face. "Have *you* ever tried to qualify for a second Olympic team?"

He beamed at the camera, mostly to reassure himself, because walking into that gym, facing the team, facing *Sol*, was the biggest risk he'd ever taken, and he still wasn't sure he was up to the challenge. If that PR guy from the USA Gymnastics men's program hadn't kept hounding him, he'd probably still be running from it. "Here's the thing, though, folks. Privacy in the USOPTC is pretty intense, so I won't be able to share my training with you, or post videos of the other athletes. But I'll update you when I can. And who knows?" Another cheeky grin. *Sell it, Thomas. Sell it good.* "Maybe I'll have good news next month when the selection committee names the team. For now, Xtremists—" He tapped his chest over his heart. "Peace out."

Tony huffed out a breath and stood up. *Now or never.* And never wasn't an option—he'd tried that, and it hadn't worked nearly as well as he'd hoped. He faced the entrance, his heart doing a Yurchenko in his chest. *Sol's in there. I'll see him again.*

But Tony seeing Sol wasn't the issue. It was the fact that Sol would see *him*—and Tony wasn't entirely sure Sol would like what he saw.

He'd thought about texting Sol, calling Sol, hell, sending Sol a fucking telegram, about a hundred times a day since Rio. He'd thought that it would get easier, the farther Rio faded in his rearview. That as soon as he'd put enough space—both in time and actual distance—between him and that epic betrayal, he'd be able to face Sol again, beg his forgiveness in person.

He'd been wrong.

Because every time Tony imagined how the joy would die in Sol's fathomless eyes once he learned the truth? That was the deal-breaker. *I'm just not strong enough for that.*

So as time went on, as he'd thrown himself into one risky stunt after another, it got harder and harder to initiate contact. Even though he ached from missing Sol, the man who'd been the other half of his soul since they were boys, throwing himself off a cliff in a bat-winged suit was easier than making the call.

Yeah, anybody who ever said "time heals all wounds" was a fucking idiot.

By the time he'd checked in, gotten his credentials, and was headed to his dorm room, the heart-Yurchenko had turned into a double layout Tsukahara with a full twist. He'd be sharing the suite with another gymnast. Odds were slim that his roommate would be Sol, but what if it was? What would their first words to each other be? Shit, maybe Tony should have gotten over himself and called before now.

He stopped outside the suite door. *I've been cave diving in Australia. Surely I can say hello to the guy who was my best friend for half my life.*

He took a breath, keyed open the door, and stepped inside—and nearly got knocked on his ass when someone charged him and wrapped him in a bro-hug.

"Tony T!"

After getting his back pounded—and gymnasts could pack a punch—Tony pulled back enough to see that the pounder was Isaiah Daniels—Danny to his buddies—who'd been one of Tony's friendly rivals back in their NCAA competition days, and who was a regular commenter on Tony's XBL videos. He'd been on the men's national team for two years, and the USOPTC was his home base.

The muscles in Tony's neck lost a little of their tension. He'd hoped for a friendly face or two (okay, so one in particular), but he hadn't counted on an all-out enthusiastic welcome. "Danny! Great to see you, man."

Danny draped an arm across Tony's shoulders and turned him to face the rest of the guys in the room. Although gymnasts weren't tall, they were all broad across the chest, so the place felt crowded with only five guys in it. Hell, they needed another room just for Danny's biceps.

"I thought all the suites were doubles. Do, er, all of us live here?"

"Hell, no. Just you and Eddie, there." Danny pointed to a guy with a shy smile and a shock of black hair. "Eduardo Campo, Tony Thomas." He leaned closer and mock-whispered, "I've been showing Eddie your best XBL videos. That's why he looks so star-struck."

Eddie's chin jerked up. "Hey!"

Danny laughed. "Eddie's a Sooner, like you, but after your time. The guy holding up the wall is Jason Steffens." Jason raised his hand in greeting, revealing a flash of KT tape on his triceps. "And the one circling the snacks is Chad Horton."

Tony held out his hand to Chad. "We've met. You were on the World Cup circuit this year."

Chad shook briefly. "Yeah. You kicked my ass in Stuttgart."

"But you qualified at Birmingham, so no harm, no foul, right?"

Chad's smirk held the cocky arrogance Tony remembered from meeting him at competitions. "For now, anyway."

Danny towed Tony across the room and pointed to an open door. "This is you. The living room is shared—no kitchen, because apparently they don't trust us not to set the place on fire—but you've got a bedroom and bathroom all your own."

"Awesome." Tony tossed his backpack on the bed. "And for a change, we're not stuck in twin beds that are narrower than our shoulders."

Danny chuckled. "Yep. The place got refurbished a few years back. They did it up right. Decent beds. Blackout shades. The whole nine."

Tony pretended to admire the wardrobe, the desk, the chair. "So… Are these the only guys who're here already?"

"Nah. There's Rahul Laghari. He's from Stanford, but we don't hold it against him. Sometimes we can even get him to stop studying long enough to relax."

"Studying? Isn't Stanford's semester over?"

"Yeah, but he's an engineering student. They're all nuts."

"What about…" Tony's voice faded, and he cleared his throat. "What about Sol? Is he here yet?"

"Sol?" Danny peered into the common room, as if he was surprised that Sol wasn't there. "He's— Yeah, he arrived a couple of days ago. I thought he'd be here to welcome you. The two of you were tight."

Tony rubbed the back of his neck. "'Were' is the word."

Danny's cheerful, open face clouded. "Something happen between you two?"

Tony scoffed. "Other than me letting the team down in Rio?"

"Are you fucking serious? You won two medals. How is that letting the team down?"

"We didn't make the podium."

Danny glared at him. "That was hardly your fault."

"If I hadn't tried to throw that extra release into my high bar routine—"

"You caught it in the event final."

"But I flubbed in the team final. It was my fault we didn't place."

"Bullshit. There were five guys on that team. That's why it's called a *team* event."

But if the right *person had been on the team...* "Still—"

Danny squeezed Tony's biceps. *Ow.* "Dude. You need to get over that. Nobody blames you. You've been busting your ass for the last four years to build awareness and increase visibility for men's gymnastics."

That PR guy kept harping on the same thing, but Tony wasn't entirely convinced. "If you say so."

This time, Danny punched him, and not gently. "I do. And so does everybody else. You'll see. Besides, other than you and Sol, none of us has any Olympic experience. Whatever anybody else may say, the team needs you."

The team. Yeah, the team. That's why Tony was doing this, wasn't it? Why he'd given in to the PR guy's push. Why he'd sweated bullets to get back in competition shape, why he'd signed on with a bulldog coach who could get him spots in the World Cup events, why he was here. The sport. The future of men's gymnastics. *The team.*

But there was one person on the team whose opinion meant more to him than anybody else's.

"So, Danny. Can you point me to Sol's room?"

Time to brave the brewing shitstorm and take the consequences.

Sol fidgeted on his yoga mat in the corner of his bedroom. Damn it, he couldn't center himself, and he knew why. *Tony's arriving today. He'll be in the dining hall for dinner. He'll be in the gym tomorrow.*

Sol still wasn't ready, and he needed to be. The selection committee would choose the Olympic squad in less than a month. Just because Sol's record was solid over the last two seasons—he and Danny were tied for wins and placements—didn't mean he had a lock on a team berth, not with the crazy new rules in place.

If he expected to make the team, to perform his best, he needed to *focus*.

But he could swear eyes watched him from every corner—limpid dark eyes set in a face he knew better than his own, since he'd spent more time looking at Tony than he ever had in a mirror. Because when he looked in a mirror, he saw the differences between him and his parents, his Korean features a constant reminder that his bio-parents had rejected him. Looking at Tony was easier.

Easier? Hell, looking at Tony was a freaking delight. The older they'd gotten, the more Sol had looked. And looked. And *looked*.

And at one time, not too long ago, he'd wanted nothing more than to *touch* and be touched.

Did Tony know that? Is that why he ghosted me?

Sol shifted into the cobra pose, still unable to get his brain to shut down. Since Rio, he'd learned how to manage without Tony in his life. Sure, he'd done it through the magic of denial, but he'd done it. He'd found a new equilibrium—the whole team had. Tony hadn't been a part of that and throwing Tony back into the mix could upset the balance they'd worked so hard to achieve.

Is it the team I'm worried about, or myself?

At this point, Sol couldn't make the distinction. *Or maybe I just don't want to try.*

He sighed and pushed himself to his feet, but before he could assume downward dog, a soft knock sounded on the door.

Sol frowned as he stood up. The athletes' living quarters were off-limits to anyone but other athletes and USOPTC staff, and none of his teammates ever knocked that tentatively. He crossed the common room and peered through the peephole.

And fell back a step, sucking in a breath.

Tony.

Sol's middle was suddenly full of dive-bombing butterflies, and the last four years might not have existed. He closed his eyes for a moment, steadied his breathing, and just like that he found his center—and what burned in his center was anger.

Anger and betrayal and loss. Everything he'd felt when Tony had walked out of his life. Xiao would probably tell him that he should focus on the positive rather than the negative, but at the moment, Sol didn't give a shit. Anger would get him through this first meeting, so that's what he'd take.

He gritted his teeth and cracked the door open.

Tony startled, blinking as if he hadn't expected Sol be on the other side of the door. *It is my room. What did he expect?* Sol stood with his hand on the door knob, his body blocking the way into the suite, and waited, unsmiling and unspeaking.

Tony licked his lips. "Hey."

Sol didn't reply.

Tony's gaze flickered away, and he ran a hand over his hair. "Do you have a minute to talk?" Sol shrugged. "Is it, um, okay if I come in?"

Sol hesitated, but then stood aside so Tony could enter.

Tony glanced around at the common room. "Nice place."

"It's exactly the same as yours."

He flashed a grin. "I know. It still beats the OU dorms, or that cramped suite in Rio."

Heat rushed up Sol's throat, settling behind his eyes. *Seriously? His first words about Rio are about the living arrangements?* "What do you want, Tony?"

"Are you alone?"

"Rahul's here, but he's studying in his room."

"Rahul. The Stanford engineer, right? Danny said he liked to hit the books." Tony shoved his hands into the pockets of his sweats. "I don't want to disturb him. Maybe we could go out, grab a cup of coffee?"

"I don't think so."

Tony blinked again. "No? But—"

"If you didn't have anything to say to me for four years, I can't imagine what you'd have to say now."

"Aw, come on, Solly—"

Sol jerked back a step. "*Don't* call me that."

Tony held up his hands. "Sorry. Look, I know I've made mistakes—"

"You think?"

"I *know*. But we're going to be training together. We're on the same team."

"We're not."

"What?"

Sol took a deep breath through his nose. "We're not on the same team. We're training in the same gym. But you're not part of the team."

Tony's eyes narrowed. "Yet here I am."

"Not for long."

"What's that supposed to mean? Did they give you blackball power over who gets invited to the USOPTC?"

Sol ground his molars together. "Don't be an asshole. Of course not."

"Then explain yourself, because I got asked to come here, same as all of you."

"This isn't your kind of training, Tony. We spend time on basics. On consistency. On mindfulness."

"Gymnastics 101? You think I can't hack that?"

Sol met his gaze. Held it for two seconds, the same as if it were a strength move on still rings. "No."

Tony rocked back on his heels. "You... *Sol.*"

The devastation in Tony's voice almost made Sol relent. *Almost.* But *almost* didn't win medals. *Almost* didn't count when the team missed the podium again. "You're all about risk. The big skills. The flashy moves." He snorted. "The *Thomas flair*. But that's not what we're about anymore, Tony, because it *doesn't work.*"

"Business as usual doesn't work either, not when USA Gymnastics is trying to reinvent itself after its massive fuckups." Tony's eyes flashed as he took a step toward Sol. "Do you think playing it safe will pull men's gymnastics out of its downward popularity spiral? Do you think consistency will pull in the fans? No. They want to see the big scary moves. They want the adrenaline rush."

"You think we're all here because of *ratings*?"

"No. I think you're here because you love the sport, just like I do. We want the same things, Sol. We always have."

No, I don't think that's true. Because once I wanted you. But I'm not so sure anymore. "Do we?"

Tony's nostrils flared. "We do. Fans in the seats. Team USA on the podium in Tokyo. Are you saying you don't want that?"

"Of course I do. But the way we get there isn't through grandstanding and showboating. The judges won't care about those risky skills if you can't complete them. If you've come here thinking your way will get us on the medal stand, you're wrong." Sol heard Rahul's bedroom door open behind him. "The training regime here, the team dynamic—it's different from what you're used to. You don't belong here, Tony. Team USA needs athletes who don't quit."

Tony's breath hitched, as if he'd taken a punch to the gut. "Not gonna lie, I'd hoped for a different reception, but I suppose from your point of view, I don't deserve it. Good to know how you feel." He pivoted and opened the door. "But I'll prove you wrong. See you in the gym." He walked out, closing the door firmly behind him.

Sol let out a breath, his shoulders sagging.

"That was a little harsh, don't you think?" Rahul's voice was as calm and measured as always.

"I meant what I said. The guys here have been focused on *legitimate* training. Making the Olympic team *means* something to us. Hell, it means everything. Ever since Rio, Tony's been playing celebrity and jumping out of planes or off cliffs or off buildings, and now he's back as if he deserves a place on the team like Danny or Eduardo or you. Guys who've sacrificed everything for this chance. What has he sacrificed?"

Rahul tilted his head. "I can't speak for him, of course, but from the expression on his face when he left, I don't think he's a stranger to sacrifice. It may simply not be the one you expect."

Sol scowled. "Are you on his side?"

"I'm on the side of Team USA, the same as you claim we all are. But I intend to reserve judgment until we see how he behaves in the gym. You might want to do the same."

Too late for that. But Sol jerked a nod and retreated into his room. *Fuck yoga.* He pulled up Galaga Wars on his iPad and started blowing shit up.

CHAPTER FIVE

After a week of Sol's cold shoulder routine—never speaking to Tony at meals or in the gym, pointedly avoiding any apparatus Tony was working on, keeping a minimum of six guys between them during conditioning workouts—Tony was about to climb the walls without the benefit of a rope.

Because it wasn't a coincidence—or subtle.

Just now, Sol had veered off at a right angle, cutting an unnecessary detour around the vault table so he wouldn't have to walk past Tony. Danny, who had just finished his still rings exercise, sweat glistening on his brown chest, stared after him.

"What gives with you and Sol, man?"

Tony stuffed his grips in his gym bag. "Ask him."

"I'm asking you."

Tony sighed. "What can I say? History."

"Well, drop history and sign up for communications, dude, because I'm starting to get frostbite from the chill. This is our gym, not a cold war zone."

Morning training was over, and although the guys were starting to straggle out of the gym, the tension was as thick as chalk dust in the air.

Fuck this. Danny's right.

Tony sprinted across the spring floor and cut Sol off by the foam pit.

"Hold up."

Sol didn't respond, didn't even glance his way, although a few of the guys paused by the gym doorway.

"Sol." Tony lunged to block Sol's path. "I said hold. Up."

Sol stared at him, unsmiling, his dark eyes hard. "I don't have anything to say to you."

"Yeah. And that's the problem."

Sol hitched his bag further up his shoulder. "I've got a meeting with Xiao."

"No, you don't."

Sol's jaw tightened, his knuckles whitening around the strap of his bag. "You don't know—"

"Yeah, I do. Xiao's tied up with the UOC. Which you'd know if you hadn't high-tailed it out of the dining hall this morning when I sat down at the table."

"That had nothing to do with you. I was done eating."

"You left half your eggs on your plate. That's not just childish, Sol, that's irresponsible. You need that protein."

"Since when do you care about my health?"

"Oh, I don't know. Maybe since the minute you walked into Central Gymnastics fourteen years ago."

Sol's shoulders rose with a huge breath, and Tony could imagine him counting the seconds in his head—*one one thousand, two one thousand*—the way he had when he was learning his first still rings skills. "If you think bringing up the past will change my opinion—"

"The past is past, Sol. I can't change it. You can't change it. But this here?" Tony jabbed his finger toward the floor. "Now? *This* we can change." Out of the corner of his eye, Tony saw Danny whisper something to the other guys and start toward them. "You claim to be totally vested in the team dynamic."

"I am! You're a disruptive influence. You—"

"Really? Because from where I'm standing, *you're* the one doing the disrupting. You're making the guys choose sides. Team Sol or Team Tony. Don't you think we should focus on gymnastics? On being Team USA?"

Uncertainty flickered across Sol's face, but then his expression hardened again. "I am. If I'm more serious about my training than you—"

"Bullshit. I'm just as serious. We all are. But if we want to be a team, we need to *be* a team. I admit I've fucked up in the past. I let the team down in Rio."

Sol blinked. "You—"

"But I'm doing my best to fix it, all right? Have you seen me doing anything to pull focus in the gym?"

"N-no."

"Mouthing off to the coaches? Slacking off on conditioning?"

"No."

"Then don't you think it's time—" He leaned forward and lowered his voice, since Danny was only a couple of yards away. "—to give me a fucking break?"

Sol swallowed, and for an instant, Tony saw the shadow of the shy, uncertain kid who'd walked into the gym looking for something to anchor him after his life had been turned upside down by his medical condition.

But then the moment passed, and Tony could see it coming— the denial, the rejection. And he couldn't really blame Sol, because he had really, truly fucked up. He'd hurt Sol in ways Sol didn't even realize yet—*and never will, if I can manage it*—and failed the team. But this was a new team, and he wasn't about to fail them, whatever it took. As Sol drew breath to speak— probably to tell Tony to go fuck himself—Tony cut him off.

"How about this? Handstand contest."

Sol blinked again. "What?"

"A handstand contest, same as we used to have at Central. If I win, you start treating me like your teammate."

"And if I win?"

Tony straightened his shoulders and looked Sol square in the eye. "If you win, I'll withdraw from the program. Go home and let you all get down to it. Because you're right. This isn't about you or me. It's about the team. So what do you say?"

Sol glanced over Tony's shoulder, where Danny had arrived in time to hear the challenge. "A-all right."

Tony clapped his hands. "Then let's do it."

"What? You mean now?"

"No time like the present." He nodded at Danny. "Wanna be the ref for us?"

Danny's expression could best be described as *WTF, dude*? And Tony couldn't honestly say he had an answer. He'd worked his ass off to earn this second chance. But he'd wanted the chance *with Sol*. And he was about to risk it all on a bet that would be over in under three minutes.

And I thought I'd sworn off taking stupid risks.

But if his presence hurt the team, hurt the reputation of US men's gymnastics, hurt Sol *again*, then it wasn't worth it, anyway.

Danny stuck his fingers in his mouth and blew an ear-splitting whistle that nearly got lost in the cavernous gym. "Yo, guys! Come on back. There's a challenge on deck." As the rest of the team trotted over, Danny grabbed Tony's biceps and towed him into the middle of the spring floor. "Are you out of your fucking mind? You're not seriously going to quit if Sol wins, are you?"

Tony shrugged, the twinge in his shoulder from his earlier rings workout hinting that he'd probably picked the wrong time for this particular challenge. "Like I said. We need to unify the team."

"The team'll be plenty unified. Shit, we don't even know who the team *is* until the selection committee makes their decision. Why are you letting Sol push you into a corner? Why is it *your* job to make him act like a fricking adult?"

Tony glanced over at Sol, who was surrounded by the guys who'd migrated to his anti-Tony group. "He's got a point. My track record sucks. I guess I want to let him know that I'm willing to put everything on the line for the team." *Everything on the line for him.*

Because being near Sol, seeing him every day, yearning for the closeness they'd once had—*and more, if I'm honest*—yet having Sol further out of reach than when he'd just been a figure on a screen at some far-off competition? Well, apparently medical science was a bunch of horseshit, because Tony was living proof you could function—more or less—with a hole the size of a discus in your chest.

He slapped Danny on the shoulder. "No risk, no reward, right?"

Danny shook his head, but beckoned to the other guys. "Handstand face-off between Tony Thomas—" Danny glared at Tony. "Salute the judges, fool." Tony snorted, but raised his arm in the gymnasts' salute. "And Sol Ashvili." He lowered his eyebrows until Sol saluted. "First one to fall, roll out, or tap out is the loser. Ready?" Tony grinned and Sol jerked his chin down. "Hands down."

Tony bent over and placed his hands flat on the spring floor. Sol did the same next to him, and Tony couldn't resist a glance at Sol's face. He looked serious and determined—but that's how Sol always looked before an exercise.

"Aaannnd…" Danny stretched the word out like taffy. "Go!"

Tony kicked up, pointing his toes and tightening his abs, because if this was his last time in the gym with these guys, the last time with the team, the last time with Sol, he was going out with the old Thomas flair.

"Fifteen seconds," Danny said.

Tony's shoulders were already burning, his biceps quivering with the effort, because damn it, he'd just finished a four-hour workout with the coaches' evil conditioning regimen.

"Thirty seconds."

Steady. Steady. This is for all the marbles.

He and Sol used to do this all the time when they were kids. It had been fun then. Tony's breath started to saw in his lungs. *Yeah, and Sol always won.* Why hadn't he remembered that? Tony had always gotten impatient at about—

"One minute."

Yeah, at about a minute in, and started to pull stunts like lifting one hand, or pirouetting, or scissoring his legs, which always resulted in him losing his balance and flopping onto the mat while Sol, with his incredible focus and intensity, could probably have gone on for hours.

"Ninety seconds."

Tony's muscles were cramping, sweat dripping off his forehead to splat onto the floor. *I'm not going to make it. This is it. It's all over.*

He started to bring his feet down when next to him, Sol tucked his head and rolled out.

The team erupted into cheers as Tony collapsed onto the floor, chest heaving, staring up at the fluorescent lights on the ceiling so far away.

Then, Sol's face swam into his view. He held out his hand. "I guess you win."

Tony hesitated for a fraction of a second, then grabbed Sol's hand and let him pull him to his feet. For an instant, they stared at one another, hands clasped, as a couple of the guys turned handsprings around them.

Then Sol hugged him, slapping his back, and whispered, "I'm sorry."

CHAPTER SIX

It was amazing what letting go of anger could do for your morale.

A week after the handstand contest, after Sol had finally quit acting like an asshole to Tony, the team was really pulling together. The tension had drained away like bathwater. Sol hadn't realized until Tony had called him on his behavior that he'd been turning the gym which should have been the team's safe space, the place where they could support each other's challenges and successes, into something with worse tension than a qualifying event.

But now, meals were raucous and entertaining. Training was rousing and constructive. Even conditioning was—well, conditioning would never be *fun*, but the friendly rivalry and ribbing got them through the grueling sessions with a lot more cheer.

The weird thing was that the lightened atmosphere was having a real effect on everybody's progress. They were all improving. Eddie had finally mastered his second vault, and unless Sol missed his guess, he'd make the vault finals for sure. Danny hadn't missed a skill on p-bars since Monday. While part of his success was because he'd been working on the routine for weeks, Sol hadn't missed how Tony huddled with Danny after each run-through, face serious, and hands moving in that expressive way that had always mesmerized Sol from the day they'd met.

Sol couldn't deny that having that tension lifted off his shoulders made a huge difference to him too. Instead of dreading his flairs on floor and horse, he relished them now, and Xiao had noticed, but hadn't pushed when Sol had evaded his questions about why.

Yes, everyone was improving, upping their skills, gaining consistency.

Everybody except Tony.

For some reason, Tony was backsliding. He hadn't stuck a dismount on anything for three days—not that Sol was watching. Not all the time, anyway. But he'd seen Tony wobble on his still rings strength moves, bend his elbows on his p-bars handstands, miss his grip on his easiest high bar releases. It was as if the tension that had paralyzed Sol before the handstand contest had shifted onto Tony, making him heavier and heavier as the week went on. Or as though the rest of the team was absorbing all his ability and leaving him empty.

"Sol." Xiao's voice startled Sol out of his reverie.

"Sorry, Xiao. Did you say something?"

"Many times. I still hope that you will hear me, even if you won't *listen*."

Right. The trials are only days away. I need to focus. "I'll do better."

"Good." Xiao motioned Sol over to the edge of the spring floor. "I want to increase the start value of your exercise."

"Now? This close to the trials?" Something stirred in Sol's belly—was it alarm or excitement? Tony had always accused him of playing it too safe, of not competing up to his ability. But for Sol, perfect execution had always been the goal, whereas Tony had always gone for the glory of the risky move, even if he didn't land it all the time.

Xiao simply gazed at him, calm and imperturbable as always. "Yes."

"Oookay."

"You will add another tumbling pass."

"A sixth pass?" Sol gulped. "I thought you said I didn't need it."

"Not for NCAA competitions or US meets. But it will stand up better internationally."

"Do you think I have time for that?"

"Yes. After your third pass and before your flairs. A tucked front with a twist and a triple-twisting layout. Skills you have had for years, but you'll get a connection bonus."

That was true. The elements weren't difficult for him. But... "A sixth pass?"

"Visualize it now and you'll see what I mean."

Xiao was big on visualizing routines before executing them and had turned Sol into a believer. So Sol stood at the corner of the floor, outside the boundary lines, and let everything else in the gym—the creak of the p-bars, the sound of someone's feet pounding toward the vault, the shouts of the other coaches— fade away, imagining each step of his floor ex. *Xiao's right. I can do this.*

He took a deep breath, then launched into the routine.

One element at a time. Don't project. Don't look back. No negative thoughts. He nailed the first three passes, then lined up in the corner for the new one. Somewhere to his left, someone shouted, followed by a thud, and feet slapping against the mats, but he ignored it, allowing the tunnel vision that descended whenever he competed to tune out everything nonessential. *I'm pausing too long.* But this wasn't a meet. On his first time with this new pass, he could be forgiven for taking a little extra time.

Another deep breath and he took off. *Run. Full twisting tuck. Punch into the triple-twisting layout.* He didn't nail the landing, but he could fix that. *Don't look back.* He moved on to his non-acrobatic sequence, and even though Xiao hadn't mentioned it, he added spindles to the flair section, as he'd been practicing with Tony. *Xiao's gonna give me hell about that.*

So when he completed the exercise, sticking the landing on his dismount—*yes!*—he wasn't surprised to see a very solemn Xiao waiting for him next to his gym bag.

Sol grinned at him. "I know, I know. I should have run those spindles by you first, but—"

"Sol." When Xiao's voice didn't include the expected rebuke, Sol looked closer. That wasn't censure in his expression—it was regret.

Sol's hands shook as he accepted a water bottle from Xiao. "What is it? What's wrong?"

Before Xiao could answer, Danny ran over, chest heaving. "Did you see?"

"See what?" Sol glanced around wildly. Several gymnasts were huddled together near the still rings, but he didn't see any of the other coaches. "Did something happen?"

"Oh, man." Danny ran his hands through his hair, leaving streaks of chalk in his black curls. "It's Tony."

The water bottle slipped out of Sol's grip, falling to the floor and spilling water onto the mat. "What about Tony?"

"He had a bad landing on rings. He might have torn his ACL again."

Sol stared at the puddle at his feet, the fluorescent lights of the ceiling reflecting in its trembling surface. *Why is the water moving?* Then he realized—*It's not the water. It's me.*

Danny gripped Sol's shoulder. "Barry and Volya took him back to his room. He's there with the doc and the physios."

"But… But the trials are only three days away." If Tony had re-injured his knee, there's no way he could be ready for the trials or the Games. Something in the darkest corner of Sol's mind, the corner that still hadn't forgiven Tony for leaving, whispered, *Isn't this what you wanted? To clear the way for the guys who've been committed to the team all along?*

Danny's grip tightened. "The doc will figure it out. She's the best."

"I should go to him." Sol stared at the water again. "But I should mop this up. It's a safety hazard. Somebody could get hur—" His breath caught on something that might be a sob.

"I will take care of the spill," Xiao said. "It's time for you to eat something."

"But Tony—"

"Will be with the medical team and the coaching staff for a while. They will not appreciate any interruption." Xiao studied Sol, his head tilted to one side. "Perhaps Tony would prefer some time alone afterward. He may have some difficult decisions to make."

Sol nodded, his feet seemingly glued to the mat. "God, his dad. Has anyone called him?" Sol wasn't a fan of Glen Thomas —*understatement*—but Tony had dropped comments in the last week about how invested his father was in his comeback. *"He thinks I might be worth something again."*

"I'm sure the appropriate people have been notified."

Danny patted Sol's back. "Yeah. Barry'll handle it. Head coach and all." He glanced over his shoulder at the other guys who were collecting their stuff and heading toward the door. "He told us all to take a break. That goes for you too, I guess. See you later?" Sol nodded jerkily, and Danny buffeted his shoulder once, then strode away.

I never wanted him to get hurt. I never wanted that. Besides, he and Tony had started to reestablish their friendship. If Tony were to disappear again…

Sol started to shiver as sweat dried on his back and chest. He yanked a T-shirt out of his bag and pulled it over his head. "I've got to go."

Xiao finished mopping up the spill. "Yes. To eat."

"Right. Eat. I'll do that."

But first, he needed to make sure Tony was okay. If that meant lurking outside his door until the coaches and medical team left, then Sol was ready to camp out all day if necessary. *I've done it before.*

As he walked out of the gym, the floor seemed too far away for his feet to reach and black spots danced in the corners of his vision. *Okay, maybe I need to eat first. And check my levels.*

But afterward? He had a door to stake out.

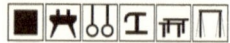

Tony lay on his bed, an arm thrown over his eyes, as the Center's doctor held a murmured conversation with the physical therapist at the door. *Maybe it's not a* physical *therapist I need right now.* Because his headspace was more cluttered than his overstuffed gym locker.

He hadn't been living under a rock since Rio, for fuck's sake. Granted, until this season he'd only seen the team compete in broadcast events, and other than Chad, he hadn't encountered any of them in the meets he'd attended this year.

Up close and personal though? *Oh my fucking God.*

Danny's p-bar skills were stronger than Tony's had ever been. Eddie's vaults had so much amplitude that Tony had jokingly checked his shoulders for wings. Although Rahul's high bar routine didn't have Tony's—*say it, asshole*—flair, it was solid. More than solid enough to stand up internationally.

Then there was Sol, and *damn*. Just *damn*. Sol on horse and floor was a thing of such beauty that Tony wanted to drop to his knees.

So he did.

And if he let everyone believe it was for another reason? All the better.

Dr. Song arranged a whole freezer full of ice packs around his knee. "I'll want to do an MRI later. How does it feel?"

Tony lowered his arm and manufactured a wince. "Could be better." *Noncommittal. That's the ticket.* Besides, it wasn't a lie—although his surgery had been successful, his knee still wasn't 100%. That's why he'd scaled back his floor and vault skills to the minimum he needed to make the team.

"Rest for a bit, then we'll take you down for the scan. Keep it iced and elevated until then." She pointed at the crutches that the PT had leaned next to Tony's bed. "And stay off it. Those are just for bathroom emergencies, understand?"

"Sure, Doc. Thanks."

Dr. Song patted his shoulder. "Try not to worry. It might be nothing more than a strain."

"Right. Got it. No worrying." Tony swallowed against the lump in his throat as she left the room. *Don't have to fake that.*

After the last days training with the other guys here at the Center, seeing their focus, their seriousness, their spirit, Tony felt about ninety years old and as deflated as his last flat tire—and delivered performances to match.

Why the hell did I fall for that PR bullshit? These guys are the ones who should be seen, who should be celebrated. I'm a fucking dinosaur. He snorted. *A fucking driven dinosaur.*

Bailing before the trials was the only sure-fire way to clear the path for everyone else, because his fingers twitched with the need to feel the rings, the high bar, the p-bars—all so different, but all of them etched in the calluses on his palms. Once he mounted the competition podium, excitement and adrenaline flooding his veins, he wouldn't—he *couldn't*—deliberately throw an exercise.

Of course, the way his practices had been going, he couldn't hit a routine with a sledgehammer. But he also couldn't take the chance that the selection committee would swallow the PR hype too. Selection committees got swayed by drama and internal politics all the time.

He grabbed a pillow and heaved it across the room. *Fuck!* When he was out there in the gym, on the apparatus, he felt whole and alive in a way he hadn't since Rio.

Of course, he'd been with Sol for the first time since Rio too. *He's gonna hate me even more now.*

Tony poked at the mound of ice packs covering his knee. Maybe Sol would accept the injury and let it go. *Maybe I can go to the Games, anyway. Watch and cheer on the team.* He clenched his fists. *I may be strong enough to step aside, but I'm not strong enough for that.*

He glanced at his cell phone. Andrei hadn't been in the gym this morning, which was why Tony had needed to stage his little farce today. He should call and give him the news. Tony winced for real. Andrei would be pissed. *Romanian* pissed, which was ten times worse than regular pissed.

Because Andrei had worked hard too. He'd followed all the regs, petitioning to get Tony a spot at the trials. He'd swallowed his pride to beg Barry for an associate coach's job at the USOPTC. He'd beaten Tony into shape on routines that could stack up in international competition—and gymnastics hadn't stood still in the last four years. The Japanese team in particular were doing some *phenomenal* skills that really pushed the limits of the sport. Tony couldn't help a grin. *If anyone's up for pushing the limits, it's me.*

But his grin faded, and he sat up, scattering ice packs over the comforter. *They don't need me, not really. Time to let the dream go.* It had really vanished in Rio—Tony just hadn't wanted to admit it until now.

He stood—on his completely uninjured knee—and grabbed his earbuds. He'd pack first, *then* call Andrei. By then, maybe he'd have figured out how to dodge the MRI. *I'll tell Dr. Song I want to see my specialist instead.* If he was lucky, she'd buy it.

He dialed up a head-banging playlist and retrieved his suitcase from the closet. As he grabbed handfuls of underwear and socks, he tried not to think about what would happen next. He could hardly pick up his XBL activities right away, not if he was supposedly recovering from a torn ACL.

Shit. What am *I going to do?*

He'd never thought beyond the Games, which was absolutely moronic. He'd just blithely assumed he'd make the team, that they'd medal, that things would proceed the way they *should* have four years ago with the sport gaining the popularity that came with success. But none of that was guaranteed, anyway. *Maybe I should have thought this through a little more.*

Sol at least had plans for after his gymnastics career. He was taking a year off, then diving back into academia. *He's going to be a freaking biochemist, for fuck's sake. The guy's a flipping genius— and not just at actual flipping.*

Tony had never had that going for him. It hadn't been a hardship for him to drop out of college before he'd gotten his degree in Health and Exercise Science. He yanked open the bottom dresser drawer, the one that always stuck, and pulled out an armful of sweatpants. *If I—*

"Jesus!"

Sol was standing in the bedroom doorway, jaw sagging. "What the *fuck*, Tony?"

Tony let the sweatpants fall out of his arms and yanked his earbuds out. Belatedly, he remembered to lift one foot off the floor as if he were favoring his knee. "Um. Hi?"

Sol stalked over to him, flip-flops *thwack*ing, and kicked the sweats out of the way. "What are you doing?"

Tony made an attempt at bravado, flashing his trademark cocky grin. "Packing."

Sol's nostrils flared, and Tony could almost hear him mentally counting *one one thousand two one thousand.* "Why?"

Tony shrugged. "Dodgy knee went out on me again."

Sol nudged the fallen sweats with a bare toe. "That didn't seem to stop you from doing the dance of the seven sweatpants. *Are* you injured?"

Tony sighed heavily. He pushed the ice packs aside and sat down where they'd lain. *Jesus! Cold!* "What if I said no?"

"Then I'd say get your ass back to the gym and work on your fucking dismounts."

Tony set his jaw and glared up at Sol. "Really? That's not the song you were singing the day I arrived. Weren't you the one who said I didn't deserve to take the place of a more *committed* athlete?"

Sol had the grace to look embarrassed. "I was angry. I didn't know then that you... That we..."

"That I what? Don't hold it in, Sol." Tony leaned back on his elbows. "God knows you never have before."

"Me?" Sol crowded closer, standing almost between Tony's spread knees, which was giving parts of Tony's anatomy the completely wrong idea. "I didn't have a *chance* to hold it in or not because *you fucking left*. Just like you're doing now."

"Mixed signals much? First it's *get out, you don't belong here*. Now it's *don't leave, because I need to be able to rag on you whenever the fuck I want*. Which is it, Sol? Go, so you can rail on me for being a quitter, or stay so you can rail on me for being undeserving?"

"That's not what I—" Sol huffed a breath. "Look, I know I gave you shit when you first arrived—"

"You think?"

"But you hadn't spoken to me for almost *four years*, Tony. You *ghosted* me. You *changed your fucking cell number*."

Tony couldn't help the little seed of satisfaction that sprouted in his swamp of guilt. "So this is all about you and me, is it?"

"I thought we were friends. We *were* friends. *Best* friends." The anger in Sol's eyes drained away to leave behind a hurt so deep Tony wanted to howl. "But you didn't even say goodbye." His voice broke on the last word.

Tony sucked in a breath. "Ah, Christ. You're killing me, Solly."

Sol clenched his eyes shut. "I asked you not to call me that. Only my best friend calls me that, and he left me behind."

Tony straightened, which made Sol back up a few steps and turn away. "You and me, Sol. We were on a different trajectory back then. You were on your way up. And you got there." Tony smiled, his pride in Sol's accomplishments bleeding through. "Three-time NCAA All-Around champ. Two-time US national All-Around champ. More event medals than I can remember"— not true: he remembered every one—"both nationally and internationally. Me? I was going the other direction fast." *Unless my father threw money around his fucking old-boy network.*

Sol whirled to face him. "That's not true. You could have come back to OU for your last year. Don't you remember? *You* were the NCAA champion before me. You could have been again."

"And then what? I didn't have your grades. I don't have your ambition. I don't have your *brains*."

"Bullshit. You've got ambition. You've got drive." A smile glimmered on Sol's full lips. "You've got one point two million YouTube followers."

Tony jabbed a finger toward Sol. "Exactly. But I wouldn't have them if I'd gone back to school and finished my mediocre degree with my mediocre grades and embarked on my mediocre life."

Sol blinked. "Mediocre? You couldn't be mediocre if you tried."

Tony snorted. "What happened in Rio suggests otherwise."

Sol's eyes widened. "Is *that* what this is about? Injured pride? People not appreciating the notorious Thomas flair?"

"Are you kidding? Pride has nothing to do with it."

Sol crossed his arms. "Right. Prove it then. Stay and compete at the trials."

CHAPTER SEVEN

Sol surprised himself. He was doing a pretty convincing impression of righteous indignation when he wanted nothing more than to fall on his knees and beg Tony not to go. *Okay, I wouldn't mind doing other things on my knees, but this is so not the right time to think about that.*

He glared at Tony. "Come on. I dare you."

Tony tilted his chin and looked up at Sol with half-lidded eyes. "Oh, you did *not* go there."

"Yes, I did." He leaned down, the better to look straight into Tony's face. "I double-*dog* dare you."

Tony threw back his head and laughed. "We're not still kids diving into the foam pit, Sol."

"Really? Because you're acting like a six-year-old who's refusing to eat his vegetables. Come on, Tony. You can't seriously think I want you to leave now." Something fluttered in Sol's belly. Was that guilt? Anxiety? Pure unadulterated terror? "Do you?"

Tony propped his elbows on his knees and threaded his fingers through his hair, the platinum-tipped curls contrasting with his dark skin in a *very* distracting manner. "I don't know. But what you said about the guys here working so hard for their chance…" He looked up, his dark eyes bleak. "What right do I have to take that from them?"

Sol sat on the corner of the bed, leaving a safe distance between the two of them. "But you've been working too. With Andrei. With the rest of the team."

Tony snorted. "And look how well that's gone. I haven't landed a dismount in a week."

"I think you're psyching yourself out."

"Is that so?" He grinned crookedly. "Abandoned biochem for psychology, have you?"

"I know you're not a fan of our mindfulness sessions, but they really do work, if you give them a chance. To paraphrase Yogi Berra, gymnastics is 90% mental and the other half is physical."

Tony chuckled. "Stick to biochem. Math is clearly not your strong suit."

"I was *paraphrasing*. That math is all Yogi's. Personally, I'm an ace at precise mental computation after years of calculating my carbs." Sol traced the weird paisley pattern in the comforter. "The only thing you're getting now is a chance to compete. To show what you can do at the trials, the same as the rest of us. If you don't deliver..." Sol shrugged. "The coaches aren't stupid. They want us to win maybe more than we want to win ourselves."

"I doubt that *very* seriously," Tony said dryly.

"You know what I mean. US gymnastics is at a crossroads." For some reason, that made Tony flinch, but Sol carried on. "The men may not have the scandal hanging over us that the women's team does, but we don't have their star power either. We need the best possible team if we expect to turn our program around."

Tony met Sol's eyes, and his expression was almost painfully hopeful. "You really think the best possible team includes me?"

"It could. *If* you get your head out of your ass and back in the game."

Tony barked a laugh. "Tell me how you *really* feel."

Sol turned sideways so he could face Tony. "I really feel that the best competitions, the best meets, the best *results*, are when everyone performs at the top of their ability. When we don't depend on mistakes from other teams or other gymnasts to put us on the podium."

"You always were an idealist. I see that hasn't changed."

"Do you disagree?" Sol leaned forward, reminding himself that inhaling Tony's scent wasn't appropriate in this conversation, especially when Tony was bare-chested and Sol was wearing nothing but a T-shirt and his compression shorts. *Where's an industrial-strength jock strap when I need one?* "Do I need to remind you that *you* were the one who said that? To me? At our very first competition when I was just a level four and you were a level six?"

"Are you really going to base your whole sports philosophy on the words of a twelve-year-old? I was probably talking about a World of Warcraft arena match."

Sol frowned. "For God's sake, what's wrong with you?"

Tony raised his eyebrows. "Other than a bum knee?"

"There's nothing wrong with your knee." Tony opened his mouth to respond, but Sol held up his hand to stop the stupid words. *Time for a little tough love.* "Nothing more is wrong with it *today*. You've jumped out of airplanes and off cliffs as well as off every piece of apparatus in the gym so you can tell the difference. You know what I think?"

Tony pressed his lips together, but even that didn't hide their fullness. "I'm sure you're about to let me know."

I think I know your triggers, Tony, and here's Number One. "I think you're so afraid of losing, that you refuse to even *try*."

Tony jumped up and whirled to face Sol. As Sol had expected, he didn't favor his knee at all. *You are so busted.* He jabbed a finger toward Sol's face. "I am *not* afraid of losing."

"Yet you're taking yourself out of the running before the competition even starts. With a totally bogus injury. 'Oh, poor me. I could have been a contender, but my knee, my knee.'"

Tony scowled and crossed his arms. "Shut up."

"Why, Tony? Isn't that what's happening? You're giving yourself an excuse? A legitimate reason to give up?"

"I told you." Tony's eyes flared with anger, something Sol didn't know was actually possible. "I'm not afraid of losing at the trials."

"No?" Sol made a point of looking around the room, at the half-filled suitcase, at the clothes scattered on the carpet. "Because it sure looks like you're running scared. For no reason."

"Fuck you, Sol."

Ah ha. We've fallen back on generic insults. We must be getting close to the real reason. "That's not an answer, Tony. That's avoidance."

"Look, I'm *not* afraid of losing the trials, okay?" Tony turned and smacked the flat of his hand against the wall. His shoulders sagged, and his head drooped as though it were too heavy to hold up. "I'm afraid of winning." His voice was so soft that Sol wasn't entirely sure he'd heard it correctly.

He moved to Tony's side. Carefully. Slowly. As if Tony were a wild animal who might attack—or bolt—at the first sign of a threat. "Afraid of winning? But that doesn't make any sense. You love to win. You *live* to win."

Tony's laugh was strangled. "Yeah. Lot of good that did in Rio. What an epic failure."

"Failure? Are you kidding? You won two medals. That's two more than anyone else on the team managed. Two more than almost everybody else on the planet."

Tony whirled, shame distorting his face. "Exactly. The only thing I managed was for *myself*. I didn't help the team. I didn't help the other guys. And I certainly didn't help *you*. If I was such a hotshot *winner*, the team would have stood on the podium that day."

"Tony." Sol ached to touch him, to hold him. "You can't seriously blame *yourself* for the team not medaling in Rio."

"No?" Tony's lip lifted in a sneer. "Who else should I blame?"

"Oh, I don't know." Sol moved closer, crowding Tony until his shoulder blades hit the wall. "Maybe the Japanese team with their incredible execution and sky-high difficulty scores? Maybe the Russian team, who I'm convinced are all part avian or they couldn't fly that high? Or maybe the other four guys on the team, none of whom matched your scores?"

Tony turned away, a scowl replacing his sneer. "That's not the point. I could have done more."

"How? That's the thing about the team competition, Tony. Gymnastics isn't like soccer or basketball or, God forbid, football. You can't, I don't know, pass Danny your biceps so he can hold his Maltese cross longer."

A smile softened Tony's mouth. "Danny doesn't need anybody's biceps but his own. They're already bigger than a small country."

"My *point* is that we call it a team competition, but we're still performing individually. There's no *defense*, no *assists* in gymnastics." Sol gripped Tony's shoulder. "We can cheer for one another, encourage one another, *support* one another. But when it comes down to it, all of us are alone up there on the apparatus. You did your job in Rio, Tony."

"You don't understand." Tony's muscles were like granite under Sol's hand, his voice rough. "It shouldn't have been me at all, Solly. It was supposed to be you."

Sol blinked, relaxing his grip enough that Tony ducked away from him. "What are you talking about?"

"The coaches wanted you after John was injured. But my fucking *father* found out and waved his donation money at them. If you'd been on the team in Rio—"

"Stop. Just stop, okay?" Sol edged closer to Tony until they were practically wedged into the corner. "The coaches aren't idiots and they're not toadies. Any payola from your dad couldn't offset the funds they'd get from a winning team."

"But—"

"They might have listened to him out of respect—he's the parent of one of their gymnasts—but they made the choices they believed were best for the team."

Tony wouldn't meet Sol's eyes. "Yeah, right."

"First, there's no way I could have filled John's place on the team, especially back then—and I told you so that night in Rio." Sol grabbed both Tony's shoulders this time and gave him a tiny shake. "You need to stop letting your dad's voice be the loudest one in your head."

"Not only in my head," Tony muttered.

"And second, you scoff at my math skills, but I was keeping track of the scores. Without all the other guys upping their combined execution and difficulty by at least three-tenths, you'd have had to be better than perfect to pull the team onto the podium." Sol raised one eyebrow and allowed a little snark to creep into his tone. "You're good, pal, but nobody's *that* good."

Tony laughed, and from the surprise on his face, he hadn't expected to. His mouth relaxed into a grin and suddenly Sol realized they were only inches apart, within kissing distance, the place he'd dreamed of for so long. Continued to dream of, even after Tony disappeared, proving how little Sol meant to him. *Only it turns out I was wrong about that.*

So he did what he'd been wanting to do since he was thirteen and realized he was gay and in love with his best friend.

He leaned forward and finally—*finally*—kissed Tony Thomas.

CHAPTER EIGHT

Tony couldn't move. He couldn't breathe. He couldn't think.

Strike that. He could definitely think because his entire brain was lit up like Times Square, all the marquees flashing a single message: *Sol Ashvili is kissing me.*

Tony was so stunned he almost forgot to kiss Sol back, and after more than four years of cowardice and regret, that would never do. But as he was angling his chin to get better traction against Sol's sinfully plush lips, Sol broke away and backed up.

"Sorry. I'm sorry. I didn't mean—"

"Oh, hell no. Come back here." Tony grabbed Sol's wrist and reeled him in. He laced his hands behind Sol's neck. "Bailing on our first kiss is worse than me faking a knee injury."

As he hoped, Sol gave him a *cut-the-bullshit* look. "They're hardly in the same class."

"You're right." Tony grinned, allowing himself to toy with Sol's hair. It was just as silky as it looked, as silky as Tony had always dreamed. "The kiss is way more important."

Sol snorted, a ridiculously adorable sound. "You—"

Tony stopped Sol's mouth with his own, because really, he couldn't possibly have anything to say that was more important than the feel of their lips touching, pressing, tasting. *God, it's better than I imagined.* And Tony had imagined a lot.

He'd been the opposite of celibate over the last four years as he'd tried to purge his guilt from his system, knowing he'd never be worthy of Sol. But Sol had always been there in the back of his mind, the gold standard against whom every hookup had been judged and found wanting.

Near the end, when the XBL stunts were becoming more and more risky just because he'd become numb to everything except the hole in his heart where Sol used to be, he finally realized he needed to make a change before he fucked up something worse than his ACL, something that wouldn't be reparable.

Like my heart.

So he'd given in to that PR guy—and how ridiculous was it that Tony couldn't even remember his name? Ori had dealt with him mostly, passing the essentials on to Tony and later Andrei, but considering he was serving up Tony's heart's desire on a platter, you'd think he'd be a little more memorable. Or maybe the memories had gotten lost in the anticipation, the sweat, and the dread.

Because getting back into competition shape had been cake compared to the courage he'd had to dredge up from the bottom of his soul to face Sol again. He'd barely let himself dream that Sol might speak to him, that Sol might forgive him, that Sol might *want* him. *I may not deserve him, but fuck if I'm gonna let that stop me.*

He cupped Sol's face, tilting his chin up with both thumbs until he could tease Sol's lips with his tongue. Sol ran his hands over Tony's pecs—*gah!*—and opened, letting Tony in, meeting Tony breath for breath, stroke for stroke, moan for moan.

Then Sol pulled back, gasping. "We can't—"

Tony let go. *Too much. I shouldn't have assumed he'd want me as badly as I want him.* "Right. Sorry. I'll just, um, clean up, I guess."

Sol gripped Tony's biceps. "I was going to say, we can't do this without locking the door."

Tony blinked. "The door?"

"Yes, the door. If I could walk in, so could anybody else. Your roommate. The doctor. Barry."

"Oh, God. Barry. I should let him know that I'm feeling *much* better now." Tony leered at Sol, who just laughed and sauntered over to the door to flick the lock.

"You can tell him later. Right now, you have something else to do."

Tony widened his eyes in mock innocence. "I do?"

"Yes." Sol pointed imperiously at the pile of ice packs. "If you think I'm getting in an ice-chilled bed, you can think again." He matched Tony's leer. "And the only wet spots are gonna be the ones we make when we come."

Tony nearly choked on his own spit, then gathered all the ice packs and chucked them on the floor. They landed on his discarded sweatpants, but so the fuck what? They'd dry. Besides, he didn't plan on wearing them—or anything else—for at least the next hour.

When he turned around, Sol had shed his shorts and T-shirt and was standing there in nothing but skin. Miles and miles of lovely golden skin, because yes, gymnasts manscaped. Chest hair under their skintight competition shirts was *not* comfortable—or attractive. "Nnngh."

"What?" Sol looked down at himself. "You've seen my body before. We've been in the same shower room hundreds of times."

"Yeah, but I couldn't spend too much time looking at you or, you know..." He jerked a thumb toward his dick, which was reaching for Sol from behind his shorts, its agenda clearly the same as Tony's. "*Issues* would have come up."

"Issues, huh?" Sol moved closer and tucked his thumbs under Tony's waistband, then let it go with a snap. "Is that what you call it?"

Tony licked his lips. "What I called it then was torture. What I call it now?" He shucked his shorts down and kicked them aside, letting his cock spring free. "Is about fucking time."

"Tony." Sol's voice was choked with some kind of emotion. Tony didn't want to waste any time analyzing it now because he had shit to do. Namely getting them both horizontal on the bed.

Tony stepped closer, running his hands over Sol's pecs and down his ribs, letting his thumbs map Sol's six-pack. Then he dropped to his knees.

"Tony! Your knee!"

Tony grinned up into Sol's worried face, although he was definitely distracted by Sol's dick—long, cut, perfect—bouncing next to his cheek. "My knee is fine. Didn't you hear? I faked that injury."

"I don't care." Sol grabbed Tony's arms and hauled him to his feet. "I'm taking no chances." He laid both palms on Tony's chest and backed him up. "Now sit down before you fall over."

"Hey." Tony circled Sol's wrists, stroking the crease at the base of his palm with his thumbs. "We're gymnasts. We don't *fall*." He grabbed Sol around the waist and toppled over, twisting so they landed on their sides, facing one another. "We stick the dismount."

Sol's dark eyes gleamed with amusement. "Is this one in the Code of Points?"

Tony ran his finger along Sol's lower lip. "If it's not, it should be."

"Uh huh. With a 4.6 difficulty value."

"4.6? No way. It's a 6.1 at least. It's not *everyone* who can master it, you know." Tony followed his finger with his tongue. "It's very advanced."

"Of course." Sol's voice was breathless. "What's it called?"

"The Thomas-Ashvili, of course." Tony rolled so Sol was under him. "Haven't you always wanted a skill named after you?"

Sol's chuckle vibrated Tony's bones. "Maybe. Although I'd hoped it would be something that could be done in public and in mixed company."

"Bah." Tony nuzzled Sol's neck at the point where it met his shoulder. "At the moment, I don't care if we're ever in public again." He trailed kisses along Sol's clavicle. "Right now, there's nowhere else I'd rather be."

Sol ran his hands down Tony's back, his calluses rough against Tony's skin. *Gymnast's hands.* They'd never be smooth or soft, but God *damn* they were magic. "I'm so glad you came back, Tony."

Tony's breath caught as Sol's hands reached his ass. "Fuck, I've missed you." He lifted his head to gaze into Sol's eyes. "You have no idea."

Sol's lips quirked up, but his eyes remained somber. "Oh, I do. Trust me. I do."

■ 🎪 ᛯᛯ 工 ᚦᚦ ⬚

Tony's skin. Tony's heat. Tony's mouth. *God, Tony's mouth.* Sol's breath was trapped somewhere below his throat—the exact spot Tony was treating to searing kisses.

"You know," Tony said, tracing Sol's collarbone with a feathery touch, then following it with his tongue, "now that I think of it, it's *your* fault that I haven't been hitting my routines."

"My fault?" Sol croaked, because Tony had traveled south to his nipple. "Wha—?"

"How am I supposed to concentrate when I'm distracted by your ass in those fucking compression shorts?"

A chuckle escaped the gridlock in Sol's chest. "For that matter, I'm surprised I didn't run headfirst into the vault table the first time you took your shirt off and I saw your chest with all the ink."

Tony lifted his chin and grinned. "You like it?"

"Mmmhmmm. Although—" Lightning zinged straight to Sol's balls and his back arched because Tony's teeth closed on his nipple. "Shit!"

"Is that a good shit or a bad shit?" Tony mumbled against Sol's skin.

"It's a *shit* shit, because if you do that, I'm gonna come before… before…"

Tony slid lower, his grin absolutely wicked. "Before you can count to *one one thousand*?"

"I'm going to murder you, Tony Thomas." Sol grabbed a handful of Tony's tight curls and yanked. "Get back up here."

Tony winced. "Ow. But I was just getting to the good parts."

"Well, I want *your* good parts too, and we don't have a lot of time before somebody comes looking for you. You really want to get your knee scanned with a hard-on?"

Tony mock-shuddered. "God, no." He crawled back up Sol's body. "The Thomas flair would never survive an MRI-as-sex-toy rumor." Tony's expression softened as he gazed down at Sol. "This timing sucks. I don't want our first time to be rushed, Solly. I don't want it to be a disappointment for you."

Sol stroked Tony's cheek. "It won't be. It couldn't be." He rolled them onto their sides, shivering as his cock slid against Tony's. "I think—" He sucked in a breath when Tony wrapped one big hand around them both.

"If you can think—" Tony nipped the curve of Sol's shoulder. "—then I'm not doing this right."

Sol thrust into Tony's hand, then added his own for more pressure, more friction, and was rewarded with Tony's moan.

"God, Solly, your hands." Tony clenched his eyes shut. "I've waited so long to feel your hands on me."

Sol couldn't have spoken even if he had any words. He tucked his head in the hollow of Tony's throat and looked down, breath hitching. *Tony's hand. My hand. Tony's cock. My cock. Tony and me. Together.*

Lightning built again, sizzling down Sol's spine. "*Unnngh! Tony!*" Sol came, splattering his belly, Tony's abs, both their hands.

"I've got you. I've got you. I've—*gah!*" Tony added to the mess between them, and Sol held onto Tony as he shuddered through the intimate release.

After a moment, Tony chuckled. "The Thomas-Ashvili gets more interesting all the time."

Sol laughed too. "I don't know. I think we need to put in the numbers. It still needs some work."

Tony's back muscles tensed and he pulled away. *Uh oh. What's coming now?* "But here's the thing."

Sol lost all desire to laugh and his belly bottomed out. "One and done? Is that what you're about to tell me?"

Tony's eyes widened. "What? God, no. Trust me, the Thomas-Ashvili will be getting lots of practice. But, um, only privately."

Sol's heart came back online. "I should hope so."

"No, I mean we need to keep this on the down-low. At least for now."

Sol searched Tony's face. "Is it because of your dad? I know he never liked me much."

"Yeah, well, he never liked me much either." Tony took a deep breath. "I'm not ashamed of this. Of us. I'd like to shout it on every YouTube channel and sports broadcast from here to Tierra del Fuego. But it's like you and your diabetes—we don't want our success—"

"Or failure?"

"Our *success* to be overshadowed by our relationship. Just like we don't want any failure to be blamed on it. The focus should be on the Games. On the team. Agreed?"

"Agreed. But, Tony." Sol gripped the back of Tony's neck. "Are you listening to me? You need to leave Rio behind you. No holding back. To be on the team, you need to *be* on the team."

"I'm not on the team yet."

"You will be." Sol traced Tony's cheekbone.

Tony turned his head to kiss Sol's hand. "So you've given up psychology and math to join the psychic hotline?"

"Don't be a jerk. It's not your job to carry the team. The team can help you too."

"I should tell you something else." His dark eyes were somber. "It wasn't my idea to return to competition. This PR guy—"

"I know the one you mean."

"What the fuck is his name?"

"I can never remember it. Let me guess." Sol nibbled on Tony's shoulder. "He was after the Thomas flair."

"Pretty much, yeah." Tony peered into Sol's eyes. "Do you resent that?"

Sol shook his head. "Trust me, US men's gymnastics needs the all the positive hype it can get. The Chinese and Japanese are like rock stars in their countries. Here? I think curling gets a wider audience."

"But…" Tony's gaze drifted downward, and he traced a circle over Sol's heart. "… I didn't start training again just to qualify for the Olympics."

"Of course not. It's every man's dream to spend countless hours in the gym every week, covered in sweat and chalk dust, busting his ass to master skills that nobody in their right mind would expect the human body to accomplish."

"Smart ass." Tony kissed him again. "I started training again so I could qualify for *you*."

Sol's heart did a double layout. "You didn't have to go to so much trouble. All you had to do was come back. All you had to do was this." Sol pushed himself up onto one arm—then had to catch himself when his head swam. "Whoa."

"Solly?" Tony scooted up onto his butt and grabbed Sol's shoulders. "What's the matter?"

"Just a little lightheaded." Sol gave a shaky laugh. "Don't let it swell your ego, though. It's not you—or not entirely. I was supposed to eat before, but I didn't want to miss the chance to talk to you alone."

"What the fuck?" Tony's expression hardened. "Where's your glucometer? Your insulin pen? We need to get you down to the dining hall *stat*. Or do you have snacks in your room? We have to—"

"Calm down, Tony. It's not that dire."

Tony ran his hands through his hair, trailing jizz through his curls like X-rated hair gel. "Jesus, Sol, you can't take risks with your health like this."

Sol raised an eyebrow. "Says the man who jumps off cliffs and out of airplanes."

"That's different. I can take chances with myself. But you?" Tony grabbed a T-shirt off the floor and started mopping semen off Sol's belly. "I don't take chances with you."

There went that heart double layout again. "I guess you do care."

Tony tossed the shirt aside and sat on the edge of the bed. He laced his rather sticky fingers with Sol's equally gummy ones. "You can doubt anything else. Doubt the world is round. Doubt that the Japanese team will invent six new elements by Friday. Doubt Rahul will pass quantum mechanics. But never doubt that. That—" He leaned in and pressed a soft kiss on Sol's lips. "—you can take straight to the bank."

CHAPTER NINE

The neoprene sleeve on his knee had bugged the hell out of Tony on the plane from Colorado Springs to St. Louis, and he'd picked at it through his pants until Sol elbowed him in the ribs. The damn thing had been a semi-permanent fixture for the last three days. Yeah, nobody had been more surprised than him when it turned out his injury wasn't completely faked after all. Turns out all the reps Andrei insisted on came at a cost—although catching Sol in equipment storage and dropping to his knees to swallow him down hadn't helped. *Worth it, though, for the look on Solly's face when he came.* And since that had been the only time they'd managed to get their hands on one another's skin since the inauguration of the Thomas-Ashvili? Doubly worth it.

He'd worn it during their training sessions out on the floor at the Enterprise Center, but fuck it. *I'm not wearing it for the trials.* He sat on the bench in front of his locker and stripped it off.

"Hey, Tony." Danny strolled over and straddled the bench next to him as Tony was stepping into his warmup pants. "I saw Quinn Urquhart in the stands during podium training. You got another interview with her after the trials?"

Tony forced himself to grin at Danny, even though his mind was apparently circling somewhere over the Mississippi, because it certainly wasn't in his head. "Nah. I just told her we always practice shirtless. Her fans insisted on evidence."

Danny flexed his biceps, which made it look like he was smuggling bowling balls under his warm-up jacket. "Tell her we'll be happy to put on a show anytime."

Rahul scowled at Danny from his spot on the other side of Tony. "Think about showboating later. It's the Olympic Trials. You should be concentrating on your routines."

Danny laughed as he rose to his feet. "Not all of us prepare by reciting the periodic table of elements."

"I'm an engineer," Rahul muttered. "Not a chemist."

"Whatever. Get ready. March-in is in five."

March-in is in five. Five minutes before Tony was on the competition floor with his team for the first time since Rio. He'd gotten used to the adrenaline buzz from his XBL stunts over the last few years, but this was different. *Is this what it's like to be afraid?* He'd never been afraid in a gym before—not for himself, anyway. He'd nearly pissed himself the first time Sol tried a Gaylord II on the high bar when he was a sophomore in high school, but that was different. That was *Sol.*

He fumbled with the zipper on his gym bag and pulled out his water bottle to ease his dry mouth. *Just take it one exercise at a time. One skill at a time.* That's what Xiao told them in their mindfulness sessions. But Tony couldn't help projecting, indulging in a what-if. Six routines today and six the day after tomorrow. Those were his only chances—his *last* chances—to prove to Sol that he was all in.

What if I can't do it? He hadn't stuck a dismount in practice all week despite the knee support, and in podium training, he'd missed the bar after his easiest release move.

What the fuck is wrong with me? I don't get nervous. But that's what it felt like—a low-level vibration under his skin, keeping him from concentrating.

He jerked when Rahul slammed his locker and stalked after Danny. The rest of the guys had already wandered off to line up for the march-in, leaving Tony alone in the dressing room, staring at his locker as if he could open it up and pull out some fucking courage.

"Hey." Sol sat next to him, facing the other direction. "You okay?"

"Beats the hell out of me." Tony closed the locker with a soft *click*. "I thought you'd be out with the guys by now."

"Nope. Had to check my levels."

Tony whipped around to stare at Sol. "Are you crashing? Do you need to—"

Sol laughed. "Calm down. I'm fine. The schedule is just weird, so I had to adjust my meal timing today. It's all good."

Tony heaved a huge breath. "Thank God."

"Why are you still in here? Based on how you've been behaving in the gym for the last week, I'd have expected you to be out there already, pumping Eddie up and calming Jason down. Joking with Danny, the two of you trying to get Rahul to smile."

Tony shrugged. "I don't know. I just feel… off."

"Tony." Sol inched closer, so their hips touched, a comforting warmth even through uniforms and warm-up suits. "You've got this."

"Do I?" Tony huffed a laugh. "Whatever *this* is, I seem to have misplaced it somewhere over the last week."

"Nah." Sol nudged Tony's shoulder with his own. "You've just got stage fright."

"Stage fright?" Tony turned an outraged glare on Sol. "You're talking to the guy who bared his ass for all the world to see. The guy who jumped off a cliff in Acapulco wearing a helmet cam. The guy who—"

"Who hasn't faced judges at the Olympic trials for nearly four years?"

Tony deflated like a pricked balloon. "Is that what it is, Solly? Am I really that terrified of judgment? I put myself out there on the XBL channel all the time, and trust me, the commenters can be brutal."

"Yes, but none of them control your destiny."

Tony stared down at his feet. "And the judges do?" *Let's not even think about my father.*

"No." Sol leaned into him, shoulder to shoulder, arm to arm, hip to hip. "Your destiny is your own. Whatever the judges say, their marks aren't going to be the only things the selection committee considers. Yeah, they're a component, but the committee wants to build the best possible team." Sol glanced around at the empty room and then raised one finger to angle Tony's chin for a kiss. "So go out there and show them the fabulous Thomas flair."

Sol's kiss sent a different kind of zing along Tony's skin, one that went a long way toward calming his earlier nerves, like that physics phenomenon, whatever it was called, when two frequencies canceled each other out.

He stood up, the bench the only thing that kept him from grabbing Sol in an NSFW hug. *I'll have to ask Rahul about that wavelength thing later.* Although he'd probably say he was an engineer, not a physicist.

Sol smiled crookedly at him. "Ready?"

"Born ready, baby."

"Then let's do this."

They joined the other guys in the tunnel leading to the arena. The two of them were on different rotations—Tony starting on vault and Sol on pommel horse—so they lined up with their appropriate groups. The instant they marched out onto the floor, the familiarity of it all settled around Tony like a well-worn bathrobe, further soothing his nerves. The applause of the crowd as the guys walked to their apparatus. The smell of chalk. The chill of the air conditioning. The lights, the long table with all the commentators, the judges in their regulation navy blazers, stone-faced at their stations.

This I know. This I can do.

But the first time he stepped up on the podium for his run at the vault table, he almost missed the green light from the D1 judge because this was *it*. Regardless of how or why he'd gotten here, he was back. Back in the place where he belonged. He almost choked up, which would be the worst possible thing to do when he was about to sprint for twenty-five meters and then fling himself into the air.

God, the vault table looks farther away than the moon. But he took a steadying breath, remembered Sol's kiss, and with a little hop, launched himself down the runway. *Rebound off the springboard. Half-twist onto the table. Push off into a double-twisting layout.*

Then the mat was there, under his feet, almost before he'd registered being in the air. It surprised him so much that he took a hop. *Hell. There goes at least a tenth.* But he raised his arms in his final salute and then jogged off the podium.

Andrei confronted him at the stairs, his habitual scowl deeper than usual. He was still pissed that Barry had pulled rank and overrode him on Tony's training intensity since the fake-injury-that-was-not-actually-fake. "You crossed your feet. We will work on that."

Tony raised an eyebrow. "My knee feels fine, thanks." Then the other guys in the rotation approached, slapping his hand in congratulations. Tony walked over to the chair where he'd parked his gym bag and took a swig from his water bottle. As he waited for his score, he checked the leader board. As he watched, Danny was knocked down a notch and Sol took his place at the top. *I knew he could do it.* Sol was a magician on horse, his arms just a little longer, and not nearly as beefy as Tony or Danny. His flexibility and fluidity were the best in the world.

Tony's score flashed up. *Not bad.* The difficulty on his double-twisting layout Tsukahara was lower than the vaults some of the other guys were doing, but his execution score was... decent. Andrei was right—there was room for improvement, but vault wasn't his event, so he'd take it. Hell, yeah, he'd take it. And with Solly up there on the top, this was shaping up to be a good day.

A very good day indeed.

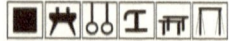

Today was a terrible day.

Sol huddled in his chair next to the pommel horse. Yeah, he'd come out in the lead after the preliminary rounds. Danny and Rahul were right behind him, as expected. Tony, however, was in sixth, trailing Eddie by less than a tenth. In fact, only two tenths separated second through seventh places, even though Sol's lead had grown to over two points after the first five rotations today.

I wish I knew what the coaches were thinking. But the men's program director and the high-performance director could flash their poker faces in a high stakes game in Vegas and walk away with the pot.

He downed a couple of swallows of water—not too much. It wouldn't do to have his stomach sloshing around on the horse. A cheer went up from over near the p-bars. The stands were a lot fuller today than they'd been on the first day of the trials, and Sol knew why.

Tony.

Well, indirectly it was Tony's doing. After Quinn posted that footage of podium training, with all the guys shirtless, ticket sales had picked way up. Six weeks ago, Sol would have copped an attitude about Tony drawing attention away from the team for his own benefit. Except Tony wasn't the only one benefitting. Danny had his own entourage. Sol did too, for some peculiar reason. He glanced into the stands, amazed at all the fans flashing signs of encouragement with his name on them.

He'd had no chance to see Tony alone since they'd checked into their St. Louis hotel. Sol was rooming with Rahul, and Tony was in with Danny. Andrei had kept Tony apart from the other guys at practice yesterday, and Sol had wanted to kick the damn man in the balls. Even though Barry had imposed limits on Tony's training, Andrei pushed it right to the edge. At the end of practice, Tony was exhausted—the day before a major competition was *not* the time to put in the high numbers, especially for Tony. Repetition was not his friend—he got bored, and then he got sloppy, and then he made mistakes and hurt himself. *He'd do better with Xiao.*

Who was frowning at Sol. *Oops.* Sol stood up. He still had two more guys on horse before him. He closed his eyes and visualized his routine. He'd seen video of himself doing this— his arms flapping at his sides like he was doing a penguin impression. So what if it looked stupid? It worked.

After two mental run-throughs, he opened his eyes and shouted encouragement to the man who was just mounting the horse—Brandon, one of Sol's fellow Sooners. He winced when Brandon faltered, his foot brushing the horse as he struggled into his dismount handstand. The judges didn't even count it as a dismount because his momentum had stopped, so he had to repeat it.

"Come on, Brandon," Sol called. "Aggressive!"

Brandon managed to fly up to his handstand this time, but his expression when he saluted the judges was grim. Sol met him at the foot of the stairs and slapped his hand anyway, then climbed the stairs to the podium as another cheer erupted from near the p-bars. But Sol didn't let it distract him. Not now. Once his feet hit the mat, his tunnel vision set in.

He chalked up his hands and the pommels, running through the routine in his head again while he waited for the judges to post Brandon's score. Then he stood next to the horse, eyes on the D1 judge until the green light flashed for him to begin.

He raised one arm in salute, then grasped the pommels and levered himself up into the first skill. *One element at a time. Don't look back. Don't look forward.* One move after the other, Sol kept his hips open, his legs glued together, and then suddenly he was flying up to a handstand, doing an extra pirouette, and sticking the landing.

Yes! He raised both arms in salute, pumped his fists, then trotted off the podium, grinning like a fool, as the crowd cheered. He slapped palms with the rest of the guys in his cohort. Xiao was waiting for him, but before Sol joined his coach, he checked the leader board.

It was wonky right now, of course. Since this rotation wasn't completely over, Sol's score hadn't posted, so he was showing up in fifth. Earlier, Tony had posted a phenomenal score on p-bars, only three hundredths behind Danny, who was a beast with those biceps of his.

Tony had faltered on high bar, though, his best event, nearly missing the bar after a Cassina release. He'd caught it with one hand, and though he hadn't fallen, he'd gotten hammered by the judges. He'd taken a totally unnecessary step—in Sol's opinion—on his layout double-double dismount too. He was finishing up on rings, and Sol was in a perfect spot to observe.

I'm not sure if that's a good thing or a bad thing.

Sure, he wouldn't have to wait for the replay to see Tony's routine, which was good. But… he wouldn't be able to wait for the replay, so his heart would be in his throat the entire time. *Not good.*

What is wrong with me? Before Tony barged into the Training Center, I'd have been praying for him to make a mistake, to take himself out of the way of guys who'd spent the last four years preparing.

But hadn't Tony spend the last four years preparing too, even if it was in a very different way? Sol edged down the floor toward the still rings just as Tony saluted the judges and Andrei helped him up to grasp the rings.

If Sol had been afraid of choking on his heart before, that was nothing to actually watching Tony compete. From the first iron cross, Tony's muscles bunching as he opened his hands to show the judges he wasn't leaning on his wrists, through every swing, every transition, Sol hardly breathed. He counted out each strength hold in his head—*one one thousand two one thousand—*

the way he had at Central when he was learning his first rings skills. Tony used to tease him about it. *"I can see your lips moving, Solly."* Even then, Sol had dreamed of his lips moving over Tony's skin.

Not that he'd ever said anything—not then. *But I could say it now.*

Then Tony threw a triple pike dismount—and took a step. Even with that error, though—only a tenth   deduction—Sol could tell the routine would post a big score. A really big score.

When the rotation was over, Sol was still comfortably in the lead, with Danny in second by a good margin over Rahul in third. Eddie was still in fourth. Tony had moved up to fifth again, his rings score compensating for the high bar error. But that didn't mean anything.

None of it meant anything, actually. Nobody was guaranteed an Olympic berth—nobody except Eddie, who had won an individual berth in the World Cup event series. But his spot was nominative—in other words, it was only for him. If the Olympic selection committee decided to put Eddie on the four-man team instead of leaving him as an event specialist, team USA would lose a quota spot and they'd only be able to take five guys to Tokyo.

But that didn't mean the committee wouldn't do it, not if they thought it would build the best team. Just because Sol, Danny, and Rahul were the all-around finishers didn't mean they'd be named to the team either.

Sol marched out of the arena with everyone else, returning to the dressing room so they could clean most of the chalk off themselves and try to stay calm while they waited for the team announcement.

Sol joined Tony, who was sitting in front of his locker, his head bowed and his elbows propped on his knees. "Hey. Your rings routine was awesome."

Tony looked up with a crooked smile. "Thanks. High bar, though, not so much."

Sol sat down, not so close to him that their hips touched, not with the rest of the guys milling around. "But it was great yesterday."

"Consistency's important, though. Isn't that what you always tell me?" Tony grabbed his warmup jacket out of his locker. "You, Danny, Rahul. You proved you could handle it today."

"That doesn't mean we'll get tapped for the team."

Tony lifted one eyebrow in a display of skepticism that rivaled Mr. Spock at his Vulcan best. "They'd be idiots not to take you. And none of them are idiots."

"Still—"

"Can I have your attention, please?" James Ferguson, the men's program director, stood in the doorway. The chatter in the dressing room died down. Ferguson smiled tightly at them. "I know all of you want to hear the committee's decision, so without further ado..." He glanced down at the paper in his hand. "The 2020 Olympic team is Sol Ashvili.

Tony grinned at Sol, buffeting him on the back. "Told you."

"Isaiah Daniels. Rahul Laghari."

Sol held his breath. They were going in alphabetical order, and they hadn't named Eddie, so maybe they were planning on him staying as a specialist.

"And Tony Thomas."

Sol let his breath out in a whoosh and turned toward Tony, who was goggling at Ferguson as if he didn't believe it.

"Eduardo Campo and Chad Horton will round out our squad as event specialists. Congratulations, men." Cheers and applause broke out, some of it more enthusiastic than others. "Barry has your team warmups. Please change and wait in the tunnel for the on-camera announcement."

Ferguson left. Sol stood, but Tony just stared at his locker. Sol nudged him with his knee.

"Come on, Thomas. Get your ass in gear. You're going to the Olympics."

CHAPTER TEN

I'm going to the Olympics. Tony's hands shook as he folded his jeans and stuffed them into his duffel bag. *Why did I think this was a good idea? Whose idea is it really?* Did the committee pick him because he deserved the spot for his gymnastics? Or because of his internet celebrity? *Goddamn Thomas flair.*

What if he let the team down? What if he fell all the way off the high bar this time? What if he landed on top of the judges' table in his vault the way Paul Hamm did in 2004?

"I should have stuck to jumping off cliffs," he muttered, and wadded up two T-shirts to jam them into the last spare inch. Who cared if they were a wrinkled mess? He was only going to visit his dad, and if Dad couldn't find something convenient to rag on Tony about, he'd invent something. Maybe if Tony looked like a slob, it would head off any comments about his performance at the trials.

"Tony?"

Tony jerked at the sound of Sol's voice. "Jesus. Way to sneak up on a guy."

Sol chuckled as he walked into Tony's room and leaned against the dresser. "You'd have heard me if you hadn't been so busy talking to yourself."

"Oh yeah. That." Tony zipped the duffel. "Maybe I'm *visualizing* my packing."

"Visualizing doesn't involve words—otherwise it would be called verbalizing." Sol smirked at him. "And you should try it. It really works."

"Uh huh." Tony peered out the door. Most of the team had already gone—they were all taking a week off before training camp started. But his roommate Eddie was still around, although Tony hadn't heard him come back from lunch yet. "Your parents picking you up?" Sol's family still lived in Arvada, so they didn't have far to drive.

"Yup. They'll be here in about an hour." Sol scuffed the carpet with one sneakered foot. "You could come too. They'd love to see you. They've missed you."

Tony sighed. He'd missed them too. Sol's parents, Pavle and Marika, were awesome. They were originally from Georgia—the one in Europe, not the one in the US. Tony had loved teasing them about it when he was a kid, running in and out of their house as freely—more freely actually—than he did his own. *Making a peach pie today, Mrs. Ashvili? I hear that's a specialty where you're from.*

God, I was an annoying little shit. But Marika had just laughed. She'd actually started making peach pie whenever Tony was expected for dinner. And Pavle hadn't ever complained about driving Tony home from the gym when Dad forgot because he was too busy reliving his gridiron glory days.

"I'd much rather hang out with them than my dad. But if I don't let him yell at me now, it'll be hanging over my head all the way to Tokyo."

Sol frowned. "What's he got to yell at you about? You made the Olympic team, for crying out loud."

"Yeah, but I didn't come in first." Tony sank down on the bed. "Ol' Dad is all about being top dog, and since he never managed it, I have to be the one to carry the flag. He thinks I need to up the risk level on my XBL channel to attract more subscribers."

"Bullshit." Sol plopped down next to Tony. "That's not why you do it, is it? The risky stunts?"

Was it? A part of Tony had never stopped trying to please his unpleasant father—probably never would, since habits learned in childhood were fucking hard to break. But the truth? "I'm an adrenaline junkie, Solly. I always have been." He smiled wryly. "I should probably take advantage of being fit enough to indulge my addiction while I can."

Sol's scowl deepened. "Also bullshit." He drew one knee onto the bed so he faced Tony. "*You're* more important than the next routine, the next stunt, the next risk. Stop taking chances with your body, Tony. The next time might not be reparable."

Tony glanced at the open door. Still no movement in the rest of the suite, so he allowed himself to take Sol's hand. "You almost sound like you care."

Sol's grip tightened on Tony's fingers. "Of course I care, you jerk. I thought we covered that the other day."

Tony squinted one eye, peering up at the ceiling. "We did? My injury, you know... The pain makes everything a little muzzy."

Sol raised an eyebrow. "You didn't have an injury. Or not as much of one as you pretended. You faked it, remember?"

"Did I?" Tony blinked in faux innocence. "I thought for sure I was heading for the light."

"You did no such thing, and you know that perfectly well."

Oh, but I was. Just not the one most people meant. "Maybe you could jog my memory?"

Sol chuckled, low and dirty, then got up, closed the door, and flicked the lock. "How's this for a jog?"

He stalked over and straddled Tony's lap, spreading his legs in the kind of wide splits that only a gymnast could manage, his groin snug against Tony's. "Ringing any bells?"

Somewhere, Tony dredged up enough breath to speak. "Maaaybe?"

"How about this?" Sol flattened his palms on Tony's pecs and pushed him backwards. Then he leaned forward and pressed his chest against Tony's, his dark hair flopping over his forehead.

"Christ, Solly," Tony growled. "Put this move in our warm-up and I'll never get off the mat. This should totally be an Olympic event. Pairs gymnastics."

Sol chuckled again, vibrating Tony's bones and, er, boner. "I doubt anyone else on the team would go for it."

"Well, *I* certainly would. This is—" Sol flexed his hips and Tony had to bunch the comforter in his fists to keep from grabbing Sol's ass. "This is another element they'll name after us. The Thomas-Ashvili 2."

Sol flexed again and Tony moaned. "Why is your name always first? I think this should be the Ashvili-Thomas. After all, you *are* on the bottom."

Tony shouted with laughter, but Sol cut it off with a kiss that was a solid 10.0 on execution. Tony let go of the comforter—why the fuck would he want to grab fake down and fabric when he could run his hands along the taut muscles in Sol's back to palm his ass. *God, that ass.* Quinn and her fans went crazy over gymnasts' chests and arms, but they were missing out on perfection if they weren't checking out Sol's ass. Not that anyone could get a good look with their stupid retro uniforms in the way.

Tony cupped one of those perfect cheeks in each hand. *On second thought, maybe I'm the uniforms' biggest fan. Because nobody should be allowed to ogle* this *but me.*

Sol nipped at Tony's lip as he drew away. *Damn. Kiss dismounts should not be allowed.* "I've got to go. My parents will be here any minute."

"You said they were coming in an hour." Tony forced himself to release Sol's ass, but couldn't let go altogether. He threaded his fingers through Sol's silky hair. "It hasn't been that long."

"Yes, but we're talking about my parents. They've never been less than forty-five minutes early for anything in their lives." Sol dropped one more lingering kiss on Tony's lips, then rolled off him. He sat, smiling gently, one hand stroking Tony's forehead before veering off to tangle in his curls. "I want you to remember something."

"The feel of your ass in my hands? Your dick against mine? Your tongue in my mouth? Because trust me—those aren't things I'm likely to forget."

Sol grinned. "Good to know. But I'm not talking about us right now. I'm talking about you." Sol sobered, his hand cupping the back of Tony's head. "You earned your spot, Tony. If the committee didn't think you were the best fit for the team, the best chance for a medal, they wouldn't have called your name."

"How—" Tony swallowed. "How did you know I needed to hear that?"

"Because I can almost hear those gears grinding away." Sol tapped Tony's forehead. "Give 'em a rest."

Tony grabbed Sol's hand and laced their fingers together. "What if I snowed them? What if the fan reaction clouded their judgment?" He grimaced. "Maybe they were just victims of the infamous *Thomas flair.*" Tony couldn't keep the revulsion out of his tone.

"Gymnastics judges are notoriously resistant to snow, clouds, or flair." Sol's fingers tightened, almost to the point of pain. "You took first on rings, Tony. Second on p-bars. You deserve your place. You deserve this chance. Furthermore, the team *needs* you. *Men's gymnastics* needs you, for everything you bring to the table."

Tony couldn't meet Sol's dark, intense gaze. "But is that what the other guys think?"

Sol's lips quirked, and he leaned over until Tony could feel the puff of Sol's breath on his cheek. "That's what *I* think. Do you really care about anybody else?"

Tony hooked a finger in the neck of Sol's T-shirt. "No. Actually, everybody else in the world can take a flying fuck with a goddamn double twist."

And he pulled Sol down into another kiss.

Man, a week with his parents had never felt this long. Normally, Sol loved visiting with them—warm, loving, funny, and his biggest supporters. But this time, he was aching to get back to the gym, back to the team, back to training.

Back to Tony.

Sol waved to his parents as they drove away from the training center. He pulled his USOPTC credentials out of his duffel and then hitched the strap onto his shoulder. The June sun was hot on his head and shoulders, and the air-conditioned coolness of the center beckoned to him, but he stood on the sidewalk looking up at the building for a moment. Once he stepped through the doors, he'd be on the path to the Olympics.

Who am I kidding? Every time I walked into the gym since I was ten has been a step on that path.

Tony had been by his side almost the whole time, except for the last few horrible years. *How did I live through almost four years without seeing him, without touching him?*

Well, the touching would mostly need to wait until after Tokyo, because they'd agreed—this time was for the team. They'd play out their own personal story after the Games.

Hell if I'm going to wait any longer for the seeing, though.

Sol sprinted to the doors and through check-in. He dumped his duffel in his room. Rahul's door was partway open, so Sol knocked softly and poked his head in. "Hey. You're here."

Rahul looked up from a hefty textbook. Sheesh, the guy *never* stopped studying. Sol was serious about his biochem work, but Rahul's dedication to engineering was off the charts. "Got in yesterday." His gaze flickered back to the page. "Got a test coming up."

"A test? But it's the middle of summer."

Rahul shrugged. "Summer term. I'm trying to get ahead on my coursework so I won't have to do as much during the Games."

Sol grinned. "If you manage anything during the Games… What am I saying? If anyone can do it, you can." He rapped his knuckles on the doorframe. "But don't spend all your downtime with your nose in a book. It's the Olympics, man. Experience the dream."

"Mmphmm." Rahul bent his head over the book. "See you at dinner tonight."

Sol shook his head, chuckling, and headed toward the door. He paused with his hand on the knob. He'd been running around like a maniac after sweating in the sun for longer than necessary—and the AC in his parents' old Honda was more a suggestion of a breeze than actual cooling. *I should take a shower.* Tony certainly wasn't any stranger to the smell of Sol's sweat—and vice versa. But for their first time after a week apart—and why did a week feel so much longer than nearly four years?—Sol wanted to make an *effort*.

So he grabbed his toiletries, a towel, and some clean clothes and zipped into the bathroom for the quickest—but most thorough—shower he could manage when his head was urging him to find Tony right freaking now. He snorted as he pulled on his underwear, hampered by his other head—the one between his legs. "You know what you want, don't you, buddy?" He slapped himself on the forehead. *I did* not *just talk to my dick.*

He struggled into his T-shirt, swearing when the fabric clung to his still-damp skin, and then yanked on his shorts. Forget sneakers—he didn't want to take the time to tie them. So he slid his feet into flip-flops and hurried out of the suite.

His steps slowed as he approached Tony's door. *I should have called first. Why didn't I call?* They'd texted a few times while Tony was at his dad's, but Tony hadn't seemed to want to talk much. *Maybe he changed his mind.* He'd appeared on Quinn's show again, laughing with her about the shirtless practice video going viral. He hadn't staged another XBL stunt, thank goodness. Shame washed through Sol's belly, because he'd actually checked the channel to make sure.

I need to trust him. Trust that he's serious enough about the team to not take chances. Trust that he's serious enough about me not to put himself at risk.

He took a deep breath and then knocked. And waited. Waited some more. *Maybe he's not here yet.* But Sol had gotten the impression that Tony couldn't wait to escape his dad's house and wasn't about to linger a minute longer than he had to. He tried the knob. It wasn't locked, so he cracked the door open.

"Hello? Anybody home?"

Nobody answered, but Sol could see a shadow moving in the light filtering in from Tony's window. *He's probably got his earbuds in again.* Sol slipped inside, closing the door softly behind him.

Flip-flops *thwapp*ing, he hurried across the living room. His heart was thumping in an odd syncopated rhythm and his breath couldn't quite match the tempo. *Good thing I'm a gymnast and not a musician.* He stood in the open doorway to Tony's room, and there was Tony himself.

His back was to Sol as he dragged clothes out of his duffel and dumped them on his bed. He bobbed his head in time to a song, but Sol couldn't tell what it was from Tony's tuneless humming. A smile curved Sol's lips. Tony couldn't carry a tune in a bucket, extreme or otherwise.

Tony was shirtless, his ink on glorious display. Sol licked his lips, hands twitching with the urge to run his fingers along that smooth, brown skin. His gaze traveled down Tony's spine, over his ass, hugged so nicely by his shorts, and—

"What the hell, Tony?"

Tony jerked and spun around, yanking his earbuds out. "Jesus, Sol. What have I told you about sneaking up on me?"

Sol couldn't make any words come out of his mouth. Instead he pointed at Tony's knee. At the *brace* on Tony's knee.

Tony glanced down. "Oh, that old thing?"

"Tony." Sol finally forced some air past his throat. "Did you do it? Another XBL stunt? After you—"

"Hey hey hey." Tony held up his hands, palms out. "I haven't done anything stupid." He wrinkled his nose. "Unless you call visiting my dad stupid, which would be fair. But I've been to see the team physio. He suggested I wear the heavier brace outside the gym for at least a week while we ramp up the training. Keep wearing the lighter sleeve during practice. I've been good. I promise." He eased toward Sol, his cheeky grin lighting his face. "Don't I deserve a reward?"

"God, Tony." Sol closed the distance between them and grabbed Tony around the waist. "Don't scare me like that."

Tony nuzzled Sol's neck. "Mmm. You're not giving me much incentive to behave. If you hug me like this every time I scare you, then—"

"*Not* because you didn't behave." Sol jerked away from the temptation of Tony's mouth. "Because you did. And I—" Sol lowered his gaze, focusing on the center of Tony's chest. "I didn't trust you to keep yourself safe. I'm sorry."

Tony kissed Sol's eyebrow, his cheek, his lips. "You're forgiven." He grinned. "Wanna try the Thomas-Ashvili again? Or maybe the Ashvili-Thomas?" He rubbed his knuckle along Sol's jaw. "I'm not sure I remember which is which. Until they put 'em in the Code of Points, maybe we should keep practicing so we don't forget."

Sol trailed his fingers across the washboard of Tony's abs and rested his hands on Tony's hips. "I'm pretty sure we can't have an element named after us unless we complete it successfully in international competition."

Tony's grin widened. "I'm game. We can introduce both moves in Tokyo."

"Really?" Sol's own lips twitched with the desire to smile. "I thought we agreed to keep everything on the down-low until after the Games."

"Are you telling me there's no place in the entire Olympic Village where we can find some time to be together? I thought the Village was famous for nonstop boinking. There's even a video parody about it."

Sol fixed Tony with a severe scowl—or at least as severe as he could manage when he was trying not to laugh. "No boinking in the Village for you."

"Me?" Tony pressed a hand to his chest, his wide-eyed innocent expression fooling precisely nobody in this room. "You were the one who was getting chased by the entire Brazilian team in Rio."

Sol rolled his eyes. "One guy. One. And I think Luiz was more interested in you."

"Oh, no. He hit on you. I watched." Tony hooked his fingers in Sol's waistband. "Really pissed me off. That's why I won the silver on high bar. I just wanted to beat him."

This time, Sol couldn't contain his laugh. "You won an Olympic medal because of jealousy?"

Tony shrugged. "Hey, everyone's motivation is different."

"But, Tony…" Sol's heart fluttered in his throat. "Did you really want me then?"

"Baby, I've wanted you since I figured out my dick wasn't just for my own amusement."

"Why didn't you say anything?"

Tony's gaze slid away. "I was going to. After the team won a medal. Or at least after we made a decent showing. But when I found *you* were supposed to be the one—"

"No." Sol laid his finger over Tony's lips. "We've been over this. You deserved your spot. You deserved your medals. I refuse to allow you to denigrate your accomplishment."

Tony's eyes twinkled, and he tickled Sol's finger with the tip of his tongue. "Denigrate. That's a ten-dollar word. You must be one o' them college grad-yu-eights."

"Shut up."

"I know one way to stop my mouth." Tony leaned forward until his lips were a breath away from Sol's. "Want me to show you?"

"Yes," Sol breathed. He closed his eyes. And then... And then...

The suite door banged open. "Yo! Anybody here?" Danny shouted.

Sol backed away, banging his hip on the dresser as Danny's footsteps thumped toward Tony's room. Danny stopped in the doorway and braced his hands on the door frame, beaming at them both. "Hey, guys. Miss me?" Then he launched himself across the room to land on Tony's bed. He propped his head on his hand. "When's dinner?"

CHAPTER ELEVEN

At the restaurant that night for the welcome-back dinner, all the guys were in a great mood. Tony would be in a lot better mood if Danny hadn't barged in on him and Sol, but he still felt as if he were floating about a foot above his chair. *This is it. The team. The "we" until after Tokyo.* The official training camp didn't start for two days which meant tomorrow in the gym would be all about Tony getting his ass chewed by Andrei about the mistakes he'd made at the trials. But that was tomorrow. Tonight, it was just the team: no coaches, no parents, no significant others. *Just us. Just the "we."*

Tony sipped his iced tea—no more beer until after the Games, damn it—and scanned the group. Sol was sitting next to him—and Sol's knee pressing against his own under the table went a long way toward improving Tony's mood. But Tony noticed Sol was picking at his food.

Under cover of Danny telling some kind of raucous joke about the Penn State team, Tony leaned over and murmured, "You okay?"

Sol shot a glance at him. "What? I'm fine."

"You're not eating."

Sol's glance turned to a glower. "Don't tell me you're going to channel my mom for the next month."

"Not your mom." Tony grinned. "Just someone who's very, *very* invested in making sure you're at peak performance in *all* your events, regardless of venue or… *apparatus*."

"Shut up." But Sol's smiled quivered to life, and he took a bite of his grilled chicken.

Tony's grin faltered as he studied the guy on his other side. Jason had been on the national team, and he'd been named as one of the alternates. *If I hadn't come back, he'd probably be on the Olympic squad.* His scores were decent—hell, they were more than decent. Some of them were better than Tony's. Tony had been afraid that Jason might resent him, that all the alternates might, since he'd waltzed in at the last minute as the result of a petition. *And a PR stunt.*

Jason seemed just as cheerful as anybody else except maybe Danny—and certainly more cheerful than Rahul, who looked like he'd rather be studying. Was that an act? For the sake of the "we," Tony turned away from Sol.

"Hey, Jason." He kept his voice low so he wouldn't pull anyone else into their conversation. "You cool with the way things shook out?"

Jason blinked at Tony, raising his eyebrows. "About…? Oh. You mean about being an alternate?" He mock scowled. "Hell, no. I've hired a hit man to take out everybody except Sol."

I think he's kidding… "Why the exception?"

"Because no hit man would be able to get past you to get to him, of course." Jason punched Tony's biceps. "Seriously, man. No hard feelings. We all did our jobs at the trials. The committee did their job afterward. There's no point second-guessing their choices, because it won't make any difference." He grinned, and there didn't seem to be anything other than friendliness in it. "I'm just jazzed to be going along. To be part of the training. Part of the experience." He tapped the KT tape peeking out from under his tank top. "I'm still recovering from a shoulder injury, so I'm just as glad not to have the coaches' full attention on me." He took a gulp of water. "Sucks to be you."

Tony barked a laugh. "Yeah, you've got a point. I'll be paying for that high bar routine for weeks."

"Are you kidding? Video of that has gone viral. Maybe they'll name the element after you—the Thomas, a Cassina with a one-handed catch."

Heat built in Tony's chest at the thought of the *other* elements he'd suggested be named after him. Him and Sol. But when he glanced to his left, Sol's chair was empty. "I'm, uh, pretty sure I won't be able to repeat that. Not that I want to." He balled his napkin and set it on the table. "Excuse me for a minute."

"No problem." Jason turned his attention back to Danny, who'd embarked on yet another anecdote which, judging by Rahul's scowl, probably involved him.

Tony threaded his way through the tables to the hall leading to the restrooms. Sol emerged from the men's room door just as Tony was reaching for it. Even in the dim hallway, Tony could see the way Sol's face lit up. "Oh. Hi." Then his brows drew together. "You're not checking up on me, are you?"

Tony leaned against the wall so he wouldn't be tempted to take Sol in his arms. *Not in public. That's not in the plan—not until after the Games.* "No." *Yes.* "Sometimes a guy just needs to pee."

"Uh huh." Sol's tone held buried laughter. "Then why are you standing in the hallway instead of heading inside to take care of business?"

Tony shrugged. "Business can wait." He swayed closer. "I missed you."

"I was gone for five minutes. And you were talking to Jason, anyway."

"Jealous?" Tony waggled his eyebrows. "'Cause I could get behind proving why it's not necessary."

"No, you goof. Not jealous. But also not rude."

Tony huffed out a sigh and turned sideways to rest his shoulder against the wall. "I just wanted to make sure he was okay with me being on the team instead of him."

Sol moved away from the door to face Tony in the narrow hallway. "I told you. You earned your spot. There's no guarantee that Jason would have been named to the team if you hadn't been there. He's had a problem with his—"

"Shoulder. Yeah. He told me. He also told me the same thing as you—that he's happy with the outcome and happy about having a place at the Games, even as an alternate." Tony snorted. "I almost believe him."

Sol edged a bit nearer than the close quarters called for—not that Tony was complaining. "Believe him. It's the truth. I should know, since I was in his place in Rio. It's still an amazing experience, and an alternate has been called up more than once. Do you remember—"

"Tony."

Tony straightened up at the unwelcome sound of Andrei's voice, which put him even closer to Sol, who backpedaled until he hit the opposite wall. *Yeah,* that *doesn't look suspicious at all.* "Andrei. What are you doing here?"

"I'll, um, leave you two to chat." Sol had to turn sideways to edge past Andrei, who was blocking most of the hallway and didn't bother to give an inch.

Instead, Andrei propped his fists on his hips, taking up even more airspace. "It is I who should ask what you are doing."

"Let's see." Tony tapped his chin. "I'm about to take a piss. Then I'm returning to the table to join my teammates and finish dinner." He wiggled his fingers. "After washing my hands, of course, because good hygiene is so very important."

Andrei's scowl was as familiar to Tony by now as his own face in the mirror. "You should be in the gym. You should not be wasting time, fraternizing with your competitors."

"They're not my competitors. They're my *team.*" Tony stalked down the hall to go toe-to-toe with his coach. "That's been the whole point of these last few months, remember?" He jerked a thumb at his chest. "Me hiring you—" He pointed at Andrei. "—with, you know, *money,* to get in shape to *make the team.*"

"This journey is not over. Being named to the team does not mean you will stay on it if you do not perform. Your mistakes at the trials—"

"I'm well aware of my mistakes, thanks. But here's the thing." He met Andrei's glare with one of his own. "*I'm* the one who'll be on the equipment, both in training and at the Games. You got me here, for which I thank you—and for which I've paid you. But you're gonna have to let me do the rest on my own terms."

Andrei grunted. "No matter what you think, Tony, you still need me. I've got you this far. I can get you to the medal stand. But not if you forget a very important point." If Andrei's laser glower were weaponized, it could have cut Tony in half. "In gymnastics, everyone is your competition, even those from your own country, those wearing the same colors as you. Because in gymnastics, nobody can help you once you're on the apparatus all alone. Only your coach. Only your training."

"And me. Don't forget I'll be doing the work," Tony growled.

"Then see that you do it." Andrei glanced over his shoulder in the direction Sol had gone. "And stay away from that one in particular. He's dangerous."

"You mean he's good? My *competition*." Tony loaded his voice with heavy sarcasm.

"He pulls your focus."

"He's my friend. He's my teammate."

Andrei studied him silently for a moment. "See that he remains no more than that." He turned away. "I'll see you in the gym tomorrow. Seven o'clock. Do not be late."

Tony stared after Andrei for a full two minutes, fists clenching and unclenching at his sides. He wished he could completely dismiss Andrei's comments, but he did have a point. Tony would never have gotten this far without him. *But can I go any farther* with *him?*

"Guess I'll find out in the gym tomorrow." He shoved the restroom door open. "At seven fucking o'clock."

Of all the apparatus in the gym, Sol hated still rings the most. He didn't have the upper body development that guys like Danny and Tony did, so the strength elements were always a challenge. Like now. *This planche is going to kill me.* But two seconds—the required hold time—wasn't forever. *It just feels like it.* Then swing down and up and let go—two twists in layout and *bam.*

Hold it. Hold it. Ha! He pumped his fists at the stuck dismount, grinning as Tony whistled and clapped from the sidelines. "Hey, Sol," he called. "Your lips were moving."

Sol flipped him off, returning the grin. "Shut up. They were not." He walked off the mat and grabbed his water bottle as Tony took his place under the rings.

Xiao nodded toward the spring floor as their next destination —never one to be overly sentimental, that was Xiao. But Sol had completed his routine without any major mistakes twice, and that was good enough for Xiao. He didn't believe in the endless repetition that some coaches espoused. Coaches like Andrei Nicolescu, professional dickhead, for instance.

Sol took a swig of water, frowning as Andrei lifted Tony up to grasp the rings. Tony had been on rings already when Sol and Xiao had arrived. He'd alternated with Sol, which means he'd done at least two exercises, and now he was doing more? Yeah, Tony was strong, but still rings was a brutal apparatus. On the other hand, maybe Andrei was just going to have Tony work on his dismount, which he had yet to stick. Sol pretended to look for something in his gym bag, watching out of the corner of his eye. *Nope. Full routine. Damn it.*

Sol shouldered his bag and stalked over to join Xiao. Granted, Sol wasn't a coach, but Andrei's methods seemed so contrary to Tony's brand of gymnastics. Tony had always been what their first coach at Central had called a "product" guy—he liked the thrill of competing, especially of landing a flashy element before anybody else in the gym. *The Thomas flair*.

Sol, on the other hand, was a "process" guy—he preferred the methodical training that would result in the perfect, the clean, the—well, not the flashy, because Sol wasn't a flashy kind of person. While Tony reveled in high difficulty, Sol was more focused on the execution component. The way gymnastics scoring was evolving, hitting a perfect ten in execution was as far away as the moon. Nowadays, guys aimed for an 8.5 and were thrilled. Not Sol. He still wanted that ten. Since his difficulty wasn't as high on some events as other gymnasts at the elite international level, he *needed* high execution to keep him competitive.

Tony liked to stack his routines with high value moves. Sol tried to minimize deductions. But if the team were to medal in Tokyo, maybe they both had to adjust their approach. *And Tony needs to stop letting Andrei beat up his body with all these repetitions.* "Doing the numbers," it was called. Sol called it insanity.

He dropped his bag next to the spring floor. "Xiao. I want to upgrade my floor and pommel horse routines."

Xiao raised his eyebrows. "This is not like you."

"We've been working on higher-valued skills all season. Do you think I can't do it?"

"No. I think you're capable. But you are not... an adventurous gymnast."

Sol smiled crookedly. "You mean I'm boring?"

"No. Consistency and pristine execution have always been your watchwords. However"—Xiao smiled faintly—"consistency and pristine execution are not always rewarded as they should be, particularly by the audience who values excitement and drama."

"Then what do you say we give them a little excitement and drama?" Sol held up his hands. "Not that I want to risk consistency and execution, but I'm ready to venture a little farther onto the Dark Side."

Xiao glanced over Sol's shoulder, toward the still rings. Andrei yelled, "Again," and Xiao's lips flattened. "We will only go so far as is safe. The audience's voracity for danger is not sufficient reason for me to court injury for you or any of my gymnasts." He glanced toward the rings again. "Others would do well to remember this."

Sol blinked at his coach. *Wow.* Xiao *never* criticized other coaches. He must really be feeling it today. Not that Sol blamed him. *Wonder what it would take to get Andrei booted out of the gym?* He shook his head. *More clout than I've got, that's for sure.* But Andrei was technically Tony's employee, even though he was affiliated with the USOPTC. *Temporarily. Because of Tony.* If *Tony* were to fire him... *If I were to ask Tony to fire him...*

But Sol abandoned that notion at once. He and Tony had only just repaired their relationship, had only just moved it to the next level. That didn't mean Tony would take Sol's advice if it conflicted with his own goals and ambitions.

And unfortunately, Andrei still seemed crucial to his goals and ambitions.

Maybe someday Sol would have the same kind of influence with Tony. *Assuming* I'm *part of those goals and ambitions.* They hadn't really talked about a future after the Games. Both of them had *assumed* they'd be able to go public with their relationship, but where would that be? What would their lives look like? Would Tony go back to his XBL stunts? Could Sol handle it if he did?

Resolutely, Sol pushed the thoughts aside. They had no place in the gym, when he was trying to upgrade routines that were as comfortable as old shoes to him. *Comfortable. Maybe that's my problem. I need to step outside that comfort zone if I expect to be somebody who can fit into Tony's world.*

But so much of Sol's life was dedicated to maintaining that level of comfort and safety—it had to be, not just because he was involved in a dangerous sport, but because of his diabetes. Regulating his exertion, adherence to his nutrition plan.

Monitoring and control were the organizing principles in his life.

Can I shake things up a bit? Do I dare?

He glanced at Tony, once again on the rings while Andrei harangued him from the ground. *For him, I can. For us, I will. For the team, I must.*

Xiao had pulled out his tablet and a legal pad. He beckoned for Sol to sit by him next to the wall and then motioned for Eddie and his coach to take possession of the spring floor. "Your non-acrobatic element can be upgraded quite easily with skills you already have. However, there's more potential in the tumbling passes."

"I know. The element we added before the trials made a big difference. I don't think I'd have won floor without it. Eddie was only a tenth behind me."

Xiao replied. He definitely said something, but Sol didn't catch it because at that moment, Andrei's shouts—and Tony's shouts in response—snapped his focus away from Xiao and to the drama under the still rings. Sol started to push himself to his feet, but Xiao gripped his arm.

"This is not your place, Sol." He nodded across the gym. Barry, the national team coach, and Volya, the assistant coach, were headed toward the rings. "They will take care of it."

Yeah, but who will take care of Tony?

Tony was rubbing his shoulder, and even from this distance, Sol could see the pinch between his brows. *He's in pain.* Who wouldn't be, after that kind of punishing workout? Volya led Tony aside, speaking to him quietly, while Barry confronted the red-faced Andrei. Barry gestured to the gym door. For a moment, Sol didn't think Andrei would comply. But then he snatched his jacket off the mat and stalked across the gym, Barry following with a face like a thundercloud.

Sol glanced at Tony and Volya again. They'd moved over to the warm-up mats, and Volya was directing Tony in some cool-down stretches. *At least Tony's wearing his knee sleeve.* Ice trickled down Sol's spine. God, if Tony injured his shoulder as well? You could still train certain skills and apparatus with either a knee injury *or* a shoulder injury, but with both? You were screwed.

"Sol. Did you hear what I said?"

Sol wrenched his attention away from Tony. "Hmmm?"

"I thought you wished to discuss upgrading your routines."

"I do."

"Then perhaps," Xiao said, his tone dry, "you should pay attention. You can talk to your friend later."

Sol cast one more glance at Tony. "Xiao. Do *you* think Andrei is a good coach?"

"It is not my place to judge."

"Why not? You're on the staff here at USOPTC now. Hasn't US gymnastics been hammered enough through the misbehavior of people whose first job ought to have been the welfare of gymnasts in their charge?"

Xiao fixed Sol with a stern look. "There is a difference between being a bad coach and being an abusive one. However, we do not take your welfare lightly—yours or any athlete who enters these doors. You must trust us to take the proper steps if necessary. But..." Xiao's gaze slid over to where Volya was smiling down at Tony, encouraging him to flatten himself against the mat in a wide straddle stretch. "You might wish to discuss the situation with your friend. Make sure he knows he has your support, and that we are here to listen to him should he have something to say."

"Don't worry. I will." And Sol finally turned his attention to the diagram on Xiao's legal pad. "Wait. You want me to do *what*?"

CHAPTER TWELVE

The next morning, Tony slipped out of the dorm building into the early light. The complex wasn't completely deserted—it was the middle of July and with the Olympics practically on top of them, a lot of athletes had early schedules. He waved at a Paralympic swimmer he'd met during his first week and she grinned at him but didn't stop. *Things to do. Places to go.* Or rather one place—Tokyo, the reason they were all here.

He rolled his shoulder experimentally. The twinge from yesterday wasn't all that noticeable and his knee was as good as it ever was. Andrei hadn't come back to the gym after their blowup yesterday—pretty typical behavior for him—and Volya had insisted that Tony visit the team physio and try some of the recovery techniques the other guys on the team used. That ice-water bath? *Damn.* It had taken his balls hours to crawl out from hiding. But he had to admit, he felt better this morning than he had any right to expect.

I'm sure Andrei will take care of that in about twenty minutes. He tapped his badge on the card reader kiosk and walked into the Sports Medicine and Sciences building that housed the gym, then trudged across the warmup floor next to the basketball court. *This is what I wanted, remember? To be back on the team, to have another chance to do right by them. For us to boost the popularity of the men's program together.* But with Andrei insisting that Tony work with him exclusively, never allowing much interaction with the other guys in the gym, it almost felt like the first days here, when Sol was still giving him the silent treatment. Not that Sol or any of the guys were doing it on purpose. Andrei always seemed to pop up to drag Tony away to do some advanced Romanian torture conditioning whenever any of them tried to chat. And after such intense training days, none of them had the energy to do much more than eat and fall into bed.

Alone, damn it.

Sol hadn't been at dinner last night—his parents had stopped by unexpectedly—so Tony hadn't even gotten the chance to sit next to him and indulge in a little under-the-table footsie. Somehow, he'd find a way to get at least five minutes with Sol, even if they weren't alone. *I'll hogtie Andrei to the p-bars if I have to.*

He nodded decisively and trotted the last few feet to the gym. The windowless room smelled of citrus cleaning products and chalk, the apparatus looming in the dimness of the emergency lighting. The *clang* of the door closing behind him made him wince. But once he flipped on the lights, the equipment didn't look so sinister. He patted the pommel horse on his way to the still rings. No doubt Andrei would insist on starting with rings this morning since that's where they'd imploded yesterday. He dumped his gym bag next to the wall and headed over to jog around the spring floor to get warmed up.

He'd only made a couple of circuits though when the door opened. "Hey, Andr—"

But it wasn't Andrei in the doorway. It was Sol.

Tony slowed down and grinned. "Hi. You're down early. Must be my lucky day."

Sol paced toward him, not answering Tony's grin. If anything, he looked distressed.

Tony strode toward him. "Solly? What's wrong? Is it your folks?"

Sol's eyes widened. "What? No, they're fine."

"Then what? You look like you're about to tell me somebody died." Tony's belly bottomed like he'd just missed his grip on high bar. "I'm off the team."

Sol's expression morphed from shocked to exasperated. "For God's sake, Tony, it's nothing that dire. At least…" He bit his lip, shoulders hunching. "… I *hope* it's not."

"Then tell me before I start imagining further death and untold destruction."

"It's Andrei."

A frisson skated down Tony's back. "Is he hurt? Did he crash that stupid Alfa Romeo?"

This time, Sol actually rolled his eyes. "Nobody is hurt, okay? Nobody died. Nobody's in the hospital. Nobody's off the team."

Tony's nerves settled—barely. "Thank fuck for that. Then what's wrong?"

"After your… discussion with Andrei yesterday—"

"Call it what it was. A screaming fit."

"Yes. Well after that, Barry called Andrei into his office. They're barring him from the USOPTC, pending a review. He's not allowed back until after it's complete, which isn't likely to happen until after the Games."

Tony's fingers went numb. "Am I barred from the Center too? Do I have to move out?" *Do I have to leave you?*

Sol gripped Tony's arms. "Don't be an idiot. Of course not. You're still on the team. You're still living here. You're still training here."

"But mandatory training camp starts tomorrow. And I don't have a coach."

Sol shook Tony gently. "In case you haven't noticed, the place is lousy with coaches. You worked with Volya yesterday, didn't you?"

Tony was still having trouble focusing. "Yeah."

"You could continue to work with him, but I'd like to suggest something else."

Tony shook his head, trying to bring his brain back online, because for some reason he was still stuck on the fact that Andrei was de facto no longer his coach. *I don't even know how I feel about this. Shocked? Outraged? Relieved?* But Sol was gazing at him, concern in his dark eyes. "Uh, what?"

"I think you should talk to my coach. To Xiao. I think the two of you would work well together." Sol gave him another shake. "And he can help you with your dismounts, because frankly? They suck."

Tony was surprised into a laugh. "Yeah, they do. But..." He disengaged from Sol's hold and paced across the mats, his feet sinking into the padding like he was wading through mud. "I don't know, Solly. Andrei's gotten me this far. What if... What if..." *What if this is as far as I can go?*

Sol smiled crookedly. "What have you got to lose? Andrei can't be here for training camp. You'll be working with the team coaches anyway, and Xiao is one of them. I'd just like you to work with him specifically." His smile grew to a sly grin. "It'll be like we're back at Central, the two of us challenging each other, trying to top one another."

"Top one another, eh?" Tony matched Sol's slyness and raised it by a double dose of innuendo. "I don't think I want to try that in the gym."

Sol's jaw dropped. "I can't believe you went there. This is serious, Tony."

"I'm being serious." He stalked toward Sol, who took a step back. "The Thomas-Ashvili needs serious work. So does the Ashvili-Thomas. If we expect to unveil either one of them in international competition—"

"Stop. Just stop." But Sol was holding in a laugh, Tony could tell. "*Will* you work with Xiao?"

Tony dropped the swagger and the attitude, but he moved closer to Sol, close enough to twine their fingers together. After all, nobody else was around. "Do *you* want me to work with him?"

"Yes. But you shouldn't do it just for me. You should do it because it's best for you."

Tony raised Sol's hand to his lips and kissed the palm, then closed Sol's fingers around it, wrapping his own fingers around Sol's fist. "What's best for me is being with you. At this point, you're probably a better judge of what I need than I am." He grinned wryly. "After all, you're the guy who took the all-around at the trials *and* the US Championships. If Xiao helped you get there, I'm willing to give it a go."

Sol gripped Tony's wrist with his other hand, keeping them latched together. "If it doesn't work out, you've got other options. But I think it will." He smiled. "I volunteered to break the news about Andrei to you, but Xiao's waiting for us in the coaches' office."

Tony blinked. "What, now?"

"Yes, now. He wants to discuss a few things with you first." Sol mock-scowled. "Changing coaches isn't something to do lightly. He wants to make sure you're choosing this of your own free will and not because I strong-armed you into it."

"I wouldn't mind you strong-arming me a bit."

"Tony." Sol's voice was laced with warning.

"Okay." He dropped another kiss on Sol's knuckles. "I'll be good. But I'll want a reward later." He waggled his eyebrows.

Sol smirked at him. "Start landing your dismounts and we'll talk."

"Hey!" Tony puffed his chest out, lifting his chin in mock-outrage. "Don't offer me sex for performance. I'll feel so cheap. Motivated, but cheap."

"Shut up." Sol tugged Tony toward the door but didn't drop his hand. "Xiao's been watching you since you arrived here at the Center. He's got a *lot* of notes to go over before this morning's practice."

With a chuckle, Tony let Sol lead him. "I think I'm regretting this already."

■🏋︎◌◌工₸₸⊓

Sol gazed up at Tony, suspended in a perfect Maltese on rings, and counted in his head. *One one thousand two one thousand*. Tony swung forward into a handstand—which he hit *cold*, no extra movement in the straps. Working with Xiao during training camp had burnished this routine to a freaking shine. Sol held his breath as Tony released into a Whittenburg dismount. *Triple pike. OMG*. And took a step on landing.

"Shit," Tony muttered.

"You could have stuck that." Xiao was imperturbable as usual, no censure in his tone. Simply facts. "You need to be more patient."

"Patience. Right." Tony winced and cleared the mat so Eddie could mount the rings. "I'll get right on that."

Sol stopped him with a touch on his arm. "Are you okay?"

Tony raised his eyebrows. "Nothing that a little patience wouldn't cure, apparently." He shot a cheeky grin at Xiao. "Why?"

"You winced."

"That was because our esteemed coach wants me to do something I'm not sure I'm capable of. Patience has never been one of my strengths. I'm more a 'Charge of the Light Brigade' kind of guy."

"Well, you know what happened to them."

"No. What?"

"They were decimated. Besides, it wasn't patience that was their problem, was it? It was incompetent leadership or bad communication or something."

"Don't ask me. I was an Exercise Science major—and never finished the damn degree, anyway."

Xiao joined them, studying his tablet closely. "I am pleased with your work this morning." He tilted an eyebrow at Tony. "Other than Mr. Thomas's persistent desire to court deductions on his dismounts."

"Hey!" Although Tony's voice held indignation, he was grinning at Xiao. *Had he ever grinned at Andrei?* "I don't do it on purpose."

"Then perhaps you should attempt to purposely avoid them instead." Xiao tapped his tablet screen. "Patience."

"Uh huh." Tony shouldered his duffel. "Will we be working on patience this afternoon?"

"No. This afternoon we will be discussing possible upgrades to your routines."

"Really?" Tony immediately perked up, but Sol wanted to shout, *No! Wait!* "I thought you didn't want me to throw anything risky."

"I still don't. Not inordinately so. I had to assess you first. I have some suggestions, but we will talk. After lunch. Go eat."

Tony saluted. "Aye aye, captain."

Xiao joined the other coaches in the corner of the gym for their usual post-session debriefing. The rest of the team was straggling out of the gym to clean up before lunch—there was nothing worse than chalk dust in your salad, and the smell of sweat didn't exactly enhance the flavor of grilled chicken.

Tony dawdled, fiddling with his duffel strap, until everyone else but Sol had left. Sol paused by the door. "Coming, Tony?"

He glanced up. "In a minute. I figured I'd give Eddie first chance at the hot water for a change. He always defers to me, and I don't want him to get to lunch last again."

Sol clucked his tongue. "So chivalrous."

Tony grinned. "Maybe I'm just learning patience. The anticipation of lunch is so much better when it's drawn out."

Sol nodded at the coaches as they passed, leaving the two of them alone in the gym. He sidled toward the door. "Yeah, well, sorry. I've got to go—"

Tony strode forward, his grin disappearing. "Are you all right? Your levels?"

Sol shook off Tony's hand irritably. "I'm fine. But meals are one thing *I* can't be patient about."

Tony crowded him, herding him away from the door and against the wall, out of sight of anyone in the outer gym. "You know one thing I'll *never* be patient about?"

"No. Wha—"

Sol's words were cut off by Tony's lips on his. His mouth was cool from his last drink of water, his skin damp with sweat that added a little salt to the kiss. Tony didn't press too close, using the tips of his fingers to angle Sol's chin because they were both workout-funky. Although Sol allowed himself to trail his fingers down Tony's bare chest.

When Tony disengaged, he grinned. "That."

Sol blinked at him. "Uh… What was the question?" Tony just smirked, so Sol jabbed him in the pec with one finger. "You know, it's a good thing nobody forgot something and came charging back in, if you're still serious about keeping this on the down-low."

"Are you kidding? With lunch calling? The guys are already in their rooms, and the coaches never break out of their gab session for at least twenty minutes." Tony's grin faded. "I kinda wish we didn't have to hide. I'm not ashamed."

"I'm not either. But it's distracting enough for me. I don't want it to affect anyone else."

"Really?" The grin was back. "I'm a distraction?"

Sol snorted. "Have you *seen* yourself?" He traced the stylized sun in the center of Tony's chest. "Are you ever going to tell me what all your ink means?"

"Someday. Maybe. But for now?" He swatted Sol's flank. "Let's go eat."

Tony dodged away before Sol could return the slap. Sol flipped him off, then hurried away to his suite, his nerves still thrumming from the kiss.

And the feeling didn't fade. Not through lunch, and not through afternoon practice. In fact, it escalated as Sol watched Tony in conversation with Xiao after working on a new high bar release sequence—serious and focused as the two huddled over Xiao's tablet, nodding at whatever Xiao was pointing out.

Tony didn't even complain—much—when Xiao sent him off for a physio session halfway through the workout. And when the coaches ended practice an hour early, Sol decided he was done waiting.

Patience, he thought as he showered off his workout funk, *is a steaming load of bullshit.*

CHAPTER THIRTEEN

After his session with the doc and the physios—and another damn ice-water bath—Tony shivered his way back to his room and faceplanted on his bed, too drained to even crawl under the blanket. When somebody tapped on his half-open door, he didn't budge.

"What?" he mumbled into his pillow.

"Just checking on your survival."

That warm voice perked Tony right up. "Solly?" He rolled over to find Sol leaning against the doorjamb, a smirk on his face. "What are you doing here? Did practice end early?"

Sol nodded. "The coaches had some big meeting with the US Olympic Committee, seeing as we'll be leaving for Tokyo in two days, so we got a break."

Tony gazed up at him. *God, he's so beautiful.* His silky dark hair flopped over his forehead—the whole team needed haircuts. They'd all gone shaggy during training camp, vowing to get their next trims at the salon in the Olympic Village. In fact, all of them were going for highlights, too. They'd even talked Rahul into it, which hadn't been easy. Tony had finally taken him aside and convinced him that being the only one *not* blond-streaked or tipped would make it seem like he disapproved of his teammates.

"I don't disapprove. But it's not *necessary*," Rahul had complained.

"True, it's not necessary," Tony replied. Then he'd grinned, nudging Rahul in the ribs. "But it's fun."

So sometime before marching out onto the arena floor, they'd all rendezvous with a bottle of bleach.

Tony must have zoned out a little, thinking about how hot Sol would look with blond striping his dark hair, because Sol nudged Tony's foot, a frown pleating his forehead. "You okay?"

"As okay as anybody who's been poked, prodded, and dunked into a tub of ice water can be." He raised his head although it felt like it weighed about fifty pounds. "You look far too chipper for somebody who's just gone through his own post-workout recovery."

Sol shrugged and sauntered over to perch on the bed next to Tony's hip. "I don't have a bum knee or a possible shoulder strain. They don't fuss over me as much."

Tony scowled. "My shoulder is fine. So is my knee."

"What?" Sol widened his eyes in mock astonishment. "You mean those treatments actually work? Just like the mindfulness and visualization is helping your performance?"

"Fuck you, smartass. It takes more than a minute to get over a lifetime's worth of habits." He poked Sol in the ribs. "And you can't tell me you actually enjoy that ice water torture. My balls are still lodged somewhere in my lower intestines."

"Hmmm." Sol tilted his head. "That sounds serious. Maybe I should investigate." He rested his hand on Tony's thigh. "You can never be too careful about things like that."

Tony's mouth dried, and he suddenly wasn't tired anymore. "Solly. What about the guys? Keeping things on the down-low? The distraction?"

"Shhh." He rose, looking down at Tony with a *very* predatory smile. "The guys are all down in Danny and Jason's suite playing Fortnite. Well, except for Rahul. He's studying as usual." He strolled over and pushed the door closed. "After being so close to you in the gym these last weeks, maybe a little of the Thomas flair is starting to rub off on me because I'm in the mood for a little risk."

Tony's mind shorted out at *close* and *rub off. I'm so ready.* He licked his lips. "Risk, huh?" he croaked.

"Mmmhmmm." Sol flicked the door lock. "But not stupidity." He stripped off his T-shirt and prowled over to the bed, staring down at Tony with heat in his eyes. He hooked his thumbs in his sweat shorts and shucked them down his legs.

"Jesus, Solly. Talk about risk. No underwear?"

Sol grinned, his cock standing proud against his belly. "I believe in dressing for the occasion." He kneeled on the bed, straddling Tony's legs. "Now. Where does it hurt?"

"Um…" Tony pointed to his dick. "Right there?"

"Are you sure?" Sol ran a finger along Tony's waistband. "Wasn't your original complaint located a bit lower?"

"M-maybe?"

"If you can't remember, I'll definitely need a closer examination." He backed off the bed again and teased Tony's shorts down his legs, exposing his jock. He clucked his tongue. "We can't have you hiding the… affected area. That's not conducive to a thorough investigation." He snagged the straps with both index fingers. "May I?"

"God, yes," Tony breathed, his body lighting up like a million kilowatt bulb. *Who needs physio? All I need is some Solly therapy.*

Sol freed Tony's cock, tossing shorts and jock aside. "There. That's better." He glanced up at Tony's face, his eyes wicked. "You can keep the shirt on. For now." Then he slipped his arms under Tony's legs and leaned in, his breath warm against the skin of Tony's inner thighs, and then… and then…

"Solly!"

Sol stopped nuzzling Tony's balls, a faux-innocent expression on his face. "Tony, how can I gather enough data for accurate evaluation if you keep interrupting me like this?"

"Sorry." Tony clenched fistfuls of the comforter. "D-do carry on."

"Thank you." He studied Tony's straining cock. "Now where was I? Was it here?" He nipped Tony's inner thigh. "No. I don't think so. Maybe here." He licked a stripe over Tony's hipbone and smacked his lips. "Mmmm. Not quite. Here?" He teased Tony's slit with the tip of his tongue and Tony nearly levitated off the mattress.

"Nnnnggh!"

"Yes, I do believe you're correct. That wasn't the spot at all." He grinned, the fucker. "Wait, I think I remember. Please hold still. We wouldn't want to exacerbate the problem." He shifted Tony's legs further onto his shoulders and engulfed one ball in his hot, wet mouth and *hummed*.

Jesus. Tony's muscles quivered as he tried not to move per instructions. But *fuck*. Solly's mouth was a fucking miracle. And when he moved from Tony's balls to his cock? At this angle, he couldn't get much more than the head past his lips, but... *gah!*

"Solly," Tony gasped. "Stop."

Sol pulled off with a pop. "But I'm not done investigating."

"Investigate yourself up here," Tony growled. "If not your mouth then your cock."

Sol shook his head, but he climbed onto the bed with his hips by Tony's head and rolled onto his side. "I've heard of this skill. I think it has a 6.9 difficulty in the Code of Points."

Tony barked a laugh. "Since you're all about perfect execution, Ashvili, show me what you've got." He eyed Sol's gorgeous dick. "Let's start with this."

Tony didn't waste time with tentative licks, not now, not when Sol's breath on the damp skin of his cock head made him feel like he was about to launch into a triple double with no mat to catch him.

He took Sol in his mouth, took him deep as Tony had wanted to do for *ages*, the weight of that perfect cock heavy on his tongue with the bitter salt of pre-come. Sol gasped when Tony swallowed and then he sucked Tony's cock down. Not into his throat, but the way his tongue circled the head was like... *Unngh. 10.0 execution.*

Sol pulled off, gasping. "Tony. I'm about to come. You need to —"

But Tony gripped Sol's hip, keeping him right where he belonged until his muscles tensed and his cock throbbed in Tony's throat. Tony eased up, so he could taste Sol as he swallowed every drop, then gentled his tongue as Sol shuddered through his release.

Before Tony could take a deep breath, though, Sol gripped Tony's cock, jacking it as he sucked the head, and heat sizzled down Tony's spine and in his balls and he was coming and Sol was swallowing and licking and right *there*.

"*Solly*." He breathed Sol's name like a prayer.

Sol dropped a kiss on Tony's cock and another on his hipbone, and then rolled onto his back, chest heaving. "Wow. Talk about risk-reward."

Tony flopped onto the pillows, keeping his hand on Sol's bare flank. "And the reward, my friend, is why the risk is worth it."

Sol pawed at Tony's leg, as if his muscles weren't quite working yet, his hand coming to rest on Tony's thigh. "No shit." Then he started to laugh. "So when can we do it again?"

With the intensity of their last training days and the frenzy of getting ready to leave for Tokyo, Sol hadn't been able to snatch any more time alone with Tony. He didn't hold out much hope for tonight either, because their flight for Tokyo was leaving from Denver at 4:00 am.

At the moment, all the guys on the team were running in and out of each other's suites like maniacs, all of them so excited they were practically jumping out of their skins.

Well, except for Rahul. The only thing he was stressed about was whether his textbooks would put his luggage over the weight limit.

Sol finished packing and parked his suitcases in the common room. "I'm, um, going up to see if Tony or Eddie need any help," he called. He didn't expect a response from Rahul and he didn't get one, so he zipped out of their suite and headed up to Tony's.

Danny was just leaving as Sol arrived. "Dude." He jerked his thumb at the door. "See if you can talk some sense into Thomas. He hasn't even *started* packing."

Sol chuckled. "He never does. Not until the last minute. I think it's part of his pre-competition ritual—an extra adrenaline rush from the chance he might be late."

"Well, do something. The team bus leaves for Denver in two hours and I am *not* missing the flight to the Olympics because Thomas is trying to choose what underwear to bring."

"Don't worry." Sol patted Danny's shoulder. "I'll take care of it."

"Awesome." He grinned. "See you on the bus." He trotted off down the hall.

When Sol stepped inside, Eddie was sitting on the sofa in the common room, staring at the wall. "Eddie? You okay, man?"

Eddie turned wide eyes on Sol. "The Olympics, Sol. It's the *Olympics*."

"Not quite yet." He hauled Eddie off the sofa by one elbow. "Why don't you go grab a snack? You've got time before the bus leaves for the airport."

Eddie groaned and pressed his hands to his belly. "Please don't mention food. Or the bus. Or the airport."

"What can I mention?"

Eddie just shook his head and sank back onto the sofa, muttering, "The Olympics. It's *the Olympics*."

So much for getting some alone time with Tony. Sol sighed and strode to Tony's bedroom door. As expected, he had his earbuds in, bopping to an unheard tune as he rummaged through a giant Walgreen's bag. Sol edged closer and touched Tony's shoulder.

He jerked, spilling the contents of the bag onto the bed next to his still empty suitcase.

"Jesus, Solly! I've told you—"

"Yeah, yeah. Don't sneak up on you." Sol cast a glance at the door, making sure they were out of Eddie's sightline, then pressed a kiss to Tony's mouth.

Tony smiled under Sol's lips, the smile turning into a full-on grin when he drew back. "You can sneak one of those on me anytime, though."

Sol glanced at the bed and did a double take. "Oh my God, Tony. If you pack all that lube, you won't have any room for your clothes. Overkill much?"

He shrugged. "The Olympics might hand out condoms by the truckload, but I'm not betting my ass—or yours—on the availability of Olympic-branded lube."

Heat rushed up Sol's chest. "Do you, um, intend to... you know?"

Tony's grin widened. "I told you. Once our competition is over, so's the secrecy. And I'm not waiting a minute longer than I have to."

"Good to know," Sol croaked, his dick trying to punch through his shorts.

"What?" The grin faded. "You mean you don't want—"

"No! I mean yes." Sol swallowed convulsively. "It's just... Wow. A long time coming, you know?"

Tony waggled his eyebrows. "A long time, huh?" His voice dropped to a suggestive murmur. "Now that you mention it, I'd love to edge you for a couple of hours. Get you sweaty outside the gym."

"A couple of *hours*?" Sol's voice broke. "Are you kidding me?"

"Sol, Sol, Sol," Tony said, shaking his head in mock disappointment. "You shock me. You've been working with Xiao much longer than I have. Have you learned nothing of *patience* by now?"

"Shut up." He punched Tony's shoulder, then allowed his hand to drift lower, down his pecs and over his abs to rest on his hip. "We'll see how you feel about patience when we won't be able to touch each other like this for the next three weeks."

Tony groaned and sat on the bed, pushing the pile of lube aside so he could pull Sol down next to him. "Ten days' training on site. Then the opening ceremonies. Then eleven days of competition, from qualifying to the last event finals. It's for-fucking-ever."

Sol took Tony's hand, toying with his fingers. "Do you suppose that's one of the reasons fans have lost interest? Because the competition goes on for so long? Qualifying, then the team event, then the all-around, and *then* three days of event finals? Not to mention alternating days with the women?"

"Maybe." Tony shrugged. "It's not like the format has changed much, not like scoring has. I don't know. Seems like attention spans have decreased at the same time sports and entertainment options have increased." He nudged Sol's shoulder with his own. "We just have to give the audience something worth watching."

Sol smiled wryly. "The Thomas flair?"

"Team USA Flair." He brushed Sol's floppy bangs off his forehead. "You'll look so hot with highlights."

"I can't believe we let you talk us into that."

"Embrace the new brand, baby. All for a good cause."

"Right. The team. Our sport." Sol tugged a curl at Tony's nape. "Does that mean more shirtless training sessions?"

"If it gets the fans excited? You bet your ass."

"My ass or yours, that's a bet I'll win either way." Sol picked up a handful of lube bottles and tossed them into Tony's suitcase. "But as much as I appreciate you naked, you still have to pack more than this." He stood, offering his hand. "Come on. The bus is leaving soon, and despite your penchant for last minute arrivals, I refuse to let you cut it close this time."

Tony took Sol's hand and pulled himself up so they were chest to chest just as the door to the suite banged open and Danny's cry of "Dude!" filled the air.

"Fucking cockblocker," Tony muttered. "C'mere." He pulled Sol over to the corner behind the door and cupped his face with both hands. Sol's heart stuttered at the heat in Tony's eyes, and he had to bury the moan when Tony took him in a searing kiss.

"Dudes," Danny called. "Isn't Thomas packed *yet*?"

Tony shook his head and kissed Sol quickly again. "Be ready, Solly. Our next kiss will be in Tokyo."

CHAPTER FOURTEEN

In the bathroom of their Olympic Village suite, Sol peered at his reflection. The stylist at the Village salon had shaved his undercut really close, but she'd left the hair on top longer than he liked. She'd convinced him to use this new hair product to keep it from lying flat or flopping into his eyes.

"Show off the highlights more," she said, rubbing her fingers through his hair. "Star power."

"Star power, my ass," Sol muttered. But he had to admit, he was starting to like it. She had laid blond streaks into his forelock but left the back alone.

She'd done something a little different to each of the guys. Tony had his usual cap of blond curls crowning his fade. Danny had platinum racing stripes carved from his temples to behind his ears. Rahul... Sol snorted when he thought of it. Rahul's jet black hair now sported frosted tips.

Tony hadn't insisted that the specialists or the alternates submit to the same treatment, but they'd chosen to do it anyway. Eddie now had platinum bangs. Chad, who had light brown hair anyway, now had some serious blond highlights. Jason normally shaved his head, but he'd had the stylist dye blond stripes in the middle of his eyebrows.

Someone pounded on the door. "You fall in, Sol?" Danny shouted. "Come on! We'll be late for training."

"Keep your shirt on." Sol took one final glance and opened the bathroom door.

Danny stood there in the hallway—shirtless—grinning like a loon. "Are you kidding? This is *training*. We don't wear no stinkin' shirts."

Eddie pushed past him on the way to their common room. "That's because if you wore one, it *would* stink."

Danny pressed a hand to his chest. "You wound me. My honest sweat is—"

"More than we want to smell." Tony poked his head out of the room he was sharing with Danny and rifled a Team USA T-shirt at him. "You can't walk around the Village that way. Save the beefcake for when we're in the gym."

"I feel so objectified," Danny moaned, but he was grinning as he pulled on the shirt. "Do we have to wear our team warmups too?"

"Not the competition ones. But deck yourself out in the Team USA gear they gave us for training. This is our first official outing and we want to make a statement."

Sol grabbed his stuff out of his room—he got the single because the coaches always wanted to be sensitive about his diabetes management privacy. He joined the rest of the guys in the common room.

"Ready?" Tony grinned at them, with a wink at Sol. "Let's go make that statement."

They headed out into the Village to meet the team bus, the sun catching in all the blondness. It was already hot—Tokyo didn't cool down much overnight—and while the humidity wasn't as intense as summer in Oklahoma—yet—Sol was still glad of the wicking action of their team outfits.

This early, the Village wasn't completely populated, but it wasn't empty either. They'd already met up with gymnasts from other countries in the dining hall, guys they'd competed against in World Cup events all year. The women's team was already on site too, and they'd had breakfast with them this morning, which involved a hell of a lot of giggling—on both sides.

When they got to the Ariake Gymnastics Centre, Sol just stood in front of it and stared. *It's like a spaceship moored in place by giant chopsticks.* He wasn't the only one who was speechless—for once, Danny didn't have anything to say, either. The coaches didn't rush them—they knew what being here meant to everyone.

I want to remember everything. Every moment. Especially now, when all of it was new, and the competition was nothing but potential—a gift waiting for them to unwrap. *Maybe it'll be the legendary and iconic Red Ryder BB gun with a compass in the stock. Maybe it'll be a pair of tube socks.* But right now? It was nothing but magic and wonder.

With nine days' worth of training to get through before they got to rip open the package.

They crossed the plaza and followed the coaches into the training gym.

"Niiiice." Danny dropped his bag next to the spring floor. "Everything all pristine and shiny."

Eddie pointed to a chalky footprint. "Not all that shiny. Someone must have beat us in here today."

As most of the guys started stripping off their outerwear, Tony tugged on Sol's sleeve. "Come on."

Sol glanced at Xiao, who was waiting to direct their warm up. "But—"

"Just for a minute. Do you need to do the pee-pee dance for an excuse?"

Sol scowled at him. "No. Of course not." But he still glanced nervously over his shoulder before he followed Tony out of the gym and down a corridor. "Where are we—*oh.*"

Tony stopped at the end of the tunnel, the arena vast and echoing beyond him. "You'll never see it like this again."

Sol joined him and they moved out onto the floor next to the vault runway. Sol had been competing, on both the national and international level, for years. He'd been in more gyms and arenas than he could count, some of them empty, some of them relatively new. Hell, he'd been to Rio. But it had never been like this.

This time, he wouldn't be a spectator, a passive member of the team, suited up for no reason. This time, he'd be out there— pounding toward the vault table, tumbling across the spring floor, swinging from the high bar. All of it.

For the first time, an empty arena made him feel small.

Tony moved closer, his shoulder brushing Sol's. "Intense, isn't it?" Sol nodded, swallowing against a lump the size of his fist. "Just wait until we march out on the first day of competition. It's not like any other meet."

"I get that," he croaked. *God, do I get that.* Even the World Championships didn't have this... this *weight.*

"Hey." Tony grabbed Sol's hand. "You okay?"

"Yeah." *No.* He felt off balance. Untethered, like the first time he'd tried a high bar release without a safety harness. Only the warmth of Tony's hand kept him from wobbling. But then a voice echoed from somewhere in the vast arena, and Tony let go.

"Sorry."

Sol gave him a tight-lipped smile. "Don't be. I needed that."

"I'm not sorry for touching you. I'm sorry I had to let go. After the Games, it'll be different. After the Games, we're letting our rainbow flag fly."

Sol nodded, turning to head back toward the training gym. Tony had said the same thing before, but when the team got off the plane, they'd encountered a huge group of XBL fans, all clamoring for Tony. Tony had graciously turned it into a Team USA moment, but until then, Sol hadn't realized exactly how big Tony's audience was outside of gymnastics. "Don't get me wrong. I'd like nothing better. But are you sure? What about your fans? What about your dad?"

"My fans know I'm bi." He bumped into Sol and didn't move away immediately. "Hell, I get marriage proposals from all gender identities."

Sol raised an eyebrow. "Were you ever tempted to accept one of the offers?"

"Never." Tony grabbed Sol's elbow, stopping him before he could reach for the gym door. "Not for one single minute. Because in here?" He tapped his chest, over his heart. "In here, I was always waiting for you."

Sol pressed the heels of his hands against his eyes. "Damn it, Tony. You can't make me tear up right before practice."

"In case I never said it before, I'm sorry I ran. I'm sorry I left you. And I'm so, so sorry I never told you how I felt before."

Sol's laugh was watery. "It's probably just as well. If you'd told me you wanted me and *then* left, I'd have murdered you as soon as you stepped into USOPTC."

"Really?"

Sol sighed. "No. I'd probably have run after you. And *then* murdered you."

Tony grinned. "Well, thank fuck it played out the way it did. Because if you were in prison for murder, you wouldn't be about to win an Olympic medal."

Sol grabbed the door handle and gave Tony a wink. "What makes you think I'd have gotten caught?"

"Oh, you'd have gotten caught. The cops could've followed the chalky footprints."

Both of them were laughing as they walked into the gym, which wasn't the best way to be unobtrusive. Barry frowned at them, but Xiao, who was standing in the middle of the spring floor as the team jogged around its perimeter, simply gestured for them to join the line.

Then after warm-up, while Sol watched, counting down the strength moves in his head, Tony stuck his rings dismount cold for the first time.

Oh yeah. This team is definitely making a statement.

And after the Games? He and Tony would make another one, even if it was four years late.

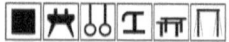

One more day until qualification. One more day before it all starts.

It was the last day of podium training before the official start of the games. They were finishing up the second set on their last rotation—the dreaded pommel horse—and fatigue was setting in for all of them. Tony, as the second one in the lineup, had already completed his two exercises. Both were identical, since he wasn't aiming for finals, just to post a respectable number for the team and go clean.

A collective groan rose from the other end of the gym where spectators—hard-core fans, the press, and judges in an unofficial capacity—were watching the athletes from Russia on high bar. Tony squinted, trying to make out what had happened. The guys from Russia had it rough enough already, since they weren't allowed to *be* their country's team—no flags, no official insignia, no anthem if they won—because of the four-year anti-doping ban that got slapped on Russia in December. They'd lost two of their top guys as a result, but their roster was so deep it almost didn't matter. *Other than the hit to their morale.*

Tony switched his attention to Sol, who was waiting his turn next to the stairs. He was their anchor on horse and had a real chance at an event gold. Sol had his eyes closed, his arms flapping comically at his sides, his upper body weaving like one of those roly-poly dolls with the round bottom. Tony buried his smirk. *Visualization.* He had to admit it seemed to work—his own routines were a lot more consistent now—but it could sure look goofy from the outside.

When Sol opened his eyes and climbed onto the podium, Tony clenched his fists at his sides. Why was he always more nervous watching Sol than he was doing his own exercises? *Maybe because I can control my own body.* But although he *willed* Sol to do well, to nail his routines, he couldn't actually *assist* in any way. That was the conundrum of a sport that was a collection of individuals performing separately rather than a team who had to interact to accomplish a scoring goal. *Sometimes I wish I'd chosen football like Dad always dreamed.*

Sol saluted, and as he grasped the pommels, Tony's mouth was so dry it was like he'd eaten the damn chalk for breakfast.

Sol mounted the horse, and just like every other time since the two of them had advanced beyond basic skills, Tony was mesmerized by Sol's power and grace. His circles were smooth, his body position straight, the extension on his flairs... God, he was perfect. He never broke his rhythm, never let his legs separate, and when he flew up to the handstand for his dismount with that extra pirouette? *Touchdown!* And not a single hop or step on landing.

Yes! Grinning, Tony punched the air, waiting for Sol to do the same. And waited. And waited.

But instead of raising his arms in the post-exercise salute, Sol slowly toppled sideways onto the mat.

"Jesus!" Tony rushed up the stairs, reaching Sol only seconds before Xiao. He knelt next to Sol and put a hand on his shoulder. "Solly, stay put. What's wrong?"

"Nothing." Sol pushed himself up and Tony steadied him with an arm around his back. "Headache. Got a little dizzy." He smiled, but it was a pathetic effort. "I'm fine." By this time, Barry and a couple of officials had hurried over. Sol winced. "Really. Let's not make a big deal out of this."

Tony raised an eyebrow. "You just collapsed in front of a crowd. It's not exactly a secret."

A medic joined Tony next to Sol. "A stretcher will be here momentarily. Can you tell me what happened?"

"I don't need a stretcher." Sol waved him away. "I need to check my levels. Probably grab a snack. I'm still having trouble timing my meals."

The medic blinked. "You're diabetic?"

"Yes. The organizers know." Sol held out a hand and Tony helped him stand. He wobbled a bit, but then straightened up. "It'll be okay. Really." He smiled again, and this one was a little more convincing. "I miscalculated the time before podium training. Stupid of me, but not catastrophic."

The medic frowned at him. "I think you should wait for the stretcher."

"No. I just need to get my glucometer and some juice. Grab a snack." Sol moved toward the stairs, Tony practically glued to his side. *He may not need a stretcher, but he's not shaking me.* "If I have permission to leave the venue?"

"I'll stay with him," Tony said, earning an irritated glance from Sol. "It's either me or the medic," he murmured. "Which would you prefer?"

"Fine," Sol growled. Barry and the other officials nodded, so Tony followed Sol down the stairs, grabbed both their gym bags, and stuck close to Sol, a hand on his lower back, as they made their way out of the arena to the murmured encouragement of their teammates.

They stopped in the restroom so Sol could wash his hands. Tony dug in Sol's bag and handed him the glucometer. Sol grimaced at the result. "I feel so fucking stupid. I ought to be acclimated to the time and schedule by now."

"You didn't eat very much at breakfast. I pointed it out, if you recall, but you snapped at me."

"I didn't snap at you."

Tony raised both eyebrows. "Dude. It was totally a snap. *'You're not my mother,'* I believe were your words."

"That's because you were *hovering*, just like you're doing now."

Tony gently gripped the back of Sol's neck. "I've got an arrears of closeness to make up. Sue me. I care about you."

Sol sighed and leaned against Tony. "I know. But I'm an adult, and I've been managing my condition for fourteen years. I shouldn't need reminding."

"Well, you might be a tad distracted. You know. Tokyo. The Olympics." He waggled his eyebrows and leered. "Me."

Sol tried to suppress his smile. He failed. "Shut up."

"I'll leave you alone to do your thing. I know you don't like an audience. But if you're not out in five minutes, I'm coming back in."

"Yes, Mother."

Tony met Sol's gaze. "I am *so* not your mother." He tightened his grip on Sol's neck and drew him into a kiss—quick but thorough. "And don't you forget it."

Tony stepped out into the hallway to find the rest of the team straggling by. "Did they call the session?" he asked Danny.

"Yep. The next subdivision is taking the floor. How is he?"

"Feeling like a fool for not calculating his carbs correctly. But he'll be okay." *He'd better be.* "You know how he doesn't like any personal drama to take away from the team."

"Yeah. About that." Danny shrugged apologetically, then handed Tony his phone. A grainy YouTube video was cued up, frozen on the image of Sol on the horse, mid-flair. Tony punched the screen, and the video played, all the way to Sol's collapse and his own frantic rush onto the podium. *Jesus, am I that fucking obvious?*

The video stopped after the medic joined the group around Sol, so it didn't include his exit under his own power. Then Tony noticed the number of hits. "Thirty-two thousand hits *already*? It only happened ten minutes ago."

Danny shrugged. "Power of social media, dude." He tucked his phone into the pocket of his warm-up jacket. "Are you gonna tell him, or am I?"

CHAPTER FIFTEEN

Sol took a vicious bite of a protein bar. *I can't believe I did that. Or rather, didn't do that.* Maintaining his levels, timing his meals and insulin injections—he'd been doing it for so long they were as automatic as breathing. Yet somehow, in the excitement of being at the freaking *Olympics*, for Pete's sake—with the team, with Tony—he'd let his attention, his internal monitoring system, slip. He'd gotten so focused on calculating the team's potential scores compared to their competition that he'd forgotten to calculate his own freaking insulin dose.

Stupid stupid stupid.

It wasn't as bad as it could have been—he didn't pass out and he didn't need a glucagon hit, thank goodness—but it was embarrassing. He hadn't slipped like this since the first couple of years after his diagnosis. He couldn't believe he'd waited until he was *at the freaking Olympics* to do it again, and at podium training, for God's sake, in front of the team, the Olympic officials—God, in front of the judges. *In front of Tony.*

For some reason, even though Tony was more familiar with Sol's condition than anyone other than Sol's parents, it was even more humiliating to fail like that in front of him. *Why? Because you want to show him you're a worthy mate who's not too high-maintenance to be a pain in the ass?*

"Well, that ship has sailed," Sol muttered. He checked his levels again. The juice he'd downed first was having an effect.

He needed to eat a full meal, because his belly was rumbling. *I shouldn't have gone all diva-fit on Tony this morning.* Because he'd been right. Sol hadn't eaten enough, not to support podium training.

He downed the rest of his water bottle. His headache was still with him, but he wasn't dizzy anymore. The guys would be heading over to the dining hall for lunch soon. *I'll be fine.*

He stood up. No wobbles. *It's all good.* When he stepped into the hallway, Tony was propping up the wall with his shoulder, gazing down at his cell phone, and looking remarkably somber. Murmurs and shouts drifted from the arena, so podium training for the next subdivision must already be underway. *Good. I didn't delay them.* That would be all he needed—to be famous as the guy who kept the Japanese team from practicing in front of their home crowd. And men's gymnastics was a huge deal in Japan, much more popular than it was in the US. These guys were superstars. *Of course, they also regularly medal everywhere they compete.*

Tony pushed himself off the wall and edged close to Sol. "Hey. You doing all right?"

Sol's annoyance spiked again. "Yeah. I'm not an invalid," he snapped. Then he winced. "Sorry. Ignore my mood. This isn't your fault." He took a deep, steadying breath. "I'll be fine after lunch. Are the coaches giving notes beforehand?"

"Ah, no. They're waiting until we hit the gym this afternoon."

Sol was glad about that, anyway. He felt okay—mostly—but he'd rather not sit through a conference with the coaches right now, especially since he'd always assured them that his condition wouldn't prevent him from delivering peak performances.

"Then I guess we can head back to our suite and get cleaned up." Sol glanced up and down the corridor which was empty at the moment, although he wasn't brave enough to dare a kiss. *But God, I'd love nothing more than a hug right now.* Did that make him weak? Maybe. But right now, he didn't much give a shit. "Are the guys waiting for us?"

"No."

Sol chuckled. "Danny wanted a chance to hog the shower first?"

"Maybe." Tony's voice was low and serious. "But Solly, there's something you should know."

Sol's belly tumbled. "Why? Did something happen? Is it my folks?" Sol always kept his phone turned off during practice, as did all the other guys. He pawed through his bag, searching for the damn thing.

But Tony laid a hand on his arm. "No. Your folks are fine, as far as I know. It's this." He touched his phone's screen and held it up so Sol could watch himself crumple onto the mat in the most ludicrous dismount in history. "The hits are up to the high six figures now, and it's trending on Twitter."

Sol stared at the phone in mounting horror. "Somebody filmed this?"

Tony nodded. "It was inevitable, I suppose. There were a lot of people in the stands, and you're a popular guy."

Sol leaned back and let his head *thunk* against the wall. "Except now I'm a popular guy who collapsed on the Olympic stage."

"Don't be a drama queen. You only collapsed at practice. That doesn't count as the Olympic stage."

Sol squinted at Tony out of one eye. "You may think you're helping, but you're so not."

Tony sidled closer until Sol could feel his heat along his arm. "Well, I won't say I told you so."

"I think you just did."

"Nope." Tony grinned. "I most certainly didn't. Doesn't mean I won't in the future if you pull this kind of stunt again."

Sol sighed. "Not exactly XBL-worthy, is it?"

"Are you kidding? It's ten times scarier—a hundred times." Tony gripped Sol's forearm. "Because it's you. Your health. Your life. Please don't scare me like that again, Solly."

Sol belly flopped again. *High-maintenance, that's me.* "I'm diabetic, Tony. I can't promise my medical condition won't affect me."

Tony's grip tightened. "That's not what I mean. You told me not to take risks with my body. Well, I'm gonna demand the same from you. Please."

Sol studied Tony's face. His dark eyes were shadowed here in the dim corridor, but the lines around his mouth were more pronounced because of the way he pressed his lips together. Sol had never seen him so serious. *So worried.* "Okay."

"Good." He gave Sol's arm a tiny shake. "Although I'm guessing this'll be a wake-up call for you, anyway."

Yeah. But maybe not in the way you mean. Because despite the intimacy he and Tony had shared—all too infrequently—since Tony had arrived at the training center, it had never occurred to Sol that Tony's feelings might run as deep as his own, that Tony might need him as much as he needed Tony, that underneath the flamboyance of the Thomas flair ran astonishing vulnerability.

Sol pinched the bridge of his nose. "God, this is going to generate exactly the kind of notoriety I wanted to avoid."

"You're trending, dude. It's inevitable. But..." Tony's gaze drifted to a place beyond Sol's shoulder. "Maybe you just need to get ahead of it."

"What do you mean?"

"Well, people want to know why you collapsed. They're gonna speculate, especially if you don't say anything." He waggled his phone. "They're already speculating in the comments and through tweets, everything from exhaustion to doping to physical abuse."

Sol goggled at him. "Are you joking?"

"Sadly, no."

"They can't—" He scrubbed his hands over his face. "I can't be the cause of more PR problems for Team USA. I won't."

"I know. And I've got an idea. Come on, though. You need to get to lunch."

Sol let Tony tow him down the corridor. "Wait. This isn't the way out."

"Secret passage. I got medical permission for you to avoid running the fucking press gauntlet in the mixed zone."

Tony led him out into the Tokyo sun, but then Sol dug his heels in. "I'm not going any further until you tell me what your plan is."

Tony screwed his face up. "It's not anything as formal as a *plan*. Not yet. But Quinn is already here. She may have been watching our subdivision train—that's the kind of thing she'd do. I can call Ori—"

"Your agent?"

"Yeah. I can have her set up an interview with Quinn."

"I don't know…"

"We can do it over at the main media center. It doesn't have to be formal, but I think it's time, Solly."

Sol tried to be annoyed that Tony persisted in using his old nickname, but if he was honest with himself, he liked it. *I've missed it.* "Time for what?"

"Keeping this secret is doing more harm than good now. You need to lay your cards on the table for everyone to see, especially people who've been dealt the same hand." Tony gazed at him, a smile playing around his lips, and Sol's brain stuttered for a moment because he was so beautiful. *Does he mean that we can let people know about us? No, he can't mean that.* "It's time for you to come out. As diabetic."

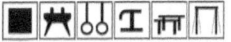

Ori came through as Tony knew she would. She had an interview with Quinn set up for immediately before afternoon training—although she told Tony that it hadn't been difficult.

Quinn had practically begged for a chance at the scoop. Ori checked in with Tony, her call coming in right after he and Sol returned to the suite after lunch. He ducked into the room he shared with Danny, who didn't care because he was playing GTA in their common room with a scowling Rahul.

"I had to hedge a little, as if it was a huge imposition to get you there so quickly." Ori's chuckle came through clearly on the call, even though she was in Los Angeles.

"Me? This isn't about me. It's about Sol."

"I know. But you're the one who has the relationship with Quinn. Besides," Ori's tone turned sly, "I figured you'd want to be there to support your... friend."

"Ori. I'm warning you. Do not even *breathe* that kind of rumor, not—"

"Chill out, my dear. I wouldn't. But I've known you for years, so don't think you can fool me. I think Sol would be more comfortable too, don't you? Especially if he wants to downplay this in favor of focusing on the team."

Tony sighed. Ori was right. Ori was annoyingly always right. "Okay. As long as Quinn knows this is Sol's show to run."

"She knows. I made it *very* clear. And I wouldn't do anything to antagonize Sol. Not when I want to sign him after the Games."

Tony plopped onto his bed. "You want him to turn pro?"

"Why not? His NCAA eligibility is up. If he medals at the Games—"

"He will." Tony had zero doubts on that score.

"Well then. His going public with his medical condition makes him an even more attractive property."

"He's not a *property*, Ori," Tony growled.

"Sorry. Agent-speak. You know I don't objectify my clients in the least." She chuckled. "Although that doesn't mean the public won't. Now go collect Sol. Quinn's waiting."

Tony emerged from his room and knocked on Sol's door. Sol cracked it open, peering out like he was expecting to get dog-piled by the press in their own suite. "Hey. Quinn's waiting for us. You ready?"

Sol nodded and stepped out of his room, a sheen of sweat glistening on his forehead. "I don't know about this."

"Don't worry." Tony rested his hands on Sol's shoulders—*that's a thing that a friend would totally do, right?* "I'll be with you the whole time."

Sol blinked. "You will? Through the whole interview?"

"Mmmhmmm. Ori pointed out to me that it made sense on several levels." Tony ticked them off on his fingers. "One, I'm the one who knows Quinn. Two, you'd probably feel better with a little backup."

"And three, you can never resist a chance to appear on-camera?"

Tony laughed. "Ordinarily, no. But for a change, this isn't about me. Come on. Let's go."

Sol was quiet on the bus ride to the Tokyo Big Sight, where the main press center was located. Quinn and her three-person crew met them at the reception area and led them into a small private studio, its cluster of tall chairs backed by a screen displaying the Olympic rings. Although the studio had seating for a small audience, it was empty except for the two of them and Quinn's staff. *Good. Less stress for Sol.*

He gave Sol's biceps a squeeze. "Don't worry. You've got this."

"Right." Sol's voice broke on the word.

Tony pulled him to a stop just inside the door. "Solly. I'm serious. Just be yourself. You've talked to the press before—"

"Yeah, but only about competitions. Only about gymnastics. Never about anything *personal.*"

"Just treat this like any post-meet interview and you'll be fine. If you get stuck, just turn to me and say, *Wouldn't you agree, Tony?*"

"But what if you don't agree?"

"With what?"

"With whatever I was saying?" Sol whispered, with a panicked glance at Quinn's crew setting up for the feed.

"Then I'll say so. But don't overthink it." Tony frowned, trying to figure out the best way to put Sol at ease. He'd appeared on-camera so often—both on his XBL channel and on other content delivery sites—that it was second nature. "I know. Imagine what you, as a newly diagnosed ten-year-old, would have wanted to know when you stepped into the gym for the first time."

Sol blinked again and nodded. "Right. Got it."

"Okay then. Ready?"

"No. But I doubt I can be readier."

Tony led Sol over to Quinn, who shook hands with both of them and invited them to sit opposite her. "I'm so glad you agreed to join me, Sol, Tony." She waited for them to adjust their mics and then gestured for her assistant to pass them each a bottle of water. "Are you ready to begin?"

Sol took a swig of his water. "Sure." The word came out garbled. He cleared his throat. "Sure."

"Any time, Quinn." Tony smiled at her and winked at Sol.

She faced the camera, and her assistant counted down until the feed went live. "Good afternoon. I'm so pleased to be here in Tokyo. With the opening ceremonies only hours away, the excitement is building as athletes and spectators stream in from all over the globe. But this morning, we witnessed a different kind of drama at the Ariake Gymnastics Centre. With me now is Sol Ashvili, one of the members of Team USA gymnastics, who had a bit of a scare today. Welcome, Sol."

Tony kept his gaze on Sol, whose throat worked a bit before he smiled at Quinn. "Thank you for having me. I'm a big fan."

Quinn pressed her hands to her cheeks, pretending coyness. "Oh, it's a good thing my complexion is dark enough not to show a blush." Sol chuckled, and his shoulders seemed to relax. *Good. He'll be fine now.* Quinn turned back to the camera. "And with Sol is his teammate, *Ringside* favorite Tony Thomas. Welcome, Tony."

"Always a pleasure, Quinn."

"Now." She settled back in the plush brown chair. "A lot of rumors have been flying around the internet about what happened this morning. Sol, can you give us the real story?"

Sol glanced his way and Tony gave him a tiny nod. *You can do this, baby.* Then he turned to Quinn. "I developed type 1 diabetes when I was ten years old, several months before I took my first gymnastics class."

Quinn raised her eyebrows. "You're diabetic."

"Yes. I have been for my entire gymnastics career. I'm not the only diabetic athlete. I'm not even the only diabetic Olympian. But I've never wanted my diagnosis to be held up as remarkable or as a qualifier to my success or failure. My coaches know. My team knows. The organizers at all the meets where I compete know, since something odd might show up in a mandatory drug test. But I've kept it quiet. Now though, keeping it on the down-low is doing more harm than good."

"So your collapse this morning was related to your disease?"

"My *condition.* Yes, but it wasn't a collapse. I just got a bit dizzy. I've worked with my doctors and trainers for years to establish clear rules about my sports participation and diabetes management, but today I miscalculated and mistimed my meals in the excitement of the Games and the intensity of our schedule." He smiled tightly. "But I'm fine now. No residual effects. And as Tony pointed out, it's been a wake-up call. I'm not likely to repeat that mistake." He looked at Tony. "Wouldn't you agree, Tony?"

Tony nearly laughed at the glint in Sol's eye. "Absolutely." He faced Quinn to pull the focus off Sol, even though he'd been doing just fine. "What Sol didn't mention was that I met him the day he took that first class. We've been friends for most of our lives. So I know the kind of commitment and drive he has, and his devotion to our sport." He leaned forward. "Do you know that he has the highest-valued pommel horse routine in the world?"

Sol rolled his eyes. "Don't let him snow you, Quinn," he said. "Tony's high bar routine is just as jam-packed with high-scoring components. But our whole team is ready to bring it. We're really looking forward to qualifications and to showing the world what we can do."

Quinn beamed at both of them. "Speaking as a long-time fan, may I say that I can't wait! Thank you both for joining me, and thank you, Sol, for sharing your story." She turned to the cameras. "Thank you all for joining us too. Tune in this evening when my guests will be the US women's soccer team, who have already won their first round game."

"And we're clear," the assistant said.

They all stood and Quinn shook their hands again, her wide grin lighting her face. "I can't thank you enough for giving me the scoop. Sol, you're welcome on *Ringside* any time. Tony?" She leaned forward—and down—and kissed his cheek. "You know I've always got a seat ready for you. Best of luck, guys. I'll be in the stands tomorrow, cheering you on."

"Thanks, Quinn." Tony gripped Sol's elbow and steered him away.

"Whew." Sol pretended to wipe sweat off his forehead. "I'm glad that's over."

"Are you kidding? You did great. Although..." Tony tapped his chin. "Since your spectacular dismount was technically performed in an international venue..."

"Stop. Just stop."

"No, I mean it. There were athletes and officials there from all over. We've got another element to add to the Code of Points—the Ashvili flop."

"I'm going to kill you," Sol growled, and chased Tony out the doors and into the sunlight.

CHAPTER SIXTEEN

Sol stood shoulder to shoulder with his teammates in the suite common room, Tony on one side and Eddie on the other, while the coaches conferred quietly in the corner. *Qualification day! This is happening!*

Jason and the other alternates were bleary-eyed and blinking after attending the opening ceremony. Sol was glad he'd opted out, along with the rest of the team. Yeah, it was awe-inspiring —they'd watched it on the big screen in the Village, together with other athletes who had events scheduled for today—but being in top form for competition was worth missing the circus, especially after his epic fail yesterday.

He'd been extra careful with his meal timing since, and didn't even gripe at Tony when he nagged—and while Tony claimed he was just *reminding* Sol, it was definitely nagging. Sol could forgive him though, because it came from a place of caring. *Annoying* caring, but caring nevertheless.

Sol's cell phone buzzed in his hand. He glanced down at it. Another spate of DMs from diabetic kids who'd thought their sports dreams were over when they were diagnosed. If nothing else, his near-collapse had done some good there. *Maybe it was wrong to keep silent about it for so long.*

"Good morning, men," Barry said, his ever-present tablet in his hand. "We'll be heading over to the arena for warm-up in a few minutes, but I want to review our strategy with you first."

Sol glanced sidelong at Tony. If Barry mandated the expected approach—conservative, clean, *safe*—would Tony go along with it? He'd been almost vibrating with energy since he'd bounded out of his bedroom this morning. In fact, Sol could feel the tremors in the shoulder pressed against his. No doubt about it, Tony was an adrenaline-and-testosterone-based life-form. *The genesis of the Thomas flair. The foundation of his style.* However, that style was miles away from *conservative* and the polar opposite of *safe*.

Barry tapped his tablet screen. "I've run the numbers. We've got the difficulty we need to make it into the team final with your conservative routines, provided we go clean. I know some of you have… opinions"—his gaze rested on Tony—"about watering down your exercises, but in qualification, it's more important to go twenty-four for twenty-four with no major errors. We are absolutely capable of that. So that's what we'll do. Understand?"

"Got it, coach," Tony said.

Sol sneaked a peek at him, but he didn't seem angry or annoyed at Barry's decree—his jaw was set, yes, and his gaze was intense, but with determination rather than rebellion. *He wants the team to succeed more than anyone.*

Barry nodded decisively. "All right. Pack up your gear. We'll meet you downstairs in fifteen."

Everybody broke to get ready. Sol made sure he had extra protein bars, apples, and juice in his bag along with his insulin pen and glucometer. He shouldn't need it—their subdivision should complete well before he'd need another meal, but delays happened. Better to be prepared than sorry.

He shouldered his bag and stepped out of his room. Tony was waiting for him, his grin lighting the dim hallway. "You ready for this?"

Sol nodded, answering Tony's grin with one of his own. "I don't have to ask you the same. If we could plug you into the electrical grid, you'd power the whole Village."

"Nah. But maybe this apartment."

"Trust me. The whole Village." Sol glanced around, but everybody else was already in the common room, so he dared to rest his hand on Tony's chest. *Is he still vibrating, or is it me?* "Just don't let your excitement goad you into doing anything..." Sol bit his lip.

"Anything stupid?"

"I was going to say anything risky, but stupid works too."

Tony rested his hand over Sol's. *It's definitely me.* "Don't worry, Solly. This is my chance for redemption. Today is all about the team." He leaned forward and kissed Sol quickly. "So let's do this."

Tony flashed another grin and then disappeared into the common room. Sol blinked, his fingers drifting up to his lips which still tingled from the kiss. *Oh, yeah.* Definitely *me. I shouldn't be worried about Tony's performance—I should be worried about mine.* Getting too distracted by the chain reaction that lit his blood whenever Tony touched him was *not* the way to win an Olympic medal.

I'll take it one event at a time, one skill at a time, same as usual. A smile tugged at his lips. *And save the Thomas and Ashvili moves— one skill at a time—for after we win.*

Sol joined the other guys, and they trooped downstairs to meet the coaches and board the bus to the arena. When they got to the training gym, the teams in the first subdivision were filing out for march-in. Team USA dropped their bags against the wall and started their general warm-up. They'd have about two hours, the length of the first subdivision's qualification round, before it was their turn—their official debut on the Olympic stage.

After a couple of laps around the spring floor to loosen his muscles, Sol sat down on a mat in the corner and pressed forward into a wide straddle. Tony sat down next to him, legs together, and leaned over to grasp his feet in a pike stretch.

Sol glanced at the other guys on the team, but they were all in their own pre-competition zone, whatever that happened to be. For Danny, it was stretching to a head-banging playlist that bled out of his earbuds. For Rahul, it was scowling at the wall, his back to the gym. Everybody had their own approach.

"Xiao says we're starting on rings in here, same as in the qualification round." Tony's voice was muffled, since he was essentially talking to his knees.

Sol pressed to a handstand and brought his legs together, toes pointed. "Makes sense." He folded to his feet rather than rolling out of the handstand and risk smacking Danny in the back. "One of your best events." Sol watched a Chinese gymnast throw a triple twisting double layout on the floor and bit his lip.

Tony peered up at him. "Are you worried?"

Sol sat and dropped into a pike of his own. "A little. Did you see that? He threw a Shirai III."

Tony's gaze met Sol's, his expression fierce. "Now who's getting psyched out? You can do that skill, Solly. You can do it just as well or better."

"Can I?" Sol turned his face to his knees. "I'm not so sure."

"Clean execution is your superpower. Nobody in this gym, nobody in this whole competition, is likelier to hit that perfect ten in execution value than you. Some of your elements, especially in Barry's famous *conservative* routines, aren't as high-valued as the Russians or Chinese, or God help us, the Japanese. But you can smoke 'em all if you go clean, Solly. So go clean."

Sol let Tony's words wash over him. In a way, they warmed him—after all, everybody liked to hear that they were good at what they loved, at what they dedicated so much of their life to. But in another way, they chilled him. *Expectations*. That was what had hobbled Team USA in Rio. They'd qualified in second place. But then, in the final, the wheels had fallen off—or rather, too many guys had fallen off the apparatus, leaving the team in fifth.

Expectations had hobbled his relationship with Tony too. *I let him carry all the weight in our friendship. I waited for him to come to me instead of following him and just having a freaking conversation with the guy who'd been my other half for half my life.* He studied the play of light on Tony's biceps, followed the line of his spine leading to the close-cropped curls at his nape. *Is history about to repeat itself? He walked away once. Will he do it again? Will I let him?*

"Not helping," Sol muttered, earning a quizzical glance from Tony.

One of the visualization techniques Xiao had taught Sol was to let the past stay in the past—as if a bead curtain separated what happened before from what was happening now. All Sol needed to stay in the present moment was to step through that curtain.

So he did.

Then, seemingly between one blink and the next, it was time. Sol lined up with the other guys behind a girl carrying the USA sign. A short march down the hall and through the tunnel and then… *God.* The roar of the packed arena hit him like a freight train. Yeah, the stands hadn't been empty during podium training, but this… *this* was different. This was the *Olympics.*

And Tony was *here*, leading the way. *Team captain.* When the guys elected him, he'd tried to decline, but Sol could tell he was secretly thrilled when they'd insisted. Now he turned and smiled at them all, with a wink at Sol. "This is it, guys. We're here. Now let's show 'em what Team USA can do."

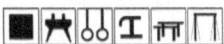

Although Tony wasn't precisely *happy* with Barry's no-risk-in-qualification edict, after one-touch warm-ups on rings, he had to admit he was okay with it. Too much adrenaline was rushing through him to keep him centered, so throwing his higher valued skills would be asking for trouble.

And this is not about me.

He was second to last in the lineup. He stood next to Sol, clapping while Eddie, first up, mounted the podium. Rahul, who was second, stood with his head bowed, scowling fiercely at the inoffensive stairs.

As Eddie pulled into his first strength move, Tony glanced sidelong at Sol. His lips were moving. "You're counting the hold, aren't you?"

Sol shot him a shamefaced glance. "Shut up. It's a habit."

Eddie landed with only a slight hop on his dismount—a one-tenth deduction at most, and no major errors. *One clean routine down.* He slapped Eddie's palms when he returned to the arena floor. "Good job, man." Eddie grinned and trotted over to confer with Xiao as Rahul mounted the podium. Sol took Rahul's place at the stairs and started his visualization routine. *Not as comical as his pommel horse show, but whatever gets the job done.* "Good luck, Solly," Tony murmured.

And despite all the grief Tony gave Sol about counting down the strength holds, he did the same for Sol. His difficulty value was lower than Tony's, but *damn.* His form was perfect. He hit every element cold, never sinking into a position, his swings never causing the straps to sway. *That's it, Solly. Just the dismount to go. Full twisting double back and yes!* Tony pumped his arms in the air and cheered because Sol just *drilled* that landing.

When Sol ran down the steps, making room for Chad, Tony not only slapped his hand, he hugged him and pounded his back. "Way to go clean, Solly."

Sol pulled out of the bro-hug and grinned at him. "Well, you told me to. How could I disobey?" He nudged Tony with his elbow. "Tell me you didn't count down my holds."

Tony grinned back. "Busted."

"Your turn at the stairs." His grin faded, his expression turning serious, but somehow tender. "Good luck. Redemption starts now."

God, Tony wanted to kiss him. But instead, he just nodded and moved toward the podium. And yes, he did his own visualization, because he was willing to do anything that helped him focus. But as he opened his eyes, he spotted two very unwelcome faces in the stands—his father and Andrei, sitting together, for fuck's sake, both of them with identical scowls on their equally florid faces.

Yeah, that's right, Andrei. I'm visualizing. *I'm cheering on my* competitors. Tony glanced behind him, where Sol stood next to Xiao. Sol gave him a subtle thumbs-up and a soft smile. *And* that *trumps the scowls in the stands any day.*

Tony congratulated Chad, then mounted the podium to chalk his hands and tighten his grips. He saluted the judges, then Volya lifted him up to grab the rings and steadied him before stepping away.

This is it. Tony rolled backwards into a planche, his first strength element, and then his training took over. The noise of the crowd faded, as did the shouts of encouragement from his teammates, allowing him to block out everything except the iron in his core and the burn in his muscles. Before he knew it, he was swinging to his triple pike Whittenburg dismount. The ground rushed up at him and he couldn't help it, he took a small hop. *I should have had more patience.*

Nevertheless, he pumped his fists in his final salute. *No major errors. I'll take it.*

Sol met him at the foot of the stairs, his grin wide, and his eyes bright. "That was awesome." He gave Tony the hand-slap/bro-hug, maybe holding it a second or two longer than the ones he gave the other guys.

"Except for the dismount."

Sol waved it off. "A tenth you didn't need to give away, and I'm sure Xiao will have words for you, but if you ask me? You'll make the event finals for sure."

Tony laughed as they both turned to watch Danny. "This is only the second subdivision. Let's not count our chickens."

"Your score's the highest one today. I'm right." Sol grinned. "And I'll remind you tonight that I told you so."

They stood, shoulders brushing, to watch Danny's exercise, and Tony was sure both of them were counting the holds this time. When Danny nailed his dismount, he hugged Sol again before they gathered around Danny. *Hey, we hit all our routines. Nobody can blame me for celebrating.*

He glanced at the stands as they marched to vault and caught the twin glowers on his dad's and Andrei's faces. *Okay, so some people can blame me.* But those two blamed him for everything, anyway, and Team USA was on fire, so fuck 'em.

The fire didn't diminish through vault, with Sol and Eddie qualifying for the vault final for sure. Then on p-bars, Danny was an absolute *beast*.

But on high bar, they ran into trouble.

Nobody fell off, thank God. Sol was rock solid as usual, and Rahul was competent but not flashy, although he took a giant step on landing. But Danny didn't hit one of his handstands clean and bent his elbows to regain his momentum.

Tony was anchoring, since high bar was his best event, so while they were waiting for Chad's score with Eddie chalking his hands and getting ready to compete, Tony sidled over to Xiao. "How are we doing? Are we holding our own against the other subdivision?"

Xiao glanced at the tablet in his hand. "We are ahead of all teams in subdivision one after three rotations, but trail the Chinese and the athletes from Russia in this round." He fixed Tony with his unruffled gaze. "We have two good events ahead of us, but your performance on high bar will be critical."

Tony grimaced. "Thanks, Xiao. No pressure, right?"

"Incorrect. There is a great deal of pressure." He smiled tightly. "But pressure is what you excel at. Just remember to have patience on your landings. There is no reason at all for you to have hopped on that rings dismount."

Xiao had a point—several, in fact. Tony lived for the win, for the rush, and pressure definitely added to that. Of course, if he had nobody but himself to worry about, he'd have been tempted to throw a higher-valued routine despite Barry's warning. But if the team needed him to go clean, then damn it, he'd go clean.

As he was waiting for Eddie to finish, Sol stepped up behind him, close enough for Tony to see him in his peripheral vision yet still allowing Tony his preparation space. Just knowing that Sol was there, at his back, meant everything. *It's like having the safety harness back on, in the days when I was first learning releases.*

As Tony mounted the stairs, Sol murmured, "You've got this," so Tony was grinning like a fool as he chalked his hands. He took his place under the bar, and when the green light flashed, he saluted the judges. *No problem. This is an easy routine. Two big releases, but not connected. Piece of cake.*

He touched his chest—*for luck*—then jumped up to grab the bar and kip up to enter his first swing. Giants to his first release —a Kovacs piked. *Keep the momentum. Hit all the handstands. Keep the arms straight.* When he released the bar for his second flight skill—a Gaylord II—Tony could swear he was floating over the bar in slow motion, with eons of time to catch it on the way down. Now the dismount. Double twisting double layout. Feet punching the mat. *Patience, patience.* Tony tightened his core to iron, circling his arms a bit for balance, but he stayed planted where he'd landed. *Yes.* A clean routine. A stuck dismount.

Sol's grin when he trotted down the stairs told the real story —he'd done his job.

The team rallied on floor, with Sol and Eddie posting outstanding scores. Although floor wasn't one of Tony's strengths—he had to make too many concessions for his knee— Xiao had helped him adjust his routine and maximize the difficulty he could manage with smart composition. Tony hit a respectable score, and other than Chad stepping out of bounds on his second tumbling pass, they didn't have any errors.

Then on pommel horse… God. Tony didn't remember his own routine—it must have been okay, because his score was decent—but Sol absolutely *smoked* it. In a sport where winners were decided by hundredths of a point, Sol's score was a full point higher than any gymnast so far. In qualification. With his lower-valued routine. Tony thought his face would split from grinning.

He's going to medal in the event finals. Gold, or I'll eat my shorts.

But in the meantime, the team had accomplished their goal—they'd posted a higher score than every country in the first subdivision and every team in this subdivision except China. With a couple of powerhouse countries still to come in later in the day, including Japan, nothing was official yet.

But Tony knew it in his gut. They'd done it. They'd made the final.

And this time, God damn it, we're gonna medal.

CHAPTER SEVENTEEN

In practice the day after qualification, Sol was still euphoric enough from the results that Xiao had to reprimand him for inattention more than once. *But can you blame me?* The team had qualified for the final in third place, only Japan and China ahead of them. He and Rahul had both qualified for the all-around, and four of them had qualified for event finals. He'd qualified for pommel horse and floor, he and Eddie on vault, Danny on p-bars, Danny and Tony on rings, and Tony on high bar.

With a week until event finals, only the four-man team was in the practice gym today—the rest of the guys were out in the stands, watching the women's qualifying rounds. Sol had no doubt the US women would be the top qualifiers again—they were just that superlative. *I wish I could see them.* But today was all about getting ready for the team final tomorrow.

Barry called them over after their warm-up. "Good job yesterday, men. With very few exceptions, you delivered the performance level we expected from you." He scowled down at his tablet. "We've drawn floor to start tomorrow, which means we'll be finishing up on high bar."

Sol glanced at Tony, who was sitting on the other side of Danny, and grinned. Tony would love that order—finishing up on his best event was exactly the kind of drama that played well with the Thomas flair. But Tony didn't look pleased. In fact, he looked as distracted as Sol had been all morning, with a little worry wrinkle between his brows.

Barry tucked his tablet under his arm. "We've analyzed the results, and our strategy tomorrow is the same as qualifying. Go clean. Errors are more costly than upping the difficulty unnecessarily. Save the fireworks for event finals." He checked his watch, muttering something under his breath. "I've got a meeting with the Olympic Committee. Why they couldn't schedule it at another time..." He sighed. "Get started with Xiao and Volya. I'll be back as soon as I can." He pointed at Tony. "No fireworks, Thomas. I mean it."

Tony waited until Barry walked away, then he muttered, "He's wrong."

Rahul's perpetual frown deepened. "He has the data. What makes you think he's incorrect?"

"The thing about data, Rahul, old pal, who's an engineer and not a chemist, physicist, statistician, or social media aficionado, is that data only tells you what happened *before*." Tony pulled a wad of paper out of his gym bag and unfolded it to reveal a complex grid with names and numbers. "Here are the results from qualifying." He pointed to their own names, with scores broken down by difficulty and execution. "We did what Barry asked yesterday. We went clean. Can we go cleaner?"

Sol and Danny exchanged glances with Rahul. *Probably not.* Or probably only by a tenth or two.

"Now here"—Tony jabbed his finger at another spot on the page—"are the scores for the other teams in the final. Only one or two major errors among them." He waved a hand dismissively. "I mean, the Japanese team could probably have one guy fall on every apparatus and still come out on top, but I guarantee you that every single one of the other teams is gonna upgrade. Assuming everyone goes clean with the same routines as qualifying, we'll end up in fourth at best. The math—" His mouth quirked up, and he slid a glance at Sol. "—just doesn't support it."

"So what do you suggest?" Rahul asked. "That we defy our coach?"

"No. It could still work, if other teams make errors and we don't. But we should be prepared, know what I mean? We've been practicing our higher-valued routines since we got to Tokyo. Let's keep practicing them today."

Danny shrugged. "I'm cool with that. I mean, better to be ready and not need the extra skills than need 'em and come up short."

Tony slapped the paper. "Exactly!"

"But Barry has already made his wishes clear," Rahul said. "He'll be back shortly and I think he's bound to notice if you're doing three consecutive releases on high bar instead of two unconnected ones."

"I'll talk to him when he gets back." Tony shoved the paper back in his bag. "I'm used to coaches yelling at me."

"Dude," Danny said, "we're a team. We won't leave you hanging."

"I appreciate it, but—"

"Danny's right." Sol caught Tony's gaze. "We're a team. You're our captain, and I think I can speak for all of us when I say that we believe in you. In your skill. Your drive. Your... your heart." Danny and Rahul nodded. "Gymnastics is always about risk-reward." Sol blinked, suddenly remembering the last time he'd mentioned risk-reward to Tony. Judging by the way Tony's eyes widened, he remembered it too. "I think..." Sol poked Tony in the shoulder with one finger to get both their minds off sexy naked times. "I think it might be time for a little risk."

"You don't say," he murmured, following up with a shaky laugh. "Thanks, guys. I hope you know this isn't just a stunt for me. I'm not doing it for the shock value or personal glory."

"We know." Sol spread his hands, palms up. "This is all about the team." It might be about redemption for Tony, at least partially. But if Sol had learned anything in the last few weeks, it was that Tony was committed to *this* team, to *these* guys, to *this* program. He wanted them to medal to raise the stature of US men's gymnastics, not because he wanted another piece of hardware around his own neck. And Sol was totally on board with that plan. "Before Barry gets back, we need to talk to Xiao and Volya, get them to agree. Barry listens to them."

"Yes, but do *they* listen to *us*?" Rahul muttered.

"More than you think. I'm sure I can get Xiao to agree—he's been upgrading my floor and pommel routines for weeks." Sol squinted across the gym where Xiao and Volya were conferring under the still rings. "I'll go talk to him now."

"I'm coming with you." Tony's jaw was set in a stubborn line. "You shouldn't have to do this alone."

Sol gripped his shoulder. *Let me carry you for a change, Tony.* "I'm not alone. You've all got my back. But Xiao has been my personal coach for years. I know him. And he's much more likely to agree to the plan if he doesn't feel like he's being dog-piled." Sol grinned at Tony. "You all just stay here and *visualize* success."

This time, Tony's laugh was full and free. "Right." He grabbed Danny and Rahul each by a forearm. "Altogether, guys, repeat after me—*oooohhhhmmmm.*"

Even Rahul chuckled at that. Sol left them chortling and crossed to meet Xiao. "Can I have a word?"

Xiao excused himself from Volya, who nodded, cheerful as always, and went to join the team. "Yes?"

Sol hadn't chalked his hands yet, so when he wiped his damp palms against his shorts, he didn't leave white skid marks behind. "We've been talking, and we think Barry is making a mistake."

Xiao's eyebrows rose. "A mistake? In the event lineups?"

"No. Those all look great." Sol bit his lip and glanced back at the team. Rahul and Danny were laughing with Volya—well, Rahul was almost smiling—but Tony's somber gaze was fixed on Sol. "The thing is, we think we should boost our difficulty for the final. Tony's done some analysis—"

"You realize Barry has many years' worth of analysis."

"Yes, but this is the Olympics. Other teams aren't going to play it safe. If we do, even if we go clean, we'll drop out of medal contention."

"If you miss a higher-valued skill, the same will occur."

"I know. But don't you think we should be prepared? Let us train both sets of routines today. If we need to upgrade, we'll be ready. If everything goes the way Barry predicts, no harm, no foul. But if we need it?"

Xiao studied Sol solemnly for a moment, but Sol was used to that—Xiao wasn't volatile like Andrei, or chatty like Volya. Then he nodded decisively. "Each of you may choose an upgraded routine for one event only, perhaps two. Then we will see."

Sol grinned, the tension in his shoulders dissipating. "Thanks, Xiao."

"I will tell Barry when he returns." Xiao's gaze intensified. "*You* will choose floor and pommel horse." Then he smiled, thin-lipped yet smug. "I would have insisted on it, anyway."

Sol goggled at Xiao until he located his voice. "You let me grovel like that when you planned to upgrade my routines already?"

"Humility is good for the soul. Nobody, least of all a gymnast, can afford arrogance. You might remind your friend Mr. Thomas of that." He glanced meaningfully at the untouched equipment. "I believe you have some work to do."

■ ⛩ ⚏ �⊥ ⛩ ⌷

Sol was wandering down the suite's hallway after his shower, a towel wrapped around his waist and blotting his hair dry with another, when somebody grabbed him by the elbow.

"Wha—"

"Shhh," Tony hissed and towed him away from the common room where the other guys were shooting the shit before heading to dinner. He hustled them both into Sol's room and then backed Sol against the door in a full-body press.

"Tony," Sol whispered, dropping his hair towel on the floor, "what are you doing? These rooms aren't exactly soundproof and we've only got ten minutes before we have to meet the women's team in the dining hall."

"I don't care," Tony growled, running his hands through Sol's damp hair. "You were so fucking *hot* today."

"Do you need glasses? Didn't you notice me fall off the horse twice?"

"I'm not talking about practice." He leaned in and nuzzled the curve of Sol's shoulder. "I'm talking about how you advocated for us to Xiao. How you got Barry to agree to our proposal."

Sol sucked in a breath when Tony licked the sensitive spot behind his ear. "To be f-fair, I think Xiao was already planning the change. And he's the one who got Barry to agree."

"Details." Tony nibbled on Sol's earlobe. "You didn't know that." He pulled back and grinned, hot and wicked. "Face it, Solly. You took one for the team. So. Fucking. Hot." He pressed against Sol, lining up their hardened cocks. "You deserve a reward for taking that kind of risk."

Sol couldn't resist flexing his hips but he stifled his moan. *Nothing but my towel and his shorts between us.* "You call this a reward? I call it torture. We don't have time for anything now."

"No?" Tony smacked his lips and hooked a finger in the towel at Sol's waist. "Want to bet?"

Sol grabbed his wrist. "Tony. I cannot go to dinner with my teammates after I've just been blown any more than you can go looking like you've just done the blowing."

Tony screwed up his face. "Fuck. You're right. That wouldn't exactly be in keeping with the plan, would it?" He huffed a breath. "Can I say for the record that I'm really starting to hate the plan? Why did we make such a stupid plan in the first place?"

"If I recall, it was *your* plan." Sol raised his palms. "But I didn't disagree. We should be about the team. About Olympic competition."

"Competition, eh?" Tony traced Sol's collarbone with one finger. "You know I never turn down a chance to compete."

He trailed his finger up Sol's throat until it rested under his chin. Then he angled his head and leaned in for a kiss—soft, unhurried, with just a tickle of tongue against Sol's lower lip.

Sol couldn't stop the moan this time—he only hoped it wasn't as loud as it sounded in his head.

Tony pulled back and leered comically. "So how was it?"

Sol tried to catch his breath. "O-okay. I only felt it about down to here." Sol touched the base of his throat.

"Really?" Tony glanced down at the tented towel at Sol's waist and lifted his eyebrows. "Because I could swear you're feeling it down—"

"Shut up." He ripped the towel off and flung it on the bed because what the hell. "You can do better. Where's that legendary Thomas flair?"

Tony's eyes glinted as his gaze traveled over Sol's skin. "Is that a double-dog dare, Solly? A *naked* double-dog dare?"

"Call it whatever you want. Now show me what you've got."

Tony threaded his hands in Sol's hair and eased closer, closer, closer—until his lips barely teased Sol's, a feather touch. "Open for me, Solly," he murmured. "Let me in."

Cock throbbing in time to his racing heartbeat, Sol parted his lips and Tony licked into his mouth, flirting with Sol's tongue. *One one thousand two one thousand.* Then he brought them together in a kiss that raised the hair on Sol's nape and made his toes curl. *Tony's lips. Tony's heat. Tony's everything.*

When Tony's muscles tensed as if he was about to disengage, Sol clutched his shirt in his fists and pulled him back, eating at Tony's mouth as if he hadn't had a meal in weeks.

I'll never get enough of his taste. Never.

Tony wrenched his head back with a gasp and a wince. "God, Solly. This fucking official Team USA gear is not designed for hard-ons."

"Then I guess you shouldn't have started something you didn't intend to finish." Sol sauntered over to his dresser, although his own erection bobbing in front of him seriously undermined his attempt at nonchalance.

"Next time, Solly, next time. Count on it." Tony grinned, his hand on the doorknob. "One one thousand. Two—"

"Shut *up!*" Sol rifled a pair of briefs at him, but they missed as he ducked out the door. Sol smiled as he snagged the briefs off the floor and tried to stuff his very disappointed cock into them. *Next time.*

CHAPTER EIGHTEEN

The team final. The day Tony had been waiting for since Rio. Four rotations in, and things were looking pretty good. They stood in third behind the Japanese and Chinese teams although the athletes from Russia were breathing down their necks, and Team GB wasn't far behind.

As they marched to their fifth rotation—p-bars for Team USA, the British on floor, Russians on rings—Tony mentally tallied the scores. The British would finish on pommel horse, which was one of their strongest events, and the Russians' last event was vault, which was easily the highest scoring event in terms of execution value because it had fewer opportunities for deductions.

But p-bars and high bar are both strong for us, especially since Barry blessed Danny's p-bar upgrade. If Tony and Rahul went clean with their original routines, they'd still be good. High bar—well, it was a bone of contention. Despite Xiao's recommendation, Barry wouldn't let Tony connect three releases and absolutely refused to let him add the Cassina back in—the skill he'd flubbed at the trials.

But it could still be okay. We've got a little cushion.

After one-touch warm-ups, Sol stayed on the podium to help Rahul chalk the bars, but headed straight for Tony after he trotted down the stairs.

"Hey." He faced the p-bars, his shoulder brushing Tony's, as Rahul waited for the D1 judge to give him the green light. "Holding up okay?"

Tony jerked his thumb at the leader board. "As long as we hold on to our spot, I'm outstanding."

Sol chuckled. "Well, you know what Tim Daggett always says at every single meet he covers. Gymnastics 101—"

"Fly high and stick the landing," they said in unison.

Masked by their position, Tony brushed his knuckles over Sol's. "Have I told you how proud I am of the way you *killed* your floor and horse routines?"

Sol's lips quirked, but he kept his gaze on Rahul. "You may have mentioned it."

"Brace yourself. Because I'll probably mention it again every three minutes or so."

Up on the podium, Rahul grasped the bars and launched off the springboard, which Volya pulled out of the way. Although Tony's attention was on Rahul, out of the corner of his eye, he could see Sol swaying in place.

"Are you getting lightheaded? Or are you just visualizing Rahul's routine as he does it?"

"Shut up. It's a—shit!"

Tony winced too, because Rahul had fumbled his grip and had to walk his hands and bend his elbows to regain his balance. *So much for going clean.* Major errors, right there, even if everything else was perfect.

They both shouted encouragement, as Rahul powered through the rest of his skills, including a double pike dismount —which he stuck. Tony didn't wait to see Rahul's score. He mounted the podium to prepare for his own turn, Sol assisting him as well.

Sol passed close to Tony as he headed off the podium. "You can do it."

I fucking hope so. Because their margin for error had virtually vanished. *Damn, Rahul must feel like shit.* But none of them could afford to dwell on it, not now. *One rotation at a time. One skill at a time.*

The green light flashed, and Tony saluted the judges. He didn't need the springboard for his mount, so he gripped the bars, blew out a breath, and let his training and preparation power him through the exercise. *Toes pointed. Arms straight in the handstands. Pivots sharp. Swings fluid.* And the dismount? *Nailed it.* But then he stood up too quickly and had to take a step to keep his balance. *Damn it! Why can't I stick the fucking dismount?*

But he pumped his arms anyway, for the team if not for himself. Danny slapped his hand as they passed one another on the stairs. "Good job, dude."

"Bring it home, man."

Danny grinned. "I intend to."

Tony accepted a water bottle from Xiao. "What was Rahul's score?" he murmured.

Xiao cut a glance at Rahul, who was sitting on the sidelines, turning his grips over in his hands. "A full point below what we had hoped for."

"Shit." Hanging onto third was going to be tough and moving up would be impossible unless every single one of the Chinese and Japanese gymnasts fell on their heads.

Tony's score flashed on the board and it was solid—a couple of tenths above Barry's data-driven plan, but not enough to make up for Rahul's error. Danny had the potential to post an enormous score if he went clean, because his difficulty value was ridiculous.

Sol joined Tony again after helping Danny prep the equipment. His smile was strained—who could blame him? *It's surprising more gymnasts don't have ulcers.*

"Four more routines," Sol said. "That's all we need to get through. One each for all four of us and it'll be over."

Tony gripped his shoulder. "One more each and we'll be—"

"Don't say it." Sol held up his fingers in a cross. "You'll jinx us."

Tony clucked his tongue. "Don't tell me you're superstitious, Solly."

"Says the man who taps his chest before every exercise."

Heat rushed up Tony's throat. "That's different. That's mental preparation. You should get that, Mr. Visualization."

"Uh huh." He cupped his hands around his mouth. "Attack it, Danny!"

Maybe someday I'll have the courage to tell him what that's really about.

But for now, he cheered Danny on. "Jesus, that Bhavsar was —"

"I know. Epic."

Because that's what Danny was—epic. No errors, perfect form, outstanding amplitude, and—

"Fly high and stick the landing," Sol said with a relieved grin when Danny did exactly that.

They rushed over to the stairs to congratulate Danny with hand and shoulder slaps as he came down the stairs, a huge grin on his face.

"Did I bring it home to your satisfaction, Thomas?" Danny asked.

"Like a boss."

They all started gathering their things in preparation for moving on to the final rotation. It would be a little while—floor ex was still going on. When Danny's score posted—four tenths higher than his previous personal best—they all pounded him on the back.

But although Tony joined in the congratulations, he couldn't keep his eyes off the leader board.

"What's wrong?" Sol murmured.

"Even with that score, we're still in danger. The Russian team —excuse me, the athletes from Russia—are insanely strong on rings, and their vault scores are always high."

Sure enough, the Russians edged Team USA down into fourth by three one-hundredths.

Sol gripped Tony's arm. "Don't think about it. Just focus on your exercise."

"I *am* thinking about my exercise. It's not enough, Solly. Even if all three of us go absolutely clean, there's no way we can top the Russians' vault scores with my watered-down routine."

"But if you try and miss, we could drop down further. All the way to eighth, if you fall."

Tony gritted his teeth. "I won't fall."

"I know you won't intend to, but—"

"I won't." Tony had never been more certain of anything in his life. With Sol there, he wouldn't fall. He couldn't. *That doesn't mean I can't screw up royally.*

On the other hand, the Russians were unlikely to miss all their vaults. And Team GB on pommel horse was a threat as well. They had to do *something*, or the fucking *math* would screw them to the wall.

As the team lined up behind their sign-bearer, Tony pulled back to talk with Xiao. "I'm putting the Cassina in."

"Tony." Xiao's voice held a warning. "Barry forbade you."

"That was before, when we still had a chance to medal without it. But we don't have that chance now, not unless other teams make mistakes." He gripped the strap of his gym bag until his knuckles ached. "If we don't medal, what does it matter whether we're fourth or eighth? This is a risk we need to take. Don't you see?" Xiao didn't respond, and Tony gripped his hair with both hands, then released it, along with his breath. "Look. Are the skills beyond my ability? Are they a risk to my person—more so than gymnastics normally is, anyway?"

"No. You are capable of doing the skills. However, you only performed them cleanly once at yesterday's practice."

"That was practice," Tony said grimly. "This is the Olympics."

Xiao regarded him for a moment. "I will speak to Barry." A small smile glimmered on his normally austere mouth. "I have the forms filled out for the difficulty review in any case."

Tony barked a laugh. "You knew." He grinned. "Or did you just *visualize* it?"

"It hardly matters. I suggest you warm up those skills in one-touch. And Mr. Thomas?"

Tony, poised to rush over to Sol's side to tell him the news, hesitated. "Yeah?"

"Be sure to stick the landing."

CHAPTER NINETEEN

When Sol's high bar score flashed up, he barely registered it because he was so focused on Tony, standing under the bar, waiting for the green light.

Danny pounded his shoulder. "Way to go, man."

"Mmmhmmm." Sol glanced at his number. *Good. At least Tony doesn't have to make up for any mistakes.* Rahul had gone clean too, although he'd caught one of his releases a little close to the bar. But Tony's routine—if it went well—could keep them ahead of the Russians, who'd already finished their vault rotation. If it went poorly…

Don't think about that.

Tony had warmed up the Cassina during one-touch, and he'd caught it—with both hands, thank God—but so late that Sol was afraid he'd miss and crash to the mat. The Cassina wasn't what he was most worried about, though—it was the three consecutive releases that happened later in the routine. They were all lower-valued, but would give him four releases in the routine, with the connection bonus giving him another three-tenths difficulty. *If he hits them.* If he doesn't…

Don't think about that either.

The green light finally flashed and Tony tapped his chest and then saluted. He jumped up and caught the bar, adjusted his grip and then kipped into a handstand.

"Let's go, Tony!" Danny shouted. "Show everything off!"

Sol managed to clap, but he couldn't force anything out of his throat because... *One giant, two giants and here comes the Cassina.* Tony somersaulted over the top of the bar, seeming to float there for an instant, and... and... *He caught it.* Sol's breath whooshed out. "Atta boy, Tony."

God, Tony was good at this. He hit every handstand spot-on, his knees straight, toes pointed. The pirouettes crisp, the reverse giants powerful. Sol's heart traveled north again because the connected releases were coming. *Tkachev. Layout Tkatchev. Tkatchev with a half twist.* Every one of them a clean catch, the amplitude insane. Sol started to laugh like a loon, clapping as Tony prepped for his dismount. *Come on, Tony. You've done everything you promised. Just one more and you're home.*

He released the bar into a triple twisting double layout, his air position perfect. His feet hit the mat, and he crouched, arms thrust out to the sides.

And didn't fucking move.

Sol leaped up, punching the air, as Tony straightened, raising both arms in a triumphant V.

"Oh my fucking God," Danny said. "He did it. He actually did it."

Tony tapped the center of his chest, blew a kiss to the cheering crowd, and trotted off the podium, his grin so wide it nearly reached his ears. The team raced over to meet him, slapping his hand, hugging him, pounding his back. Sol was last, and if he held onto Tony a little longer than anybody else, so what? *Screw it.*

"I am so fucking proud of you," Sol murmured into Tony's ear before stepping back when Danny came in for a second round.

The four of them huddled in a circle, their arms across each other's shoulders.

"It's up to the judges now," Tony said. "We've done our jobs, and we've done them well. Now we just have to wait for—"

A roar rose from the crowd and Sol looked up. Tony's score was posted. *Yes!* Enough to pass the Russians. The gamble had paid off. *We did it. We medaled!*

Danny grabbed Sol's shoulder. "Wait a minute, wait a minute. I think— Yes!" He whooped and leaped up, then wrapped Sol in a bear hug, squeezing his ribs until Sol couldn't breathe.

"Danny," he croaked. "What—"

But Danny let go, and as Sol stumbled to catch his balance, he pounced on Rahul next. God, was Rahul crying? Sol met Tony's dumbfounded stare, his belly swooping like he'd missed a catch. *God, was there a mistake? Is something wrong?* But it couldn't be or Danny wouldn't be acting like a frenetic octopus.

Sol glanced up at the leader board—then did a double-take. Because the Japanese were at the top as expected, but Team USA wasn't in third.

They were in second.

Sol's knees nearly buckled, but Tony caught his arm, steadying him. "What happened? How did we—"

"The Chinese must have made a mistake on rings. That's the only way they could have dropped behind us." Tony caught Sol in a tighter hug than Danny's. "We did it, Solly. We're Olympic medalists. *Silver* medalists."

Then Danny and Rahul were there, wrapping their arms around both Sol and Tony—and yes, Rahul *was* crying, but since Sol was tearing up too, he wasn't about to mention it.

Olympic medalists. Team USA.

He met Tony's shining eyes. *And we couldn't have done it without you.*

Was the ground under his feet? Tony couldn't tell. It must be down there somewhere, because he'd somehow moved from the arena to the dressing room. *Maybe I teleported.* He wouldn't be surprised, because he kinda felt like he could do anything.

Silver medalists. While some teams might bemoan being so close to the gold, Tony had no patience for them. Winning the silver when bronze had seemed like a distant possibility was better than gold. It was vindication. Validation. *Redemption*.

This time, Team USA hadn't fallen short of expectations. This time, they'd exceeded them. And God *damn* that felt good.

Danny was almost dancing on the ceiling, he was so excited. And Rahul had actually smiled *without* a textbook in his hand. Sol, though… Sol's dazed wonder was almost more than Tony could handle. He wanted to kiss that amazement, touch that joy. The end of the Games had never seemed farther away.

"Dude!" Danny flung his arm across Tony's shoulder. "That high bar routine. You put us on the podium!"

But Tony wasn't having any of that. "No way. *We* did it. Every one of us, with every exercise. If you hadn't *destroyed* the p-bars, if Solly hadn't nailed the horse to the wall, if Rahul hadn't stuck that vault landing cold. It's a team medal, and the team won it. End of story."

Danny grinned, apparently unfazed by Tony's reprimand. "Not quite the end. There's the medal ceremony. So put on your official duds, dude. Because we're about to go collect some bling!"

Damn straight we are.

Marching out into the arena was surreal. The Chinese team, although they had to be disappointed, was so gracious when they congratulated the Americans. The Japanese team, as gold medalists in their home country, of course got a huge ovation. But standing on the second tier with his teammates—with *Sol*—as the officials presented them with flowers and then looped the medals around their necks… Well, that was what Tony had been working for, what he'd been seeking, what he'd been missing since Rio. *What US men's gymnastics needs.*

They waved to the crowd. Congratulated the Japanese team. Stood respectfully still while the Japanese anthem played. But the sight of the US flag up there, high above their heads? That was *everything*, and it was Tony's turn to get choked up.

Sol glanced at him, then let the backs of his fingers graze Tony's, hidden by his bouquet.

Of course, that choked Tony up even more. Because as much as this meant to him, it meant even more—double, triple, quadruple with a twist—because Sol was standing beside him. *We talked about this from those first days together at Central. It was always a far-away dream then. But now we've done it.*

As the last notes of the Japanese anthem died away, and the crowd erupted in cheers, Tony met Sol's gaze, and everything fountained up inside him—gratitude, longing, love. Some of it must have shown in his face, because Sol tilted his head, brows quirked up like twin question marks.

They stepped down from the podium and took their place behind the Japanese team to march out of the arena, the Chinese men behind them. But once they passed through the tunnel, Tony grabbed Sol's arm and pulled him out of line. The Chinese gymnasts peered at them curiously, but continued on to the dressing room.

With the hallway empty, Tony grabbed Sol by the arms. "You were incredible."

"Me?" Sol smiled wryly. "I'm pretty sure you were the one who pulled us from fourth to second with that high bar exercise."

Tony shook his head. "I'm not talking about the scores. I'm talking about *you*. I'm so, so happy I got to share this with you. There is literally no one else on earth I'd want next to me right now." He edged closer.

Sol's smile turned hot. "I'm not sure we could fit anyone next to you. There's no room."

"If I have my way, there'll be even less." He leaned in, capturing Sol's lips with his as Sol's arms slid around Tony's waist.

"Whoa, dudes." Danny's voice acted like a Taser bolt, jolting them apart.

"Um…" Tony glanced at Sol, then straightened to face Danny. "That was, um…"

Danny crossed his arms, his face as rock-hard as a D judge's. "You gonna try to tell me that's not what it looked like?"

Sol edged in front of Tony and lifted his chin, meeting Danny's eyes. "If it looked like us kissing? Then no, because that's what it was, and I'm not going to apologize for it."

Danny stared at them, his medal winking with the rise of his chest. *One breath. Two.* Tony braced himself, fists bunched, the skin between his shoulder blades prickling. Then Danny shrugged. "Whatever."

Tony choked on a sharp inhale. "'*Whatever*?' That's all you got?"

"Dudes." Smirking, Danny buffeted their shoulders. "You're both about as subtle as a kick in the nuts. We've all known for weeks."

Sol shared a wide-eyed glance with Tony. "Ooookay."

"Just don't let making out get in the way of the competition." Danny grinned and beckoned to them. "Now come on. We've got some celebrating to do!"

CHAPTER TWENTY

The evening after the team final had been crazy—interviews, meetings, congratulations from the Olympic Committee and the gymnastics federations. Sol hadn't had a minute alone with Tony since their stolen kiss after the medal ceremony. Since Sol and Rahul had to prepare for the all-around competition, Barry had ordered the two of them off to bed and handled the whole dog-and-pony show with Danny and Tony.

The next day, although the whole team had spent practice time in the gym to train for event finals, Rahul and Sol had been excused from further press appearances to get their upgraded routines ready.

"There is no point in holding back," Xiao said. "You have only yourselves to consider. Any error you make will only affect yourself. So you will oblige me and do yourselves the service of presenting performances that are appropriate to your skill levels."

Sol glanced at Rahul. "That means he's going to kick our butts."

Rahul shrugged. "It can't be any harder than electromagnetism."

"I don't know about that. Exactly how rigorous is your degree program?"

Rahul shrugged again. "I practice still rings to unwind."

But since Xiao didn't believe in high numbers, after their recovery period and a session with the team physio, Sol was weary, but not exhausted. Even better, he felt confident in the upgraded routines—the fact that any missed element wouldn't kill anybody's chances but his own took a lot of the pressure off.

When he and Rahul got back to the team suite, it was empty. Sol tossed his bag inside his room. "I guess they must still be doing interviews or meetings."

Rahul nodded. "Yes. Barry is encouraging them to maximize the opportunity for team visibility and PR." He peered down the hallway, toward one of the two suite bathrooms. "At least we can have first chance at the showers. Then I have studying to do."

Sol chuckled as he collected his own toiletries and towel. Trust Rahul to be able to compartmentalize the Olympics in favor of Stanford. Sol closed the bathroom door and tossed his towel over the glass shower stall wall. *On the other hand, maybe having a way to mentally separate yourself from the competition mindset is good.* Sol often got a little too focused on his training, let it push everything else aside. *Well, everything except diabetes management.* Maybe that was his own way of compartmentalizing—gymnastics disengaged him from monitoring his condition and monitoring his condition detached him from overtraining.

He held his hand under the water until it warmed up, then stepped under the spray. *And apparently I'm not the only one who needs that kind of balance.* Since he'd done the interview with Quinn about his diabetes, he'd lost count of the number of people—both kids and adults—who'd reached out to him via social media. Sure, there were a small percentage of trolls who lambasted him for imagining he was *"just as good as a normal person."* But far more people sincerely thanked him for his example, either fellow diabetics who'd believed they couldn't follow their dreams, or people with diabetic loved ones, who wanted to support them and encourage them in a full, healthy life.

He was rinsing the shampoo out of his hair when he heard the bathroom door open and close. He groped for his towel to blot the water and soap out of his eyes, but then somebody placed the towel in his hand—and a hand on his hip.

"That better be you, Tony," Sol muttered as he dried his face.

Tony's chuckle sent shivers down Sol's spine. "Who was it who schooled me about locking doors?"

Sol turned off the water before his towel could get soaked. "I was distracted."

"I'm not sure how I feel about that. I mean, I wasn't here, so who was distracting you?"

Sol kept his towel draped in front of his groin because he was naked. And wet. And Tony was dressed in the blue blazer and red tie of Team USA's official interview wear. "I take it you were off being the face of USA men's gymnastics."

"You're dodging the question." Tony reached into the shower stall—which didn't have a door—and gripped Sol's waist. "Who was distracting you?" He tugged Sol forward. "It wasn't that Brazilian guy, was it?"

"I told you, he maybe hit on me *one time*. And I'm still not convinced he wasn't after you." He put his hand, which was at least marginally dry, on Tony's chest. "Stop. You'll get your outfit wet."

"It'll dry. Come here."

"Tony. There are other people in the suite."

"So? They all know what we are to one another by now."

"But Danny was the only one who saw us."

Tony raised an eyebrow. "You really think he kept his mouth shut? Besides, he said they'd all known for weeks."

"One of them might need to use the bathroom."

"There are two. They can use the other one or just hold it." He tugged more insistently, so Sol didn't resist—*because why would I want to?*—and relaxed into Tony's arms, Tony's muscles straining the ability of the team blazer to contain them.

Tony exhaled on a long sigh. "That's better," he murmured. "I'm sorry I barged in, but I needed to see you. It wasn't right, you not being with me while we were paraded around for the press to poke and prod us."

Sol chuckled. "I know. You'd rather be the one to poke and prod."

Tony kissed Sol's wet hair. "I wouldn't mind if you wanted to do the poking and prodding. I'm versatile."

"Good to know."

"Maybe. But what I really want you to know is that while I can't be on the floor with you tomorrow, I'll be there in the stands, every minute. Look for me when you mount the podium, before you salute." He kissed Sol's temple. "I'll touch my chest just for you."

"Your mental preparation."

"Exactly. It always works for me, so it's bound to work for you."

"That's a bit of a stretch, don't you think?"

"Hey, you can't argue with results." He kissed Sol's lips, soft and lingering. "Now put some clothes on, you exhibitionist. It's time for dinner and they frown on nudity in the dining hall."

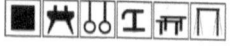

One one thousand two one thousand.

Tony's lips weren't moving, but he was counting in his head anyway. If Sol had a weak event, it was still rings, and Tony had been on the edge of his seat ever since Volya had lifted Sol into the air to begin his routine. *Damn, why does he have to start on rings?* On the other hand, that meant he'd end on pommel horse, which was a downer for most gymnasts, but not Sol. *Now if he can just keep from letting his strength holds decay…*

Danny, sitting next to him, nudged Tony in the ribs with his elbow. "Dude. Chill. You'd think *you* were the one out there."

He stuck his index fingers in his mouth and whistled loud enough to pierce Tony's eardrums. "Atta boy, Sol!"

"It would be easier if I was," Tony muttered. *It would be easier if I was on the floor with him.* For some reason, sitting up here in the stands put a greater mental distance between them than the physical distance Tony had maintained so religiously in the years after Rio.

Down on the floor, Sol swung out of a rock-solid handstand and into a double twisting layout dismount and... stuck it.

Tony leaped to his feet. "*Yes!* That's how you do it!"

In the row in front of them, the other guys in the team cheered and clapped. Danny slapped Tony on the back. "See? You need to give your boo more credit."

Tony grinned at Danny's easy recognition of his and Sol's relationship. "I give it to him. Believe me, I do. But *damn,* I wish we could be down there with him. Down there with them both."

Danny squinted across the gym where Rahul was waiting for his next rotation. He'd hit his vault with a decent score, although not the highest in his cohort. Still, he was a consistent gymnast rather than a flashy one, with no one event especially stronger than another. He just methodically built up his totals, one solid, dependable performance at a time.

Sol's score flashed on the board, better than his qualifying or team final scores by two tenths. *That's my boy.*

Tony collapsed back into his seat, grinning like a fool.

"Tony."

Shit. At the unwelcome sound of his father's voice, Tony's grin dropped off his face. His father was standing in the aisle next to Tony's seat, the belligerent thrust of his jaw doing nothing to disguise the bloat in his face and neck. "Dad."

"I expected to see you after the qualifying round. Or at the very least after the team final. We need to talk."

"This isn't a good time." Tony gestured to the gym floor, where the twenty-four guys in the all-around competition were marching to their next rotation.

"That's an understatement. *You* should have been out there."

"Whoa," Danny murmured.

Tony stood up. "We're not having this conversation in the middle of the stands." He glanced down at Danny, who was staring between Tony and his dad with wide eyes. "I'll be back."

Tony marched up the stairs to the exit and into the concourse that circled the arena. It was mostly empty now, since all the reasonable people were inside watching the meet. *Yeah, only my dad would be self-centered enough to think this was a good time for a father-son heart-to-heart.*

Tony stopped next to a pillar displaying an Olympic banner and turned to face his father. "All right. Talk. But if you make me miss the guys' next routines, I will *end* you."

His dad, several inches taller although no longer broader, crossed his arms over his ex-linebacker's chest. "What the fuck were you thinking, Tony? You kicked Andrei to the curb?"

Tony forced himself to take a deep breath. "Andrei kicked himself to the curb."

"Bullshit. You could have taken a stand. Defended him. Got him back into the Training Center to whip you into shape so *you'd* be out on that floor right now."

"I was never gunning for the all-around."

"Also bullshit. Every athlete wants to win. *You* want to win. You've never been the kid who sat on the sideline like a fucking cheerleader, for God's sake."

"Listen, Dad—"

"If they wouldn't let Andrei in the door, you should have walked. There are other gyms. You could have—"

"Are you out of your mind?" The difference in height between them had always unnerved Tony when he was growing up, especially when he realized that his father took shameless advantage of it, trying to intimidate his own son the way he intimidated an opposing football team. But Tony hadn't fallen for that since Rio and he wasn't starting now. "I was training with the Olympic team. At the mandatory camp. I wasn't about to walk out just because Andrei got his ass kicked for being an overbearing dickhead."

His dad's eyes narrowed. "I'm not paying for you to ignore your coach's advice."

"You're not paying for *anything*." Tony met his dad's glare. "*I* financed my training, and now I'm funded by the team. You've got nothing to say about it." The muffled sound of the announcer's voice bled out of the arena. "Damn it, if I miss Sol's vault—"

"Oh yeah," his dad sneered, *"Sol.* I should have nipped that in the bud the first time you brought him home. He's always held you back."

Tony's throat burned, and he gritted his teeth. "You wanna talk bullshit, Dad? That's it. Right there. *Cosmic level* bullshit. Sol has never held me back. Not once. Not *ever*. In fact, he lifts me up, and I fucking needed it with the way you always tore me down. You're not fit to even mention his name." Tony lifted his chin, staring his dad straight in the eye. "So you and me? Right now? We're done." Tony turned his back and strode toward the entrance to the stands.

"It's that fag—"

"Don't!" Tony whirled and barreled toward his dad. He shoved him hard in the chest. "Don't you say that word. Not about him, not about anybody."

His dad's laugh, a hiss through clenched teeth, lifted the hair on Tony's neck. "Not about you?"

"Not. About. *Anybody.* Now I'm going back inside to watch my teammates. I don't want to see you again."

"I've got tickets. I've got a right to be here."

"You don't have a ticket to *me*." Tony practically sprinted back into the arena. Fuck, if his dad made trouble for Sol... He dropped into his seat next to Tony. "What'd I miss?"

"One-touch and the first couple of vaults. Sol's still to go, though, and Rahul's up next on p-bars." Danny glanced back toward the exit. "Family drama?"

"Not anymore." As far as Tony was concerned, his family was right here. He glanced up at the leader board. Sol was in fifth, Rahul in seventh. Reasonable. Sol's best events were still to come, and Rahul would improve his standings event by event, as long as he didn't make any major errors.

But Tony winced and the rest of the guys groaned when Rahul had a balance check on a handstand. They all hollered encouragement anyway, and there weren't any other mistakes—and no hop on dismount.

Tony heaved a relieved sigh and turned his attention to vault. Sol was waiting by the stairs, so he was next. Tony didn't breathe again until Sol landed on the other side of the table, on his feet, in bounds, with no hop. *Trust Solly to ace the execution.*

Tony's knees wobbled so much when he stood up to cheer that he almost butt-planted in his seat again. Being a gymnastics spectator was not for the faint of heart, especially when you were watching someone you… Someone you…

God, am I going to say it?

Yes, God damn it. *Someone you love.* He'd been running from that as much as he'd been running from the Rio debacle. He could hardly have offered himself to Sol as the hot mess he'd been, not with his dad's machinations poisoning his thoughts. But if his father's fucking ill-timed interruption did nothing else, it reminded him that Sol wasn't stupid, petty, or disloyal.

He'd have stood by me then like he always did, like he still does. Tony grimaced and scrubbed his hands through his hair. *It's time to get a fucking clue and stop underestimating him.*

So the fear knotting his gut every time Sol mounted an apparatus was joined by an almost light-headed anticipation. *I'm going to tell him. And he feels the same about me.* Tony swallowed convulsively. *At least I hope so.*

By the time Sol nailed p-bars, high bar, and absolutely *killed* on floor, Tony's muscles were sporting more knots than a macramé demonstration. He couldn't even look at the leader board anymore because it just made things worse. Of course, that didn't keep Danny from nattering about it non-stop.

"Sol's holding in third." Danny scooted forward and peered down at the arena floor under them. They were right in front of the pommel horse, so they couldn't see the athletes sitting against the wall beneath them. "Rahul's dropped to sixth. I don't think he can move up."

"Uh huh." Tony gripped his armrests.

"If Sol hits this last routine, there's no way anyone can pass him."

"Uh huh."

"As long as he stays on the horse—"

"Don't!" Tony grabbed Danny's massive biceps, fear spawning a spiky ball in his belly. "Don't even *think* that."

Danny just smirked at him. "You know we can't really jinx him, right? It's not like we can send him evil mental vibes."

"I don't care. Gymnasts can't afford to think negative thoughts."

"Yeah, about our *own* routines." But Danny must have seen how close to the edge Tony was, because his mocking expression softened. "Okay. But I wouldn't worry. Nobody can touch Sol on horse."

Tony gulped and nodded. But then Sol appeared on the podium for one-touch warm-up and everything else faded from his perception. And none of Danny's snarky comments could keep Tony from chanting "You can do it, Solly" for the next ten minutes—right up until Sol drilled his dismount after a perfect routine.

Tony slumped in his seat as the other guys surged to their feet. *He did it.*

"Second!" Danny pounded Tony's shoulder. "Dude, he's taken silver. That's the best US all-around finish since 2004."

Tony swiped a hand under his eyes and pushed himself to his feet. "Of course he did it. Never doubted it for a second."

CHAPTER TWENTY-ONE

"The arena looks different from up here." Sol settled in the cushy seat next to Tony. "The lighting makes it look like a night football game."

Tony snorted. "Assuming football players wore sparkly leotards and could leap more than double their height in the air while twisting three times and flipping twice."

Sol grinned at him, letting their shoulders brush companionably. After yesterday's men's all-around—which still seemed like a fever dream to Sol—the coaches had granted the team the day off before training ramped up again for the event finals in three days. Somehow, Xiao had managed to score the men's team seats for the women's all-around competition, one of the hottest tickets at the Games. They weren't all sitting together—that would have been a miracle—but since Sol got to sit with Tony, he had no complaints.

"Hey." Tony nudged Sol's knee with his. "I'm so proud of you."

Sol smiled at him. "You've mentioned that once or twice."

"Yeah, but it's worth repeating." Tony glanced irritably at the surrounding crowd. "It'd be nice if we could grab five minutes or so in private."

Sol raised an eyebrow. "Only five minutes? I didn't know quickies were a feature of the Thomas flair."

Tony's eyes glinted, and he leaned closer. "When I get you alone next," he growled, "I'll pay you for that remark. Slowly. Very, very slowly."

Heat pooled in Sol's belly. "Promise?"

"You can take that to the bank." Tony's fingers brushed Sol's where they dangled over the armrest. "I waited up for you last night."

"I'm sorry. Barry paraded me around to about a million different press interviews. You must know the drill—you were the poster boy when the team medaled." Sol angled himself toward Tony. "Damn it. These seats were not built for two guys with gymnast-wide shoulders to sit next to one another without invading each other's personal space."

"You can invade my space anytime." Tony leered at him. "Or I could invade yours."

Sol laughed. "Our agendas are a little full for the next few days. Playing Space Invaders may have to wait for a while."

"But not forever."

Sol met Tony's gaze, oblivious to the cheers of the crowd as the women marched into the arena. He gripped Tony's hand— *one one thousand two one thousand*—then reluctantly let go. "No. Not forever."

"Good." Tony settled back, his gaze drifting to the podium where the women had started their one-touch warm-up. "Have you thought much about what you'll do after the Games?"

Sol glanced sidelong at Tony. Was his tone a little too nonchalant? "I've been informed that the gymnastics promotional tour is nonnegotiable. So that's the next few months. You did that after Rio, right?"

Tony's jaw tightened, but then he blew out a breath. "Yeah. It was kind of a shitshow. The schedule was insane. A lot of the venues weren't outfitted properly. Some of the gymnasts got injured. I was glad you weren't— I mean, it would have been tough on you."

"They brought me in for a couple of shows, you know, since I was an alternate. In Texas, so it wasn't too far from OU. But you weren't there." Sol tried to keep the accusation out of his voice, but it was a struggle. *Guess I've got a little residual resentment.*

Tony shot him a surprised glance. "They did? I didn't realize — But I guess that makes sense. I took time away from the tour a couple of times for other commitments. I never asked who they got to come in to replace me."

"It was me, at least that time."

Tony gripped Sol's thigh briefly. "I'm sorry. You know that by now, right? Sorry that I was an asshole. Sorry that I ghosted you." He grinned wryly. "I can't promise that I'd do it differently if I could, because let's face it—I *am* an asshole."

"You're not," Sol said fiercely. "You're just larger than life."

Tony's grin lost its wryness. "The Thomas flair? That's not an excuse, you know. It never should have been. And it won't be again. Not with you. I promise."

"I'll hold you to that."

They gazed at each other for what felt like forever. *I wish we weren't in an arena full of people, because I really want to kiss him.* Then Tony cleared his throat and faced the podium where the first rotation was beginning. "So the tour. But afterward?"

Sol settled back in his seat, his shoulder still pressed against Tony's. "I'm taking the whole year off before I start grad school. I've got a couple of options of where I'll go."

"Biochem?"

"Yup. What about you?"

Tony slid down in his seat, letting his legs fall apart so his knee bumped Sol's. "Oh, I've got a few… ideas."

Sol elbowed him. "So tell me."

"Shh." He pointed to the balance beam. "Show some respect. Our USA sisters are about to kick some serious ass."

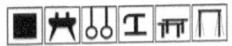

Tony tossed his cell phone on his bed and ripped off his tie. If he didn't get his hands—and mouth—on Sol tonight, he was going to jump out of his skin without benefit of a springboard. The last few days had been *intense*, the coaches relentless in the lead-up to event finals and the PR guy—what the fuck was his name?—booking them for press appearances in every minute the coaches would allow. Since Tony and Sol were competing on different events, even their training schedules hadn't coincided.

I thought the fucking Olympics were supposed to be the fucking *Olympics.* Either that rumor was completely overblown, or else the Tokyo organizers had figured out a way to minimize athletes boinking at every opportunity. *You'd think we'd have managed something in our own suite, for Chrissakes.* But no.

They'd barely managed to see each other except at meals, and no matter how much he'd wanted to sneak into Sol's room at night, he didn't want to disturb his rest.

But Sol's competition was over, now that he'd added vault gold to his floor ex silver and—*yes, I knew it*—gold on pommel horse. Tony had high bar tomorrow, but he could get by on grit and adrenaline. He could risk his own performance—he refused to risk Sol's.

His cell phone vibrated with an incoming call. *Solly? Is he finally done with whatever the fuck they had him doing tonight?* But it was only his father. Again. His dad and Andrei had been bombarding him with increasingly frequent calls in the last two days. Tony had ignored them, of course. He'd have turned off the fucking phone except he didn't want to miss a call from Sol.

Tony stripped off the rest of his official Team USA interview suit. He'd earned a bronze on still rings today and had taken his turn in front of the cameras, but Sol's medal count was higher, and those two golds guaranteed more interest.

Because Sol deserved every bit of the attention and adulation —and more—Tony couldn't have been happier. *Other than it's kept us apart for too fucking long.*

The message alarm pinged on the phone as Tony was pulling on a pair of sweat shorts. He grabbed it, grinning, because his XBL fans had been sending him congratulations since before the medal ceremony.

His grin faded, though, because the text was from Andrei. It was a picture taken at the media center after today's events—a picture of him and Sol.

Sol was smiling for the camera, his neck draped with all five medals. Tony, wearing his team silver and newly minted still rings bronze, was smiling too, but not at the camera.

At Sol.

And nobody who looked at that picture could doubt what he felt.

Heat built behind Tony's eyes as he typed in a response. If he didn't need his hands in top shape for the high bar final tomorrow, he'd have punched the wall.

Tony-> WTF, Andrei?

Andrei-> Lodge a protest. Insist that I should be with you on the floor tomorrow as your personal coach.

Tony jabbed his phone so hard he was surprised the screen didn't crack.

Tony-> Are you fucking kidding me? Just for the record—you're fired.

He turned the phone off and tossed it on the nightstand. *And I hope they nail his ass to the wall in that review.*

Still shirtless, he yanked his door open and nearly ran into Sol, who stood with his hand raised as if he was about to knock. "Solly. You're back."

Sol's gaze traveled down Tony's chest and he licked his lips. "I am. And in case you've forgotten, I've got the only single in the suite." Grabbing Tony's elbow, Sol towed him down the hall to his room and shut the door behind them. He led Tony to the bed and pushed him down to sit on its edge, then sauntered back as he loosened his tie.

"Observe me locking the door," Sol said, flipping the handle. He flung the tie aside and shed his blazer. "Observe me removing my clothes."

Tony grinned at him and leaned back on his elbows, his cock tenting his shorts. "Observe me observing."

Sol stripped off his shirt, baring that gorgeous golden skin, then shucked off his pants, leaving them in a puddle on the floor. Gloriously naked, he stood over Tony. "Why are you still wearing clothes?"

Tony levered himself up on one elbow. "Just enjoying the show." But he paused with his thumbs under his waistband and nodded at the door. "The rest of the guys are bound to be here soon, you know."

"I don't care. As you pointed out, they all know about us anyway. We both won medals at the freaking Olympics, Tony, but *this* is the reward I really want."

"Well, then…" Tony peeled off shorts and lay back. "Come and claim it."

Sol knelt on the end of the bed and then crawled up Tony's body, dropping kisses on knee, thigh, hipbone, abs, and leaving fire in his wake. He lowered himself onto Tony, fitting their bodies together, their hard cocks lined up next to one another in a slide of iron and velvet. "God, I've wanted to do this every minute since before we left Colorado. The Ashvili-Thomas. Only naked."

Tony groaned. "You're killing me, Solly. Give me your mouth."

So Sol did, and Tony devoured him in a kiss that went on for days, yet not nearly long enough. When they finally had to gasp for air, Sol undulated his hips—*God*, gymnastics core muscles weren't only good for competition—and licked a path from Tony's jaw to his clavicle. "Mmmm. Sweat and chalk. Gymnastics hors d'oeuvres."

Tony laughed, gripping Sol's hips so he didn't bounce off. *Because that would be a crime.* "Good thing you're planning to be a biochemist instead of a restaurateur, because that will never catch on. Besides, I've showered since competition. Twice."

"Shhh." Sol hummed against his throat, sending the vibration all the way to Tony's cock. "I'm *visualizing*." He trailed open-mouthed kisses down Tony's chest, and it took every ounce of Tony's self-control to hold still as Sol traced the sun tattoo with his tongue. "Eddie's going to get an Olympic tattoo. Are you finally going to add the rings to your ink?"

"I might." Tony clenched his teeth to keep his moan in. "Are you?"

"Maybe." He kissed the center of the sun's smiling face. "Are you ever going to tell me what this is for?"

Tony gripped Sol's hair and raised his head. "It's the sun."

"Yeah. That's obvious."

"And what is our sun called?"

"Other than the sun?"

Tony laughed, shaking his head. "It's *Sol*, you dope."

Sol pushed himself to his haunches, straddling Tony's hips, and stared down at him, jaw sagging. "You mean—"

"Yeah." Tony ran his hands up Sol's thighs. "I wanted you with me. Every day. Everywhere."

"So when you touch your chest before each event—"

"I'm reminding myself who's important. Who inspires me." He laced his fingers with Sol's and drew him down. "Who I love."

Sol's belly did some kind of weird roll that would never make it into the Code of Points. "You do?"

"Of course." Tony kissed him, soft at first, then more insistent, with tongues and breath and teeth. "I've been wanting to tell you, but I needed to prove that I was good enough for you."

Sol glowered at him. "Are you kidding me? I'm the one who needs to measure up to you."

"That's not so." Tony cupped Sol's face with one hand, running his thumb along Sol's cheekbone. "You've been my hero since the minute you walked into Central that first day, all elbows, knees, and determination. You have never once let me down. But I've let you down more times than I can—"

"No." Sol stopped Tony's words with a kiss. "The only time you've ever let me down is when you disappeared. When you refused to let me in. But that's over now, right?"

"Absolutely." Tony wiggled underneath him, reminding Sol of exactly where he was sitting and what kind of... *apparatus* was currently available for him to, er, mount. "I'll let you in any time. I'll let you in right now."

Sol's mouth dried. "You mean—"

"I want you to fuck me, Solly," Tony murmured, his eyes dark and hot.

Sol swallowed, his cock threatening to go off like a bottle rocket. "Seriously? Have you... have you ever bottomed before?"

Tony didn't meet his gaze. "No." He peered up from beneath his lashes. "I was waiting for you. Always for you."

"Then you'll have to wait a little longer."

Tony groaned. "My patience hasn't improved *that* much. Come on, Solly. Please?"

"Tony. You've got the high bar final tomorrow. No way am I going to be the one to screw that up for you." He smirked. "As it were."

"But the blue balls might screw it up just as badly." He kissed Sol's neck. "I've got a drawer full of lube and Olympic condoms. You can't be so cruel as to leave them unused."

"Oh, we're gonna use them." Sol rolled so Tony was on top. "The Ashvili-Thomas might have to wait until after your last event, but I'm done competing already. How about giving the Thomas-Ashvili a try?" He waggled his eyebrows. "Its international debut."

Tony's gaze darkened. "World debut. I'm so ready. But only if you're sure." His expression turned wary. "Have *you* bottomed before?"

Sol bit his lip. "Not… exactly."

"What's that supposed to mean?" Tony growled. "I think you'd be able to tell if some guy had his dick up your ass."

"Do, er, sex toys count?"

Tony's grin bloomed. "Sex toys, Solly? You?"

Sol shoved Tony's jaw aside, the better to hide his blush. "Shut up. I get horny, same as the next guy. But I'm not big on hookups, and the combination of gymnastics training and diabetes management makes me a little high-maintenance for a relationship."

Tony's expression darkened. "Did some idiot actually say that?"

"More than one, actually."

"Hmmmph. Assholes."

"Are you saying I'm not high maintenance?"

"Oh, you're high maintenance, all right." Tony framed Sol's face with his hands. "But you're worth it." His grin turned crooked. "And in case you haven't noticed, I'm a little high maintenance myself. In fact, I can't believe you've put up with me as long as you have."

"Are you kidding?" Sol tangled his fingers in Tony's curls. "How can I resist the Thomas flair, if only so I can bask in your ambient glory?"

"There you go again with those ten-dollar words." He nuzzled behind Sol's ear. "Now about those Olympic cond— Fuck!"

Sol's heart leaped sideways. "What? What's the matter?"

"The condoms and lube are in *my* dresser. I love our teammates but marching down the hall naked with my boner leading the way is oversharing even for me."

Sol chuckled and reached for his bedside table. "What makes you think you're the only one with supplies?" He pulled out the drawer. "I've made a couple of trips to the health center myself."

"They had lube too?" Tony asked, his tone both surprised and hopeful.

"You brought enough for an entire gay Olympic team." He laced his fingers behind Tony's neck. "I swiped some from your room the day after we got here."

"Solly." There was no mistaking the admiration in Tony's voice. "You've been planning this since then?"

Sol threaded his fingers through Tony's curls, so perfect for a solid grip, and gazed deep into his eyes. "I've been planning for this since Rio, Tony. Maybe since the minute I figured out I was gay and was in love with my best friend."

Tony blinked rapidly. "I— Really?"

"Really." He scrabbled in the drawer and pulled out the lube. "So don't make me wait any longer." He held out the bottle and lifted his head to kissed Tony's parted lips. "Don't make *us* wait."

Tony sat up, straddling Sol's thighs, and took it with a trembling hand. "I don't want to hurt you."

"You won't."

"But—"

"For God's sake, Thomas, I'm a gymnast." Sol snatched the lube, snicked it open, and handed it back. "I fall off every piece of apparatus an average of five times a day. I've had broken fingers, dislocated shoulders, torn palms, and bruises from one end of me to the other. You think I can't handle you prepping me with love, *for* love?

Tony's smile glimmered. "Well, when you put it like that…" Tony moved off Sol's legs and knelt next to his hip. "How do you want to do this?"

Sol sat up, biting his lip. Because as much as he wanted this, *craved* this, it was still a new skill for him. "I've heard that it's easiest if I'm on my elbows and knees." He chuckled. "I guess that's another new one for the books—the reverse Thomas-

Ashvili." He rolled over, careful in the narrow bed, propped himself on his elbows, and waited. And waited. Finally he looked over his shoulder to find Tony staring at him, slack-jawed, the lube slipping from his lax fingers. "Tony?"

"Jesus, Solly, you're beautiful." He swallowed, his Adam's apple bobbing under his warm brown skin. He ran one hand down Sol's spine and over the globes of his ass. "So fucking beautiful. I can't even…" He stared down at the bottle as if he'd never seen lube before.

"Here." Sol sat back on his haunches and wrapped his hand around Tony's, squeezing a good dollop of lube into his own hand. "I've done this part before anyway. Sex toys need slicking up too."

He resumed his position as he prepped himself—one finger, then two. But before he went any farther, Tony grasped his wrist gently. "Let me."

Then *Tony's* fingers were teasing him, entering him, stretching him. Sol dropped his head onto his clenched fists because—*gah! Right there!* "Tony," he moaned.

"I've got you, Solly. I've got you." Tony's fingers scissored inside, making Sol writhe and push back against them. Tony's chest was warm against Sol's back, Tony's lips soft against his neck. "So fucking beautiful."

"Now, Tony," Sol gasped. "Please, now."

Tony muttered something as he withdrew his fingers, leaving Sol craving more, craving *Tony*. "Fuck. I should have put the condom on first. This lube is—"

Sol reached back and grabbed his hand. "I'm clean. You're clean. We've got the tests to prove it." He peered over his shoulder. "We don't need the condom. Unless… unless you want it."

Tony stared at him, wide-eyed, then licked his lips. "But, Solly, they're *Olympic* condoms."

Heat infused Sol's face. "If you don't want to, it's okay. I know bareback is a big step, so—"

"Are you fucking kidding me?" He leaned over and kissed Sol, hard and deep. "You're it for me. You always have been. Everywhere. Every day. So if you feel the same…"

At Sol's frantic nod, Tony slicked up his cock. Sol resumed his position, gripping the base of his own cock because he didn't want to shoot too early. Then Tony was behind him, nudging Sol's entrance and Sol had to remember that he wasn't a complete ass virgin. *Relax. Bear down.*

And then Tony was there, stretching Sol wide as he pushed in, slow and steady, until the head popped through the ring of muscle. Sol fisted the blanket and groaned. *So much different than a dildo. So much better. So perfect.*

"God, Solly," Tony said, his voice like gravel, "you're so hot. So tight. I can't—" He started flexing his hips in little pulses, gaining ground with each thrust until Sol could feel Tony's balls against his. "I'm not gonna last. I can't."

"Then don't." Sol tilted his ass up, changing the angle and *oh my God.* "Just fuck me, Tony. Hard."

Tony growled and bent over Sol's back, driving in harder, deeper, hitting that spot again and again. Sol jacked himself although it was impossible to keep pace with Tony's thrusts— *gymnast abs*—and honestly, he didn't want to try, so finally he stopped and just held onto the blanket, dimly aware that he was keening into the pillow.

Then Tony hit his prostate at exactly the right angle and Sol's orgasm rolled over him like a lightning-struck tidal wave.

"Solly," Tony gasped, losing his rhythm as his cock pulsed inside Sol, flooding him with so much jizz it dripped down his thighs. Tony gripped Sol around the middle and rolled to the side with them still connected, his chest heaving against Sol's back.

"That was…"

"Yeah."

Sol dabbed his fingers in the puddle of his own semen. "We should probably clean up."

"Mmmhmmm," Tony hummed against Sol's neck. "In a while. Right now, I can't move. I'm not sure I'll ever move again."

Sol chuckled, warmth expanding in his chest despite the come dripping out of his ass. "You have to move. You've got an event final tomorrow."

"That's tomorrow. I'll worry about it then."

As he snuggled back into Tony's big spoon, flipping the dry part of the blanket over them, Sol opted to close his eyes. *Just for a few minutes.*

But when he opened them again, light was streaming in his window and somebody was pounding on his door hard enough to make it bounce on its hinges.

"Guys!" Danny shouted. "I know you're in there."

Tony groaned into Sol's ear, swearing under his breath as he peeled himself away. "Shit. Who needs waxing when you've got dried jizz to remove your short and curlies." He raised himself on one elbow. "Whatever you want, Daniels, it can wait."

Danny pounded again. "No. It really can't. I mean it, guys. You need to get out here. Now."

Tony dropped a kiss on Sol's shoulder. "He'd better not just want to tell us about his latest GTA score."

Sol sighed and rolled up to sit on the side of the bed. "I may kill him anyway." He brushed at his belly and thighs. Didn't help. "Guess we should have cleaned up last night after all. Because you never know who'll drop by at—" He peered at his travel clock. "—ass o'clock in the morning."

"Especially when they live in the same suite." Tony crawled out of bed and picked up his shorts. "Come on. We might as well see what he wants. Although to make up for the unwelcome wake-up call, he can let us have the first showers."

CHAPTER TWENTY-TWO

"He did *what*?" Fists clenched at his sides, Tony stared across the common room at Danny and the other guys on the team. *I'm going to fucking kill Andrei.*

"He outed you. You and Sol." Danny grimaced and rubbed the back of his neck. "He copped an interview on one of those conservative channels, the ones who are always on about the sanctity of sport."

"Fucking hypocrites," Tony growled. "They only care about the alleged sanctity when it conflicts with their self-righteous, racist, homophobic—"

"Tony." Sol's calm voice was the only thing that could cut off Tony's rant. "It's not like we didn't expect a backlash."

"Yeah, but it should be *our* news to share. Not fodder for some sanctimonious ratings-grubber and a pissed-off ex-coach." Tony grabbed Sol's hand, because damn it, *this* was their truth. "You know what? Fuck it. We were never hiding on purpose. We're not ashamed." Tony's belly suddenly plummeted, and he glanced at Sol. "At least I'm not."

Sol returned Tony's grip. "I'm not either. I wish we could have handled the optics ourselves, though." He edged closer and put his hand on the small of Tony's back. "You've got the high bar final today. What if the judges are swayed by the news? For that matter, Danny's got p-bars. What if it affects the rest of the team?"

"Fuck," Tony muttered. "This is exactly why we wanted to wait. Because the Games shouldn't be about this."

"I don't agree." Everyone's head turned to stare at Rahul.

"What do you mean?" Sol asked.

"I think the Games are about inclusivity. Or at least they should be." He favored them with his wintry smile. "Excluding someone, punishing someone, for something that has nothing whatsoever to do with their athletic performance, seems counter to what the Olympics are all about."

"You know," Sol said slowly. "He's right. Tom Daley participated in Rio as an out athlete. And remember what happened when Gus Kenworthy's boyfriend kissed him at the Pyeongchang Olympics? Or how Adam Rippon being so open and downright celebratory about his fabulousness made him the star of the Games? Maybe we need to do our part to make gender identity and sexual orientation a non-issue by, well, making an issue of it." Sol smiled at Tony, fond and as intimate as a caress. "Forgive me if I'm wrong, but don't we have our very own internet celebrity on this team? Maybe we should attack this with the celebrated Thomas flair."

Tony faced Sol and took both his hands. "You're sure?" Jesus, this was the second time that Sol's privacy had been trashed in Tokyo. "You weren't happy about that other interview."

"And I should have been. The support and feedback I've gotten since then proves that I was looking at it from the wrong angle. I was worried that my performance would be blamed on or excused by my medical condition. But instead, it's not my performance, it's my *participation* that's made a difference to more people than I can count. I think that's what Tom and Gus and Adam started. Unashamed visibility is the first step toward acceptance." Sol shrugged. "Our own shame gives the haters more ammunition. Maybe it's time to disarm them."

"All right. If you're sure."

"I am."

Tony took a steadying breath. "Our phones are probably blowing up as we speak. I suspect we won't even have to wait to get an interview spot with Quinn."

And Tony was perfectly right. Before Sol got out of the shower, they had a live spot booked with Quinn. Tony kissed Sol on the way to his own shower, in full view of the other guys who mostly just ignored them. "We're meeting Quinn at the main press center right after breakfast."

"Don't you and Danny have training?"

Tony shook his head. "We postponed it. The final isn't until 5:00 this evening, and Barry agreed that getting ahead of this story is more important."

"Hey," Danny called from the sofa where he was in the midst of a GTA throw-down with Jason, "should we wear our Team USA warmups?"

Tony raised his eyebrows, sharing a surprised glance with Sol. "What do you mean?"

"Ah, shit," Danny muttered, as his on-screen car careened off a cliff. He stood up and propped his hands on his hips. "Well, you don't think the team will let you face this alone, do you? We're all going. Even if Quinn doesn't ask us any questions, we'll be there to have your backs." He sauntered toward his bedroom, bopping Tony on the biceps on his way past. "That's what being a team means."

Tony glanced at Sol, who shrugged. "Why not?"

By the time they finished breakfast and met Quinn in the *much* busier broadcast center, they'd picked up more supporters —the entire USA women's gymnastics team, the captain and a bunch of other players from the women's soccer team, and several gymnasts from other countries, including Luiz, the Brazilian who'd hit on Sol in Rio.

Quinn studied their mob with her usual aplomb. "I see you've brought some friends with you, Tony."

Tony glanced at their impromptu entourage. A couple of the soccer players had rainbow flags draped over their shoulders. "Yeah. Hope you don't mind a crowd."

"Not at all. Although the larger studio was already booked so I can't offer you all chairs."

"That's okay," one of the flag-draped players said, "we can stand." She grinned. "In fact, we prefer to stand. Because we all stand together."

Quinn returned her grin and gestured for the group to take a position in front of the screen displaying the Olympic rings. "Perfect." She waited until Tony and Sol were mic'd and seated in the tall stools in the center of the studio, took her own place, then nodded to her assistant who counted down to air. "Good morning, Ringsiders. Welcome back to the Olympics, where yet another brouhaha has arisen today involving our friends from the US men's gymnastics team, Tony Thomas and Sol Ashvili. Today, Tony's coach—"

"*Former* coach," Tony corrected.

Quinn smiled like a shark. "Well, doesn't that make this even more interesting? Tony's *former* coach, Andrei Nicolescu, appeared on *In the Name of Sport* and revealed some information that perhaps wasn't his to share."

Danny darted forward and stuck his head into the shot next to Tony. "No perhaps about it. Dude was out of line." The camera followed him as he danced back to the other athletes and high-fived the soccer captain.

Quinn chuckled. "You probably recognized Isaiah Daniels from Team USA's silver medal men's gymnastics team. But Tony and Sol weren't only accompanied by their teammates today. We've got the Olympic champion US women's gymnastics team, including the two-time all-around gold medalist, most of Team USA's women's soccer team—"

"All of the team," the flag-wearer said.

"The entire team, plus a few people in the colors of other countries." She paused until the camera was back on her. "Tony, what do you think this says about the controversy?"

"Pardon me for correcting you, Quinn, but there's no controversy here. Controversy implies disagreement, and I think we can all agree that Andrei inappropriately invaded Sol's and my privacy. That I believe he chose to do this in retaliation over being fired as my coach is my own opinion, but hey—" He spread his hands and plastered a faux-innocent expression on his face. "—I'm entitled to that, right?"

The group gave a ragged cheer, but Quinn turned to Sol. "Do you have a comment, Sol?"

Tony tensed for an instant. It didn't matter that Sol claimed he was ready for this, the spotlight wasn't his natural habitat. But Sol smiled easily. "I have a number of comments. First..." Sol turned to Tony and—yes!—took his hand right there on camera. "I'm incredibly proud of what my boyfriend accomplished yesterday. I'm not sure you noticed, but he won an Olympic medal."

Quinn laughed. "I believe you've won a few of your own over the last few days. Two silver and two gold, on top of your team silver, if I recall. Congratulations."

Sol flushed. "Thank you. Second, I'm not ashamed of our relationship. The only reason we chose discretion here at the Games is because our focus was on our team and the competition. While LGBTQ+ representation and visibility in sports is incredibly important, it really shouldn't matter. The competition is about excellence and achievement in the gym, or the pool, or on the field. What happens behind closed doors between consenting adults—whether they're athletes or not— shouldn't have any bearing on the competition."

This time, the group's cheer was louder and more heartfelt. Quinn gestured for her camera operator to pan the crowd. Tony noted that they were standing with the shorter gymnasts in the center, the taller soccer players at the side, so that the iconic rings were clearly visible. *Nice statement. Couldn't have arranged it better myself.* "Apparently your friends here agree with you."

Sol shrugged. "Like Tony said, there's no controversy here. We're in Tokyo to represent our country and do the best we can, just like any other athlete. If we bring home medals, all the better." He winked at Tony. "And since our plan to stay on the down-low has been exploded, nobody should be surprised if we hold hands on our way to the dining hall."

The third cheer had Quinn's sound mixer wincing. Quinn faced the camera. "So there you have it, Ringsiders. An exclusive from Tokyo where, according to the two men who were the object of some incredibly petty and small-minded reporting today, things are business as usual for Team USA." She turned back to them. "Any last comments for our viewers?"

Sol leaned in. "Just one. Be sure and watch the last round of event finals tonight. I won't jinx anybody by making medal predictions, but I'll say this much: no matter who wins, you'll see outstanding gymnastics from all the competitors." He grinned at Tony. "My boyfriend included."

Tony rolled his eyes. "Way to put the pressure on, Solly."

"No pressure." Sol squeezed his hand. "Just facts."

Quinn beamed at them. "I look forward to it. Thank you, Tony and Sol." She turned to the rest of the group. "If any of you would like to add a few words, I'm sure my audience would be more than happy to hear from you."

Tony and Sol relinquished their mics to Luiz and the soccer captain. As the two of them settled next to Quinn, Tony drew Sol to the rear of the studio. "I know you don't like the camera," he murmured into Sol's ear, "but you were great, babe."

"It was easy, Tony." Sol gazed at him, such love in his dark eyes that Tony wanted to go down on his knees right there. "All I had to do was look at you and tell the truth. My truth." He kissed Tony's knuckles. "Our truth."

Although Tony's eyes prickled and his throat was too thick to respond, he drew Sol into his arms and into a kiss—deep, hot, and dark. After all, the cameras weren't pointing at them. But even if they were? *Fuck it. We don't have to hide anymore.*

CHAPTER TWENTY-THREE

"How can anyone stand this?" Sol gnawed on a cuticle, his knee bouncing in time to his amped-up heartbeat, as Tony completed his one-touch warm-up on high bar.

Jason chuckled. "I was sitting in front of Tony when you were competing, and he was pretty much climbing the walls. Guess you know how he feels now, huh?"

Ugh. This was worse than watching Tony do those ridiculously risky XBL stunts, because at least they'd all been uploaded after the fact. This time, Tony was *right there.* And Sol was *right here.* Close, but not close enough. *Although even if I was on the floor, I couldn't make much difference. Once we're on the equipment, we're always alone.* Sol just hoped Tony could feel the support of the team, of the crowd—a number of whom were waving rainbow flags as well as the US flag.

All the guys other than Tony and Danny were in the stands today—Danny was competing on p-bars, and Tony on high bar. The women were on balance beam—and seriously, what sadist had invented that event?—so the tension was high everywhere.

Sol had watched Tony's practice in the warm-up gym. Not only was he planning the Cassina, but he'd upgraded one of the releases in his connected series. *Great. More risk and difficulty. Just what he needs.*

But Tony was Tony, so doing a *less* risky routine in event finals wasn't even on the table, not when the event specialists from every country were upping their firepower. *As long as the additional difficulty doesn't bite him in the ass when it comes to execution.*

Just stay on the bar, Tony, please. High bar was the biggest crowd-pleaser in men's gymnastics, primarily because it was so explosive and dynamic and—yes—dangerous. The force generated by the giant swings, the distance to the mat in a missed release, the air time in the dismounts—all of it was flashy. *And one hundred percent Tony.* It was no wonder that high bar was his favorite event.

"So what did Tony do to make it through the competition?" Sol moved on to his next cuticle.

"Mostly took his seat apart with the strength of his grip. Although I think he blew off a lot of steam fighting with his dad."

Sol stared at Jason. "His dad was here?"

"Yeah. Didn't he say? On all-around day. Almost made Tony miss your vault." Jason screwed up his face. "I think he would have run after the guy and punched him out if that had happened."

On one hand, Sol was perversely thrilled that Tony had been so invested in watching him compete. On the other… God, his father. *I wonder if he's here tonight?* The last thing Tony needed was to have his dad spouting his usual win-or-you're-nothing garbage. But Tony seemed almost relaxed down on the floor, gulping some Powerade and chatting with Xiao.

The announcer called Tony's name—he'd drawn the first spot which meant he couldn't evaluate the other competitors and scale back his difficulty if it wasn't warranted. *Who am I kidding? This is Tony. If he has permission to do the risky routine, he'll do the risky routine.* Sometimes he did the risky routine even without permission.

Tony mounted the podium and chalked his hands before slipping his fingers through his grips and chalking those too. He stood under the bar, calm and apparently relaxed, until the green light flashed. He saluted the judges in acknowledgement, then, just before he jumped up to grasp the bar, he touched the center of his chest with two fingers. *"You're with me. Every day. Everywhere."*

Sol's breath whooshed out of him as Tony circled the bar in his first giant. *I'm not sure I can watch.* But if he didn't watch and something happened, then he'd have to wait for somebody else to tell him about it. *No way. I spent too long* not *knowing.* From now on, Sol wanted to know everything—like why Tony hadn't mentioned his father's visit—good, bad, and in between.

So Sol made himself watch without cringing as Tony hit every skill with precision and perfect form. *Come on, Tony. Gymnastics 101.* And sure enough, he stuck that insane triple twisting double layout. When he raised his arms in a triumphant V, he caught Sol's eye—then touched two fingers to his chest, then his lips, and winked.

Then all they had to do was wait. Danny nailed his routine, taking silver on p-bars. But cheers erupted all over the arena, accompanied by the flutter of rainbow flags, when Tony took high bar gold.

Two days after the gymnastics competition completed, Tony was still floating somewhere above the Tokyo Bay. He'd completely exorcised Rio from his personal cadre of demons, but that wasn't the real reason. No, that would be because of the man at his side as they strolled through the Village on the way to meet Ori at the broadcast center. Sol wasn't holding Tony's hand at the moment—but that was because he was signing an autograph for one of the women from the Japanese table tennis team. When Sol handed the little book back to her, she bobbed her head and giggled, then raced away.

"You're amassing quite the fan club there," Tony said as they continued on their way.

Sol shrugged. "Nothing like your one point two million XBL followers—"

"That's one point *seven* million, thank you very much."

"Oh, *excuse* me." Sol grinned at him, then laced his fingers with Tony's, right where they belonged. "Do you have any idea why Ori wants to meet with you today?"

"Not just me. She asked for you too."

Sol's brows drew together. "Me? But why?"

"Why do you think, doofus? You won five Olympic medals, two of them gold. You've got a solid social media footprint as a successful diabetic athlete." Tony grinned and swung their joined hands. "And you've got a really hot boyfriend."

Sol rolled his eyes. "Right. I almost forgot about that last one."

Tony laughed because no way would either of them forget that. They'd woken up in each other's arms since the third day of event finals—*thank you, Barry, for giving Solly the single room*—and were doing their best to up their boinking tally. "Seriously, though, your NCAA eligibility is up anyway now that you've graduated. Have you thought about going pro?"

Sol peered up at the Olympic flag flapping in the breeze. "I don't know. I hadn't really thought about continuing to train. I don't think I want to put myself through another World Cup season, let alone another four up to the Paris Games. It may be time for me to give something back instead."

"Well, just think about it, okay? Wait to see what Ori has to say."

"Don't worry. I'm keeping an open mind."

They spotted Ori sitting on a bench outside the Tokyo Big Sight, the breeze teasing curls out of her messy bun. She rose to meet them. Unlike Quinn, she didn't tower over them so she didn't have to duck to give Tony a kiss on the cheek. "Good morning, gentlemen. Enjoying the life of Olympic gold medalists?"

"More like enjoying the life of a guy who doesn't have to bust his ass in the gym for at least another week. Good to see you, Ori. You know Sol."

"By reputation, of course." She held out her hand for Sol to shake. "A pleasure. Did Tony tell you why I asked you both here?"

Sol gave Tony the side-eye, but Tony raised his free hand in denial. "Hey. I swear. I know just as much as you do."

Ori laughed. "Sorry, Tony. Didn't mean to get you in trouble. Shall we walk?" She led them on an ambling stroll through the breezeway under the conference tower. "Do you have plans for after the gymnastics tour, Sol?"

"Just deciding on grad school."

Ori wrinkled her nose. "Are you completely set on grad school next fall? Would you consider putting it off for another year, maybe two?"

Sol shot her a narrow glance. "If you're angling for me to keep competing—"

"No, not exactly. But I've heard some buzz related to your diabetes reveal. How would you feel about signing on as a spokesperson for the Juvenile Diabetes Coalition?"

"Spokesperson? What does that entail?"

"Well, in your case, they'd want you to participate in a series of sports camps for kids with type 1 diabetes. It wouldn't just be gymnastics. There'd be other athletes involved—swimmers, basketball and soccer players, track and field. So far, none of the others are diabetic themselves, although that could change as the program's visibility increases. There'd also be some fundraising events, public service appearances, and the like." She slid a glance at him. "You're planning to go into diabetes research, aren't you? That's what grad school is about?"

"Yeah." Sol's answer was measured, but more like he was considering it, not dismissing it out of hand. "I'd be interested in hearing more. I assume there'd be a good amount of travel."

She nodded. "The Coalition is based in Las Vegas, but yes, they plan for these events to take place nationwide."

"Would I sign on with you as part of this deal?"

"You don't have to. You can handle it on your own or find another agent to work with. But I'd like you to consider me." She tilted her head. "I've done pretty well by your boyfriend here."

Tony nodded sagely. "That's right. She has. And she only brings out the whips and chains if she really needs them." When Ori glared at him, Tony widened his eyes in mock innocence. "Oh, I didn't mean she uses those on her *clients*. Those are for the goons she faces across the negotiation table."

Sol laughed. "I'd like to talk to you about both things. But maybe not until we get back to the States."

"Of course. I'll set something up. Now, Mr. Thomas."

Tony edged closer to Sol at the veiled threat in Ori's voice. "Yes, boss?"

"Are you aware that scouts from Cirque du Soleil attend the podium training at most major gymnastic events?"

"No." Tony drew the word out. "So?"

"So they're interested in having you join one of their casts. Pending an interview and personal audition, of course."

Tony glanced at Sol. "Aren't a lot of the Cirque shows based in Las Vegas?"

"As a matter of fact, they are."

"Then hell yes, I want to talk to them." Tony drew Sol's hand to his lips and dropped a kiss on it. "We could get a place there. Assuming you go for the Coalition gig."

"With you there to sweeten the pot?" Sol's smile glinted in the sunlight. "I might be persuaded."

Ori clapped her hands. "Excellent! Now, the other thing I wanted to float by you is for your whole team. How do you think the guys would feel about doing their own calendar?"

Tony smirked. "A naked calendar?"

"With strategic placement of gymnastic apparatus. And perhaps kittens."

Sol barked a laugh. "Making gymnastics sexy again?"

"Why not?" Tony kissed Sol's temple. "I've got some great ideas about how to make that happen." He leaned forward to murmur, "The Thomas-Ashvili. The Ashvili-Thomas. We'll work them all out. Together."

CHAPTER TWENTY-FOUR

Las Vegas, one year later

Tony's cell phone vibrated on the coffee table while he was adjusting the camera on the corner shelf unit. He glanced over his shoulder at the screen. *Solly.* He grabbed for the phone, missed his grip, and sent it skittering onto the floor. Cursing under his breath, he retrieved it before the call went to voicemail.

"Hey, Solly. Did you get registered?"

"Yes. I had to get one class changed, but— Why are you breathless?"

"Me? I'm not breathless." *Liar.* "Knocked my phone on the floor, that's all."

Sol heaved an audible sigh. "Good lord, Tony, why did we think living in the middle of the desert was a good idea?"

"Aside from the fact that your grad school is here, my job is here, and the charity that you're committed to up to your neck is here? Can't think of a thing."

"Damn you and your logic." Another sigh. "I think my clothes are about to melt off."

"Then you better get home quick." Tony checked the clock over the TV, calculating how long it would take Sol to get back from campus. *Perfect timing.* "Because I wouldn't want to miss *that.*"

Sol chuckled. "All right. Do you need me to pick up anything? I could stop at the grocery—"

"No!" Tony pinched the bridge of his nose. *Dial it back, stupid.* "I mean, we're good. I picked up what we need for dinner this morning."

"All right." Sol's voice held a note of uncertainty. *Probably because I sound like a maniac.* "See you soon."

Tony huffed out a breath as he disconnected the call. *Half an hour. I can do this.* He froze, staring at the phone. *Unless Sol was already on the way home.* Shit! He could be here any minute!

Focus, Thomas. After years of gymnastics competition and six months of performing in a Cirque du Soleil show, Tony had had plenty of practice doing *that. But nothing prepared me for* this.

He tweaked the camera angle again, making sure it captured the full living room, plus their drop-leaf dining table with its single rose in a crystal vase. *Yeah, I'm the guy who buys crystal vases now. Go figure.*

He squinted at the balcony doors. The light spilling in from the sliders would illuminate the shot without too much glare. Tony patted the glass, unable to suppress a smile. When he and Sol had gone apartment hunting, Sol had assumed that Tony would want to be in the thick of Las Vegas action—right on the Strip, or at least close to it, because, hey, the Thomas flair was all about flash and dazzle.

But flash and dazzle weren't Sol's things. Even though they'd moved in together right after the Team USA gymnastics tour, with months still ahead of them before Sol started grad school, Tony—for maybe the first time in his life—had been thinking *ahead.* With this relationship, he didn't want to approach things one skill at a time, one moment at a time. He wanted to see his future—his and Sol's—stretching out in front of them like the view across the desert to the distant mountains.

And when Sol started grad school, the last thing he needed was the relentless light and distraction of downtown Las Vegas.

So Tony had insisted on this place in Summerlin, much to Sol's surprise—and delight, if his relieved smile and the blow job against the sliders had been any indication. *I've got good memories of these doors.* He patted them again. *These doors and I are tight.*

He checked the clock again. He'd posted that the live feed would begin at three, to give him time to chat with his followers before Sol got home. It was nearly three now. *Close enough.* He picked up the camera remote to fire up the video, and his gaze caught on his T-shirt sleeve. *Oops.* He stripped off his shirt and tossed it into the corner—his followers had *expectations*, after all.

He hit the button for a three second delay, then set the remote on the coffee table and took his place in the center of the room. "Hey, there. Welcome to the XBL channel. Before we get into today's special content, I want to thank all you Xtremists for helping to sell out the *fifth printing* of the Team USA men's gymnastics calendar." He grinned into the camera. "And considering this is August, I'm guessing you didn't buy 'em for the dates." He winked. "It's the kittens, am I right? Who can resist a good kitten?"

Tony took a deep breath and let it out slowly. "I've got some news for you today. It's a good news/bad news kind of thing. The bad news... Well... This will be my last XBL video." He patted the air with both hands. "I know, I know. But it can't be a real surprise, can it? Think about my videos since Tokyo. With the team tour first, and then the audition and rehearsals for Cirque—" He pointed at the camera. "And I expect any Xtremists in the Vegas area to grab tickets, because two words about the show: *In. Tense.* You thought I flew high in the gym? Wait until you see me launched off a springboard. And the costume?" He winked. "Way more revealing than our old uniforms."

Out in the hallway, the elevator *ding*ed, and Tony tensed, his palms suddenly damp. *Shit. He's early. I'm not ready.* But the muffled sound of multiple footsteps and a bright, definitely feminine laugh, eased the tightness in his shoulders.

"Sorry about that." He chuckled weakly. "That's what happens when you do a live feed. Anything can happen, right?" He wiped his palms on his shorts, his hands catching on the lump in his pocket. "Anyway, so that was the bad news. The good news? I'm doing one last stunt. The riskiest ever." Tony's mouth dried when he thought of what could happen if this went sideways. *It'll be fine. It has to be fine.* He forced himself to grin at the camera. "And you'll see it live. Right here." The elevator *ding*ed again, and this time, Sol's jaunty whistle announced that *this was it.* "Right now. So brace yourselves." *Because I sure am.*

He faced the door, which was out of camera range, as the lock disengaged. Sol entered, his face lighting like it always did when he stepped into their home. His gaze heated as it traveled from Tony's face down his chest to his bare feet and back.

Sol hung his messenger bag on the hook by the closet, his smile turning positively wicked. "I was hoping for a reward for getting through registration without turning into a desiccated mummy, but I was envisioning a glass of iced tea. This is way better."

"Solly—"

Sol *lunged* at him and caught all Tony's words in a kiss that would send their already sky-high AC bill into the stratosphere.

As much as he hated to disengage—because Sol's kisses were *never* to be dismissed easily—Tony drew back. "Solly, we're not alone."

Sol blinked, his eyes still dark with intent. "We're... What?" His brow wrinkled as he scanned the open plan room from the leather sofa to the obviously unpopulated kitchen where the only sound was the ice maker dropping another load of cubes. *Shit. I should have turned that off before the feed. I'm seriously off my game.* "Is someone in the bedroom?" His eyes widened. "Oh,

God. Are my parents here? They said they wanted to catch your show, but they didn't tell me—"

"Easy, easy." Tony ran his hands down Sol's arms and laced their fingers together. "We don't have any unexpected visitors." He nodded at the camera. "But we do have an audience."

Sol's head turned in slow motion—*damn, it's like special FX*—and he spotted the camera. "You're filming? Tell me you can edit this out later."

"Sorry, babe." Tony grimaced. "Live feed."

Sol winced and lifted a hand in a feeble wave. "Hi, Xtremists. Sorry for the NSFW action. I'll try to keep it clean from now on." He turned to Tony. "What's the occasion?" His eyes narrowed. "You're not thinking of staging another risky stunt, are you?"

"I am. The riskiest." Tony tucked his hands into his pockets to hide their trembling. "And I'm working without a net."

"Tony. What the actual fuck?" *Talk about a thunderous expression. I think lightning just shot out Solly's ears.* "Doesn't Cirque have rules about that?"

"They do. But there aren't any rules about this one." Tony dropped to one knee and drew the little velvet box out of his pocket.

"Tony?" Sol croaked, then snapped his mouth shut, throat working. "Is that— Are you—"

"Solomon Ashvili, heart of my heart, sun in my sky, light of my life, will you marry me?" With Sol's wide, dark gaze on him, Tony's hands shook so much he couldn't open the box.

"God, Tony." Sol dropped to both knees and closed his hands around Tony's. "Are you actually *nervous*?"

Tony laughed shakily, Sol's fingers against his sending the inevitable tingles across his skin. "Let's just say I've got a bottle of champagne in the fridge and a bottle of vodka in the freezer and I'm drinking one of them tonight. If your answer is what I hope, we'll be drinking the first together. If it's the other"—*God, please not the other*—"I'll be drinking the second alone." He scared up an approximation of his usual cocky grin. "So what's it gonna be, Solly? Champagne for two tonight or a pity party for one?" *For the rest of my life.*

Sol shook his head. *Oh, God. He's gonna turn me down.* Tony tried to pull his hands free, but Sol's grip tightened. "Are you serious right now, Thomas? In what fractured, fucked up universe would I ever say no?"

Thank God Tony was already on his knees or he'd have collapsed because his equilibrium was suddenly shot. He listed to one side and would have toppled over if Sol hadn't caught him and pulled him into a hug with Tony's hands—and the ring box—trapped between them.

"I wasn't sure," he mumbled into Sol's shoulder. "I didn't want to presume."

"Idiot." Sol's chuckle ghosted over Tony's ear. He drew back, but kept a firm grip on Tony's shoulders. "What was it you said to me once? I may be paraphrasing a bit, but wasn't it something like you can doubt anything else?" Sol kissed Tony's forehead. "Doubt the world is round." He kissed Tony's left eyebrow. "Doubt that the Japanese team will invent six new elements by Friday." *Right eyebrow.* "Doubt Rahul will pass quantum mechanics." *Cheekbone.* "But never *ever* doubt that I love you and that we're in this together for good. That—" This time, Sol planted one on Tony's mouth, and Tony dropped the stupid ring box so he could wrap both arms around Sol and lean into the kiss because *yes!* Except Sol pulled away. *No!* But then he looped his arms around Tony's neck, and his gorgeous smile dawned. "—you can take straight to the bank."

"So, um, is that a yes?"

Sol lifted an eyebrow. "Yes, Tony, you doofus. That's most definitely a yes."

Tony's shoulders sagged. "Oh, thank God."

"Oh for the love of— Is that the camera remote?"

Tony glanced over his shoulder, because he legit couldn't remember where his *feet* were at the moment, let alone something as inconsequential as tech. "Yeah."

Sol grabbed it, and with his other arm still looped around Tony's neck, he faced the camera. "You heard it here first, Xtremists. Tony and I are engaged. If we decide to tie the knot at the Chapel of Elvis, you'll be the first to know. But for now..." With the hand that held the remote, Sol tapped Tony's chest in the center of his sun ink. "Peace out." He hit the button, squinting until the red tally light faded to black, then tossed the remote across the room. "Because for now," he growled. "For now?" He laced his fingers behind Tony's neck and kissed him, teasing Tony's lips apart with his tongue until Tony moaned and matched Sol thrust for thrust as he worked one hand under Sol's T-shirt and slid the other down to his ass.

Sol broke away with a gasp. "For now, I'm taking my fiancé to bed."

"Damn right you are," Tony murmured against the skin of Sol's neck. "Because the Ashvili-Thomas and the Thomas-Ashvili will need practice—lots of practice—for the rest of our lives."

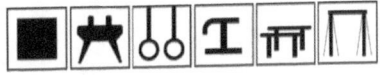

AUTHOR'S NOTE

When Darling Sons A & B were small, they had a tendency to stand on their heads on the sofa and do somersaults across the rug. So when they were about three or four, we enrolled them in tumbling classes at a local gym (okay, not *that* local—we're not close to anything except blackberry brambles and fir trees). Unfortunately, that gym only fielded a girls' team, so by the time DS A & B were eight, they'd spent a little too much time on the balance beam for my liking (seriously, *who invented that thing?*)

Almost by chance, we stumbled on another gym a bit (!) further away that had a boys' program, and DS A & B joined the team when they were nine. At about the same time, our neighbor boy, who's a few months older than my twins and was one of their best friends at the time, developed type 1 diabetes. As you can imagine, this resulted in huge changes for his family as they all learned and helped *him* learn how to manage his condition.

The learning curve wasn't always without friction, of course. When his younger sister complained that he was getting all the attention, he replied, "*I'm* not getting all the attention. *Diabetes* is getting all the attention!"

Shortly after his diagnosis, he started taking gymnastics classes, joined the boys' team at another gym—and proceeded to kick everyone's ass. He continued to compete long after DS A & B abandoned gymnastics for dance, only stopping because he grew too tall to perform the skills efficiently. As Tony tells Quinn, the physics of gymnastics tends to enforce its own implicit height restriction!

Diabetes doesn't have to prevent athletic participation and competition, but every athlete should work closely with their health professionals to develop a safe care plan for their particular sport and activity level.

A Message from
E.J.

Dear Reader,

Thank you so much for reading *The Thomas Flair*, my very first sports-themed romance. If you have time, I'd love it if you could drop a review on Amazon or Goodreads. Reviews help authors more than you can imagine!

Wondering what to read next? If you're in the mood for more M/M contemporary romance, you might like *Clickbait*, where love blossoms unexpectedly at a construction site between a prickly web designer and a big-hearted electrician. Or if a quirky paranormal story might hit the spot right now, check out my screwball rom-com *Nudging Fate*, the first in my Enchanted Occasions series: it's *The Bachelor* meets *The Wedding Planner* where mythology and technology collide! Or give my Mythmatched story universe a try. It kicks off with *Cutie and the Beast*, where a cursed fae warrior turned psychologist clashes with his determined temporary office manager. As you might expect, hi-jinks ensue!

You can see all my books on my website, https://ejrussell.com, or on my Amazon author page here: https://www.amazon.com/author/ej_russell. Most are also available at Apple, Kobo, and Barnes & Noble.

Would you like exclusive content and ARC giveaways, not to mention gratuitous dance videos? Then I'd love for you to join me in Reality Optional, my Facebook fan group (https://facebook.com/groups/reality.optional). My newsletter is the place to get the latest dish on new releases, sales, and more. I promise I only send one out when I've got...well...news. You can subscribe here: https://ejrussell.com/newsletter.

All my best,
—E

ALSO BY
E.J. RUSSELL

Paranormal Romance
Mythmatched Universe
Fae Out of Water Trilogy
Cutie and the Beast
The Druid Next Door
Bad Boy's Bard

Supernatural Selection Trilogy
Single White Incubus
Vampire With Benefits
Demon on the Down-Low

Other Mythmatched Romances
Howling on Hold
Possession in Session
Witch Under Wraps
Cursed is the Worst
The Skinny on Djinni
Assassin by Accident (part of Carnival of Mysteries)

Mythmatched Companion Stories
Rusty's Really Bad Day (free to newsletter subscribers)
Second First Date (free to newsletter subscribers)

Quest Investigations Mysteries
Five Dead Herrings
The Hound of the Burgervilles

The Lady Under the Lake
Death on Denial

Art Medium Series
The Artist's Touch
Tested in Fire
Art Medium: The Complete Collection (omnibus edition)

Legend Tripping Series
Stumptown Spirits
Wolf's Clothing

Enchanted Occasions Series
Best Beast
Nudging Fate
Devouring Flame

Royal Powers Series (shared world)
Duking It Out
Duke the Hall
King's Ex

Magic Emporium Series (shared world)
Purgatory Playhouse

Monster Till Midnight

Historical Romance
Silent Sin

Contemporary Romance
Camera Shy
The Thomas Flair
Mystic Man

For a Good Time, Call… (A Bluewater Bay novel, with Anne Tenino)

Holiday Shorts (separately)
The Probability of Mistletoe
An Everyday Hero
A Swants Soiree
or all three together in
Christmas Kisses

Geeklandia Series
The Boyfriend Algorithm (M/F)
Clickbait

Writing as Nelle Heran
(traditional cozy mystery)

Crafty Sleuth Series (with C.K. Eastland)
Die Cut
Mixed Media
Found Objects (*coming soon*)

ABOUT THE
AUTHOR

E.J. Russell (she/her), author of the award-winning Mythmatched paranormal romance series, writes LGBTQ+ romance and mystery in a rainbow of flavors. Count on high snark, low angst, and happy endings.

Reality? Eh, not so much.

She's married to Curmudgeonly Husband, a man who cares even less about sports than she does. Luckily, C.H. also loves to cook, or all three of their children (Lovely Daughter and Darling Sons A and B) would have survived on nothing but Cheerios, beef jerky, and Satsuma mandarins (the extent of E.J.'s culinary skill set).

E.J. also writes traditional cozy mystery as Nelle Heran. She lives in rural Oregon, enjoys visits from her wonderful adult children, and indulges in good books, red wine, and the occasional hyperbole.

News & Social Media:
Website: https://ejrussell.com
Newsletter: https://ejrussell.com/newsletter

ACKNOWLEDGEMENTS

I owe thanks to many people for the birth of this book. First, to Sue Brown-Moore, who wanted stories about the Olympics—your enthusiasm for my initial (very sparse) proposal is what prompted me to write the book in the first place. To Leslie Copeland, beta reader extraordinaire, for your stellar (if painful) advice—you made this into a far better story. To Cate Ashwood for the gorgeous cover—your patience, grace, and talent continue to awe me. To Meg DesCamp for editing and comma-wrangling—someday you'll stop encouraging me to put *more* innuendo into my books! To Jill Rehkopf Smith for offering advice about how type 1 diabetes affects a young gymnast—any mistakes here are of course my own.

I remain indebted to my family—Jim, Hana, Nick, Ross, and Billy—for encouragement and forbearance. Love you, guys!

And as always, thanks to you, my readers, for joining me on my writing journey. You're the reason I can continue to do what I love, and I appreciate you more than I can say.